Polar Doom
Virulent Strain

By
Jack A. Vitulli

Editor
Lynn Forgit

This work is intended as fictional. Events that
parallel reality are speculative.
All characters appearing in this work are fictitious.
Any resemblance to real persons, living or dead, is
purely coincidental.

Polar Doom Virulent Strain

Chapter 1: Warm Weather Ahead

"Today was hotter than yesterday," Tom utters mockingly from his porch bound rocking chair. His wife Kathy agrees with a slight nod of her silvery head.

The elderly couple gazes beyond their home into the hazy distance that was once their family farm. The flat plains of Iowa roast under a dry blaring sun, just days before the first of April.

"Eighty degrees is not normal for this time of year," Tom rattles. "We have no winters anymore. Back in our day, we'd be lucky to have this weather in July." A loud cough jolts his frail frame.

"Yes Dear," Kathy muses idly. "Why are you coughing so bad?"

"No reason. Don't fret about it. It ain't nothing."

"Our farm is obsolete." Kathy smiles sublimely.

Food no longer grows in the open, instead it sprouts in climate controlled domes with automation. "My father rolls over in his grave every time I hear that. Food being grown genetically in some lab is comical."

A loud rhythmic melody emanates from their old farmhouse, but only Kathy hears it. "Someone is calling us." She smiles, rising slowly from the chair.

"I hear nothing," Tom derides. "Why don't they make those things louder?"

"It's already up all the way. Besides, it's your fault for not having the surgery."

"I don't want any robot fiddling around in my ears."

Kathy waves her hand dismissively before entering the house.

Sparkling wood floors are intertwined with modern living. Bright airy rooms clean of clutter exemplify the expansive rooms.

Entire walls dance with both still and active images of loved ones. No physical frames delimit each portrait.

Kathy enters the living room where a static picture of a young man fills a thirty by eight foot wall space.

"Yes Jim," she responds, prompting the still portrait to vanish into a live image of the man.

"Mom." He smiles. "How are you?"

"Fine. Your Dad and I are fine, Dear."

"Did you see the news?"

"We don't watch too much of that these days,

Dear."

"You missed something important." As he begins to describe the report, two children scurry across the screen.

"Dad, Tommy is bothering me," says a girl of thirteen.

"I'm talking to Grandma now, you two be quiet."

"Sorry," the girl slumps before sitting politely on the couch alongside her father.

"Hi Grandma." She smiles and waves.

"Hello Alisha."

The rambunctious boy temporarily plants himself by his sister, but only for a moment before vanishing from view.

"Mom," Jim continues. "A disease is spreading throughout the world. People are getting sick and dying."

"My word," says Kathy with a concerned guise.

"Twenty thousand people in China died from it already."

Jim pauses. His finger draws a square in the air to his left. Instantly, a news cast fills the void. A well dressed man explains.

"... No one knows how to stop this. In only a week, thousands have died. Today, there were two hundred cases reported in Los Angeles alone. Estimates suggest there are many undocumented cases. Officials are mandating that those exhibiting these symptoms must be hospitalized."

The news caster narrates over vivid images of infected people. Crying faces marked with bursting sores inundate the screen while unclaimed bodies lay on street corners. People scurry past uncovered corpses wearing scarves and handkerchiefs over their mouths, hoping not to catch the vile disease.

The image returns to the commentator's stricken face, caught up in the hysteria.

"If you or those you know have these symptoms, please call 911 immediately. Now I have Dr. Solji Mudi, director of the National Center for Disease. Doctor, where did this come from?"

A dark skinned man bristles with concern. Behind him stands a large glass window depicting an opened room. White coated practitioners pass in and out of view. They parade nonstop by the window, unaffected by the live broadcast.

"The first cases surfaced just over a week ago in China," he responds hurriedly. "We have never seen anything like this before. It has all the markings of a pandemic," says the health official.

"Is there anything we can do to protect ourselves?" asks the commentator.

Dr. Mudi gulps. "Stay home and away from those infected. I'm sorry but I have to cut this interview short."

"That is quite alright Sir."

"Dad?" Jim interrupts while closing the hovering window of the news caster. The senior Tom stands behind his wife Kathy in the empty farmhouse. "You're in New York, right Jim? You have little to worry about," says Tom.

"But they said it's spreading rapidly from west to east. You should cancel all your appointments and stay isolated for a while." Jim affirms.

"That's easy," Tom chuckles. "We're in Iowa son."

"Make sure you have enough food," Jim insists. "Go to the store now and stock up."

"We're fine," says Kathy. "You're over reacting."

"No. This is going to be big."

"You know the media," Tom callously chides. "They always over dramatize things."

"Just be careful," Jim grimly asserts. He thinks for a moment. "Maybe you can both come and stay with us?"

"What?" Tom snarls. "We've lived our whole lives here. I'm not going to just pull up stakes and leave on account of some little bug. Remember the time we were infested by..."

"Don't worry about us, Dear," Kathy smiles sublimely, cutting her husband off. "We weathered many storms in our day. You just take care of those two precious grandkids of ours."

"I can't wait to see them in June." Tom smiles with an eager grin. His birthday is the 12th. Each year, friends and family descend on the farmhouse for a barbeque. But this year marks a special occasion. Tom has reached a milestone of 100 years.

Tom is young in comparison to the oldest living human of over three hundred.

"I never thought I'd live this long," Tom musters. "Imagine being healthy at 100. But it was a rough road getting here. In my youth, we didn't have all these fancy things to prolong life..."

"Dad," Jim interrupts. "June is a long ways off. If the virus spreads like they predict, none of us may make it past a few weeks."

"Nonsense!" Tom blares. "If it gets that bad, they'll find a cure. You're getting caught up in the hype. I suggest that you stop watching television."

Jim grows agitated. "I have to go, but we'll talk tomorrow. Take care."

Chapter 2: Transmutable Chaos

Dawn offers little solace to those infected with the heinous disease. Hospitals quickly fill to capacity, sending many into makeshift tents and nontraditional infirmaries.

The virus spreads beyond person to person. In mere hours it infects virgin populations without warning. Most of Asia is polluted by the tempest on its way through Europe.

Nearly half of the American continent is corrupted by the vile symptoms. It sweeps across the United States like wildfire and deep into the prairie plains, racing eastward to eventually engulf the earth.

In its wake, thousands lay dead or dying. Those who remain healthy are poked and prodded to expose their immunity. If not for them, society would collapse. Their diligence keeps the infrastructure from collapsing, but they are taxed beyond stressfulness.

"I'm declaring a state of emergency," the President asserts over the airways just days after Jim had spoken to his parents. He sits nervously at work watching the broadcast through his computer.

"Those who can telecommute must do so," he continues. "Able bodies must report to work, otherwise without your diligence, our nation is doomed. We rely on you to save us." The President coughs for a few seconds, a cough that rattles his flanking Aides.

He brushes them off.
"National Guards will be setting up food and water distribution points in those areas where stores no longer operate."

Jim breathes deeply from his small office high above New York City. The investment banker eyes the glistening sun beaming through the glass behind his desk. All seems peaceful from his perch atop the world.

Instinctively he calls home. A three dimensional image hovers above his desk.

"Hello." His little girl Alisha answers. Her crisp face glistens only a few inches in front of him. Her disembodied head floats above the desk.

"Honey, why are you home from school?"

"They closed it. Tommy and me are both home."

"Where's Mommy?"

"She went to the store to get some food."

"You two behave and don't leave the house."

"We know..." she pauses. "Daddy, I'm scared."

"We are all scared. But we'll get through this." He bites his bottom lip.

"When are you coming home Daddy?"

"I don't know." He sighs heavily. "There are so few of us here and I have to keep things going. I'll be home my normal time."

"Okay. I love you Daddy."

"I love you, too."

Jim slides back into his chair with a heavy sigh. Fright invades him. Nervous hands cover his eyes, leaving only a sliver to see through. A knock on the door startles him.

"Yes."
The door slowly opens. A pale young man enters cautiously. He lingers by the doorway.

"Sir, I'm sorry, but I'm not feeling well."

Jim looks up in bewilderment.
"How many of us are left out there on the floor?"

"Ten at most," the man utters stressfully.

"It wasn't supposed to spread this fast. They said we had about a week before it would hit us."

"I guess they were wrong, Sir."

"Go home and take care of yourself."

"Yes, Sir. I hope to see you again," the man whispers before quietly closing the door.

Jim swivels his chair to face the windows. His
eyes strain to glimpse a dark approaching
storm.   The once sunny sky turns silver then dark
gray before a streak of lightening illuminates the
office.

A crack of thunder vibrates the glass, jolting Jim
back to reality. Instantly, he places a call to his
parents.

It rings for a while before his mother answers.
"Is everything alright Mom?"

"I suppose so." Her glassy eyes say otherwise as
her head appears only inches away from Jim
sitting at his desk. "Your father is sleeping. He's
been tired lately." Her lips quiver.

"Do you want me to come there?"

"No, no please. You stay with your family."

"You're my family too."

"No Jimmy. Please do not come."

"I just can't leave you two alone. Ma please."

"Please what?" she scolds. "You stay with my
grandkids. Don't leave them for an instant." She
pauses, eyeing his office. "You're at work, aren't
you?"

"I have no choice. Many of the employees are

sick."

"You should be home with your family," she admonishes.

"I'm not sick Ma."

"You will be if you stay there."

"That's not true. There are some who are immune."

"Don't risk it. You can be a carrier and bring it home to your family and infect them all."

"If that's true, then it's too late. I've been around sick people all day. Just a few minutes ago, a worker asked to leave."

Her eyes swell with tears, unable to hold back searing emotion.
"It's your father Jimmy. He's dead."

"What?"

"An hour ago he stopped breathing. He had a high fever."

"Did you call..."

"Yes I called 911 and no one picked up. Everyone is sick. I did not want to tell you, but it hurts so much. He's gone Jimmy."

"Mamma, I'm coming."

"No! I'll hear no such thing. Don't you come here! Promise me Jimmy."

"But Ma, you need my help. I just cannot leave you alone."

"I'm hanging up now." Her eyes exhibit a stern gaze. "Call me tomorrow."

Chapter 3: Fond Illusion

Cold winter rain pelts Jim as he walks along deserted streets to the subway station under a blustery night sky. Normally at rush hour, these venues are filled with cabs and people scurrying homebound.

Instead, handfuls of scattered pedestrians glide to their destinations unfettered by congestion, an unusual sight indeed.

Dressed in a dark overcoat and brimming umbrella, Jim strolls down to the subway. An eerie feeling grips him as he spots on three people standing only the platform waiting for the train. It is normally packed with fellow strap hangers elbowing their way into the crowd.

Jim scans his metro card and proceeds through the turnstile. Other commuters acknowledge him with a brief but noticeable smile; another oddity indeed.

"Have you ever seen a rush hour like this before?" a slightly overweight woman asks. The others nod but offer no verbal response.

Soon a screeching train roars in. The doors open, exhibiting a bright but mostly empty car. Seats are plentiful. Everyone finds one before the doors swiftly close.

"Next stop is Canal Street," the automated voice eagerly blares through the onboard speakers. The train whisks into the tunnel a few hundred feet before abruptly stopping.

A small day laborer, sits parallel to Jim.
"Ah. Again. We keep a stopping," he fumes.

The others look up, but this is not your typical bunch. On most subways, especially during rush hour, people remain quiet and brandish a somber stone gaze that yells, "Do not bother me", but tonight it is different. This small group of commuters are more animated.

"Has it been doing this all day?" the woman who had made a comment earlier asks.

"Yes. All day," the small man answers.

A young Nubian teen dressed in a grey billowy coat rocks intensely to his rhythmic music leaking through the ear buds. His eyes remain glued to the floor with a detached gaze.

"What a sorry state," Jim utters. "Only eight people fill a rush hour train."

"It looks bleak," a squirrelly looking man remarks. His thick black rimmed reading glasses rest smugly on his long slender nose.

Though his hairstyle resembles a field of weathering grass, he sports a dark luxurious mustache. "I suspect that only a few people are left running the subways. Perhaps they do not even know or care to know that there are stranded passengers on this line."

"Ah, yeah. Excuse the interruption," a voice echoes through the audio system. But this time it is not automated. Instead a thick Brooklyn accent fills the car. "Ah, we're experience'n dif fa cultees on the six train bound for Grand Central. I'm gonna backs yas up to Fulton Street. Yous can wait thear for a while or find anotha line."

"Oh, that is just great!" remarks the squirrelly man.

The train abruptly moves in reverse and stops at the bright platform from which it had departed. However, the doors remain closed.

"Let me out!" the squirrelly man orders. He pounds on the door in earnest until his aching hands force him to stop.

"Calm down!" Jim insists. "Panicking will not help. The doors will open eventually."

"I feel like a trapped rat," the man whines. But he takes Jim's advice and slumps on a bench.

The group of eight sits quietly along the expansive seats in squelched anger. After ten minutes of silence, the teen removes his headphones and stands up.

He approaches the door with casual fortitude. Standing in front of an access panel, his fingers fiddle with a litany of buttons. With the dexterity of a world renowned computer hacker, the doors magically part.

He strolls out and up the stairs coolly. Squirrelly man quickly vacates the car and dashes from the station. The others follow, leaving Jim, the woman and the small laborer on the platform.

"You heard what the MTA said. This whole line is down," the woman offers. "I'm going cross town and take the number one up. Maybe the three of us can walk together."

The laborer nods, but Jim lags behind, gazing blankly into the empty car.

"Are you coming?" the woman asks.

"Yes," he whispers. "It's just. Well, it's just so empty in there. I've never seen anything like it before."

The three crest the stairs onto Fulton Street emerging from the lonely subterranean subway station. Jim unfurls his umbrella to shelter his new friends from the cold rain.

"I'm Jenny."

"I'm Emilio."

Jim reciprocates.

The three walk toward Chambers and West Broadway with Jim in the middle holding the umbrella against a buffeting windswept sidewalk.

Empty stores line the desolate streets with a sense of bleakness.

"I'm going to Grand Central," Jenny remarks.

"So am I," Jim replies. "The Hudson line is my train."

"New Haven line is mine," Jenny answers.

"I'm going to 23rd Street," Emilio declares as if not be left out to the conversation.

The three quietly press on, until reaching their intended subway line. Unlike the previous departure point, there are more than ten commuters waiting along the platform.

The train speeds in. The doors open. A meager crowd occupies the seats. The train blasts forward without incident.

Emilio winks before exiting at his stop. Jim and Jenny sit together for the short ride up town.

"I've never seen it like this," Jenny offers. "I've been taking trains all my life, nearly thirty years."

"That overshadows my twenty."

"It's going to get worse before it gets better," Jenny whispers.

Her voice carries over the meager passengers. They all look blankly at each other as if not to acknowledge her remarks.

The doors fly open to an empty Grand Central terminal. The ten strap hangers that had gotten on earlier have left, leaving only three alongside Jim and Jenny.

A short walk from the station finds the two inside Grand Central hub. The normally bustling arena resembles a lackluster weekend crowd. Large open holes remain where throngs of people usually stampede indifferently across the shiny tundra.

The gleaming golden island clock is usually manned by a group of employees eager to dispense information. However, today the lights are out and no one is home. Even the manned ticket booths are devoid of life.

Jim's gaze is drawn toward the towering message boards above the long empty ticket counters. Bold red letters signal that many departures have been canceled or delayed beyond normalcy.

Jim's expectant conveyance will not leave for another hour. However, Jenny's train is about to depart in just two minutes.

"Take care," she yells while bolting toward her gate. If she does not catch it, she'll be stranded for at least three hours until the next departs.

You would think with all these cancellations and

delays, that this expansive venue would be overrun with throngs of commuters, but it resembles more of sparse mid holiday travelers.

Instinctively Jim pulls out his phone and calls home.

"All circuits are busy," the screen blinks.

"That's happening a lot today," a man dressed in a long black overcoat remarks. A smoky hat shades an elderly man dressed in a suit while a cane umbrella curves around his left arm.

"I say it's been quite a day," he exalts with sophistication.

"Yes it has been," Jim answers wearily.

"Would you be waiting for the Poughkeepsie bound train?" the man asks crisply.

"Yes."

"Ah. I have been waiting for that one nearly two hours. They keep pushing up the departure time. I will wait no more before I find lodging. What say you?"

"I am going to stay here, thank you."

"And then what? As for me, I will find a nice hotel to spend the night."

"Thank you," Jim replies flippantly while

attempting to make another call.   The man walks
away.

The call goes through but static fills the line.
"Hello," his daughter Alisha answers.

"Honey, I'm delayed in Grand Central."

"Hello, hello?" she echoes frantically. "Is that you
Daddy? I can't hear you."

"Where's Mommy? Hello? Alisha, where's
Mommy?"

The signal fails.
"Damn it!" he swears, staring at the phone with
disgust. A flutter of hopelessness fills his
heart. He looks up into the ornate blue ceiling of
the majestic terminal. A tear rolls down his cheek.

"I have to get home," he sighs. The next train is on
the Harlem route and leaves in twenty
minutes. Though not his normal line, he
contemplates taking it and then finding a taxi
home from there.

He sprints toward the gate and spots a
conductor. The normal pristine blue shirt and
front bill cap is askew.

"Excuse me," Jim exhales, but the conductor
continues walking past him. "Excuse me, Sir?" Jim
presses.

The man stops. His glassy eyes are filled with

tenderness.

"Yes?" he slurs slowly.

"I need to get to Poughkeepsie."

"Good luck," the conductor snickers. "The last train out was the New Haven line. They're going to close the terminal shortly. I suggest you find another way home." The man coughs.

"What? Why are the trains not running?"

"Mister, isn't it obvious? There are few left to run trains or anything else. Now please leave me alone. Can't you see I'm sick?"

The conductor walks away and vanishes around a corner, but his cough lingers in the hollow like a rumbling train.

"Attention. May I have your attention," the intercom blares. "The terminal will be closing immediately. We are sorry for this inconvenience. Good luck."

Jim's arms dangle by his side. He gawks upward in despair at the elaborately decorated domed astronomical ceiling. He steps back into the main concourse to find only a few stragglers sprinting toward the exits.

There is utter silence instead of a bustling 6:15p.m. terminal.

"Now what?" Jim asks rhetorically. His words carry in the empty cavern.

Looking like a lost dog, he emerges outside onto 42nd street. A stray taxi rushes by before his hand rises. Numb with bewilderment, Jim strolls westward.

"Hey fella," a cop catechizes while shining a bright flashlight at him. "Are ya sick?"

"No," Jim utters in dripping shock. "They just closed Grand Central and I can't get home."

"Penn Station closed over an hour ago too. You might wanna try the bus terminal."

"And if that is not running?"

"Well, you can wait till morning or find a subway up to the Bronx and take your chances there. Oh wait, they've stopped running for the night too."

"So I'm not getting home today?"

"It sure looks that way Mister. I say hunker down till morning."

"Where?"

"Most of the hotels are filled with sickos. I say find a warm stairwell and settle in."

"Can I stay at the Prescient?"

"What? That's for cops," the officer balks. "You best be moving along, Buddy. Go up town but be careful."

"Are the streets safe?"

"You best be aware of your surroundings. Giv'n what's happen'n, you probably won't be bothered too much. Just stay alert."

Along an ill traveled street, Jim comes to an elegant glass building. The unlocked doors allow unfettered ingress into the main lobby. In the center sits a vacant security desk. He strolls beyond the post to a bank of elevators.

A random ride to the eighth floor opens to a lavish waiting area filled with plush seats. Jim lays his weary head upon the supple leather and falls fast asleep.

Chapter 4: Canyon Desert

The first ray of sunlight bleeds through vertical window blinds, forcing Jim to wake. He yawns deeply before sitting up on the sumptuous couch. A vending machine down a hallway flashes the words "Cash Only" indicating lost communications with the credit card system.

He pulls out his wallet and injects crumpled bills in return for a handful of candy bars. With a ravenous growl, he greedily eats his meal before sitting back down on his warm leather bed. A satisfying grin fills his face.

Jim examines his phone, but it cannot find a signal. Instead a better idea sends him down to the lobby. The security desk remains unoccupied.

He picks up an outbound phone and dials home. It rings for a few seconds, sending an anxious smile brimming around his chocolate covered lips.

"All circuits are busy," the automated voice declares. He slams the phone back onto its cradle.

Outside, the brisk air pushes him uptown. There should be more life parading on the streets at this early hour, but not even a cab occupies the lonely thoroughfare.

On a vacant sidewalk sits a solitary man propped up against the building. He doesn't look destitute, but is well dressed and adorned in a suit and tie. Jim kneels by the sleeping man.

"Hello?" Jim voices, but the man does not move. Jim taps him on the shoulder, causing the man to keel over in a locked position. Splotches of blisters fill his face. Pus oozes out of one juicy blister and dribbles onto the pavement. He is just an empty shell leaking death.

Jim backs away in shock and runs up the avenue. His legs eventually give out, forcing him to rest against a street lamp. He puffs vigorously, trying to regain his adrenalin filled breath.

In the distance, a city bus rolls up a parallel venue. Jim dashes through the block and emerges a few feet from the stalled conveyance.

He runs toward the opened door.
"Where are you headed?"

"Uptown," answers driver with a Jamaican accent.

"How far up town?"

"Are ya be coming in or not?" the man clamors.

Jim opens his wallet to present his metro card. "No, cash only," the driver insists.

Flashing bills catch the driver's eye before Jim hands over the fare. He quickly finds a seat up front. There are five others riding this conveyance. Three men sit at the back row. While a man and woman relax in separate aisles at mid-point.

"Are the subways running?" Jim asks the driver, but the man remains focused on the road ahead.

A few blocks beyond where Jim had gotten on, the bus turns right.

"What route is this?" Jim asks, but no reply is offered.

Moments later the bus comes to a halt in the shadow of a building. The driver stands up and faces the passengers.

"Now empty your pockets!" he demands. Jim turns and looks down the aisle. The three men who sat in the back are now frisking the two middle passengers.

Jim stands with a stunned expression.
"No, no. Sit down. Gimme ya wallet!" the driver insists. One of the three men walks forward. He stands as a stone pillar, breathing like a ferocious dog behind Jim.

The driver holds out his hand.
"How could you do this?" Jim sighs before handing over the loot. Bills and cards are plucked from his leather fold.

The two passengers are escorted out of the bus from the back doors.

"Move!" the driver demands while his muscular

henchmen grab Jim by the arm.

Together, the three passengers are pushed through an entrance inside the adjacent building.

"We gave you our money. What else do you want?" Jim yells. He is swiftly backhanded by one of the enforcers, rendering Jim unconscious.

Jim's eyes flutter open as he lay on his back, shackled to a cold steel radiator in a dark moist room.

At the opposite end, the other male passenger sits on a mattress with both hands tied behind his back.

"Yar wake?" the man whispers with bulging eyes.

"Yes," Jim replies. An odd thing catches his eye. Jim's pants are gone, stripped off to expose his naked lower body. His underwear dangles around one ankle.

"Yar were knocked out when they did it to ya," the man utters. He is barely visible behind shadows.

"Did what?"

"Do ya feel it? That warm creamy ooze in ya butt? They didn't want the woman. They actually let her go after slapping her around for a while. It was us they wanted."

Jim gulps with a sense of loathing. "I was raped?"

"Yeah. Both of us, four times, one for each of them."

"I have to get out of here."

"I hear ya. It looks like we've been had. I'm Ray."

"Jim. I'm Jim," he rattles grimly.

"Can ya get free Jim?"

"No. I'm tied to the radiator."

"I think I can..." Ray groans for a few minutes. "There, my hand is free." The other arm is quickly extricated. Ray runs over with is pants in hand, stumbling before adorning them in flight.

A wide Nubian face breaches the darkness. The puffy thick jowls resemble a teddy bear. He kneels by Jim.

"They sure got ya bound tightly to this thing." But the ropes are no match for Ray's brutish hands.

"Yar pants are in the corner." Ray motions. Jim hops into his trousers with a squeamish limp.

Together the two find the main door. Intrepidly, Jim twists the knob, allowing the door to glide open quietly.

"I see the bus," Jim whispers.

"Yeah, and I think it's empty."

Cautiously, they step beyond the threshold.

"Hey!" a voice blares from down the street after spotting the two.

Jim dashes inside the bus and presses the start button.
"Go, go, go!" Ray yells while flopping onto a seat.

The bus jolts ahead then streams forward, hitting one of the thugs broadside. His body bounces off the bus and into a gutter like a rag doll.

"Keep going," Ray blares. "Don't stop!"
Jim floors it, passing red traffic lights until ten blocks separate them from the gang. He pulls over to the side.

"Why are ya stopping?" Ray jeers.

"Where are we going?"

"I don't know about you, but I'm heading to the Bronx!" Ray exalts. "Just keep driving!"

"How do you get there?" Jim asks.

"Where ya from?"

"Way up state near Poughkeepsie."

"Oh, yar a long distance runner. Just go over the Henry Hudson Bridge. Here, let me do it." They exchange seats. "I live on west 232nd street just past that bridge," Ray explains.

The bus treks steadily uptown to Broadway. They meet up with stalled automobiles blocking 125th street. The abandoned cars litter the passage, forcing Ray to abruptly turn right for an impromptu detour, but he misses the turn at a high rate of speed.

The bus careens over a sidewalk and smashes into a light pole, shattering the windshield. The pole lands on top of the bus, denting the roof, but the transport continues its forward momentum before clipping a corner of a brick building. Soon it glides to a gentle stop in the middle of a desolate street, spewed with mortar and broken bricks.

Jim pulls himself up from the floor. Scrapes and bruises dot his shocked face. However, Ray is motionless, slumped over the steering wheel.

Pulling him back reveals shards of fractured glass embedded like pockmarks on his face. Blood oozes from the pores.

"Ray!" Jim yells frantically.
His lifeless expression brings Jim to his knees below the driver's seat.

"Why is this happening? Why?" Jim cries frantically.

A loud pop lingers in the cold silent air followed by three others in rapid secession from outside the bus. Jim stumbles out in fear and heads inside the smashed brick building.

"Guns?" he whispers nervously. Instead of waiting around to find the culprits, he disappears into the gashed structure and then into a hallway. Electricity is out, yet backup power illuminates Exit signs, flaunting their message in darkened hallways.

"Ouch," he winces after noticing a gash on his left shoulder. Other scrapes and gouges appear on both hands. He staggers for a moment until finding the building directory embedded on a wall. On the third floor is a Doctor's office, an Internist.

A dirty stairwell leads up through the structure. He climbs to the third floor and finds the medical office. The waiting area is dull and devoid of life. "Hello," he expounds. "Hello, anyone here?"

Each of the four patient rooms has a short but inviting bed. Jim rummages through the drawers to find astringents to sterilize his wounds. A few dabs from the moistened tonic sting his gash.

His thoughts gravitate beyond physicality toward family faces. "I hope they're alright," he voices while staring through the window. His young family crystallizes on the pane where the sun is about to set. He sees their faces as if they were all standing just outside the window hovering three floors up.

He instinctively reaches for his phone.

"All circuits are busy," it reads amidst dwindling battery power.

Jim's focus wavers while eyeing the brown upholstered exam table. "This is a comfortable place as any to sleep for the night," he remarks. "I'll cross into the Bronx tomorrow. Maybe I'll find a car and drive all the way home." His eyes close in exhaustion.

Chapter 5: Internment

Rain pelts the nearby window, prompting Jim to wake in the dark void. "Ah," he sighs. "I'm still living the nightmare."

He shuffles toward the door and into the short hallway that separates the waiting area from patient rooms. If not for the blazing Exit signs, there would be utter darkness.

His phone says 4 a.m., yet he feels as if he has only slept a few minutes. Groggily, he lies back on the bed.

Bang!

A door is slammed in the stairwell, shocking Jim to his feet. Footsteps pound the rungs like a hurried animal.

Jim stays motionless in the room until the sun lightens the windows. Though fearful of the sounds, physical hunger races through his body.

He ventures out into the stairwell corridor where a single elevator remains unusable due to the power outage. Yet not far from the elevator are a couple of office doors leading to other businesses.

One nameplate is etched with, "Walter P. Bolton, Therapist". Another offers a less descriptive label, "Acer Industries".

His inclinations are to find food. None of these names inspire such edible offerings. Jim quietly steps down to the first floor hallway.

There are four doors but only one has "Lunch Pit" etched on it. The others display numbers.

He ravenously opens the publicized ingress with hopes of finding morsels of sustenance. The door squeaks with the slightest push. A whisper from within quickly subsides.

"I'm just looking for a little food," Jim asserts fearfully. "I mean you no harm. I have a family." He enters intrepidly into a large loft with gleaming white tile floors. Large windows allow light to flood the room. Rows of plastic picnic tables fill the expanse. In a corner are small cabinets and counters.

But sitting on one bench at the far end of the room rests a large figure with meaty elbows resting on the table.

"Hello?" Jim cautiously expounds.

"Yah?" The occupant snarls.

As Jim walks closer, he notices Ray. "Is that you?" Asks Jim with a bubbling smile. "It is you."

"So ya left me?"

"I thought you were dead. I heard gunshots and ran."

"Heck, I'd do the same. For a white boy ya sure know how to run." He pauses. "Guess I was going a little too fast for the turn."

"Yes." Jim smiles gleefully. "There are medical supplies upstairs that can help with your face."

Ray smiles.
"Nothing can help this face."

They both chuckle, adding levity to their misadventure.

"What happened Ray? How did you get here?"

"I was knocked unconscious. I don't think anything is broken. When I came to, I stumbled into this room." Ray hands Jim a sandwich wrapped in plastic. He eagerly accepts.

"I plan on crossing the bridge today," says Jim between ravenous mouthfuls.

"Me too. Are ya married Jim?"

"I have a wife and two kids that I'm desperate to find."

"I have a teenage daughter. Her mom didn't make it. I lost her two days ago."

"I'm sorry to hear that. I lost my father yesterday. We were going to celebrate his 100th birthday in June."

The two sit silently eating their sandwiches. "Today is Thursday, right?" Jim asks.

"I think so."

After breakfast, Jim persuades Ray to seek medical help. The two enter where Jim had spent the night. Gauze and bandages litter his onetime bed as he tends to Ray's wounds.

"Thanks." Ray smiles.

"Were you walking around last night around 4 a.m.?" Jim asks.

"No. Why?"

"Someone slammed the door and ran down the stairs."

"It wasn't me. I just found this place when the sun came up."

Jim's eyes widen with fear. "I think we should leave now."

"Yeah, I'm with ya."

Outside, the two ponder their advance under a golden sun. The air is crisp, hovering just above freezing.

"We gotta find a car," Ray insists while blowing into his cupped hands for warmth. His eyes search the environment in preparation for a dubious undertaking. Like a skilled sprinter, Ray scurries across the street and into another block, where abandoned cars had caused his ill-fated avoidance stunt.

Jim follows a few yards back until they stand together at the end of an automobile conga line. Three lanes of cars stretch one full block in a mini traffic jam.

Ray hops into one unlocked vehicle, finding it poised for duty. The sleek car comes to life while Jim enters the passenger's seat.

Ray throws it in reverse then pulls forward down another street, spinning the wheels around a corner. "Sorry. I'll keep it under thirty this time," he remarks, heading northwest toward the Henry Hudson Parkway.

Their short sprint comes to an abrupt halt. A sea of gleaming abandoned cars pack the northbound viaduct. Ray backtracks northward through Harlem in an effort to avoid obstacles.

They pass beneath active traffic lights. In bygone days, traffic was controlled by three distinct indicators hung by cables across a road or erected on poles.

But that was then. Today large flat panels serve as both billboard and traffic control. They hang across the road like stoic flags anchored by a single pole at the right, where it supports an identical display facing another direction.

These marketing tools have replaced those iconic tri-colored fixtures of yesteryears. Only in small towns and out of the way places can they still be found.

Today, the highly visible image radiates with messages. On the right side of the flat colorful display are stationary advertisements rotating every eight seconds. To the left is a large red circle with the words STOP sparkling inside. The circle resembles concave glass with beveled edges on a flat panel screen.

The advertisements depict products and services to a captive audience waiting at the light, but the abandoned cars do not move when the images cease, and the entire display radiates a large green circle at its center.

Ray passes beneath the traffic sign by rolling up the sidewalk. He manages to push beyond 125th street, weaving in and out of city blocks like a master cabbie.

"What's that?" Jim asks as they come to an odd sight.

Stacked in the parking lot of a red bricked hospital are rows of bodies. Some are wrapped in plastic while those farther from the building are not. Hundreds of corpses fill the lot, exposed to swooping birds eager for a quick meal. Crows and vultures fight with other aviators to pull flesh from ripe corpses.

"If that's what I think it is," says Ray, "I'm not stopping to get a closer look."

He drives past the grisly sight expeditiously, while flocks of vultures fly overhead for an easy banquet.

The journey uptown is slow and arduous, hampered by deserted cars. They explore bridges out of Manhattan, but all are blocked.

Their journey has taken most of the day. The sun is about to meet the horizon as they stop on Dyckman street where a long line of desolate cars disappear over a distant bridge. Only a half mile separates them from their initial destination.

"We're so close." Ray sighs. "What did these people do? Did they just abandoned their cars and walk across?"

"How much farther?" Jim asks.
Ray thinks for a moment. "About a mile from here I suppose."

"Then we will do the same and cross by foot."

"No, not at this time of day. It's gonna be dark soon."

"Alright, then tomorrow. Let's find a place to spend the night."

Chapter 6: Resourcefulness

Neighborhoods coalesce within the grander scheme of a metropolis. In upper Harlem, the community of Inwood sports a collection of commercial and residential high-rise buildings all concentrated within just a few square miles.

A coughing man echoes his affliction from across the street where Ray and Jim have just parked their car.

"Looks like we have company." Jim motions.

"I'd stay away from him and anyone who coughs."

"Good advice."

Life sporadically dashes near buildings in an attempt towards normalcy. The once vibrant streets that had brimmed with car horns and the calm of human exuberance have conceded to the whisper of nature.

"So are ya hungry?" Ray asks.

"You better believe it."

Restaurants, delis and fast food franchises line the street with a smorgasbord of variety. A sandwich shop catches their attention just a few paces away, but on the door, a hastily scribed sign dangles behind the glass, "Closed 4 illnesses".

The pair continues their pursuit for sustenance with a stop at a deli. The door is unlocked.

Inside the dark market, a bouquet of rancid meat lingers in the air near a dormant refrigerator display case. But all the contents have been previously extracted.

While Ray examines other cases, Jim strolls down the mostly bare aisles. He spots something on the shelf. Behind cans of tomato paste, a yellow treasure catches his attention.

A single bag of crushed potato chips hides inside its protective fortress. Jim pushes the cans aside and wraps his hands hardily around the noisy wrapper, sending shockwaves throughout the store.

"Who's thar?"
A gravelly voice emanates from the stockroom.

A large greasy man emerges carrying a baseball bat. Two eyes breach his thick brown beard to catch Jim holding the chips.

"Wair did ya find that?"

"Behind these cans. You are opened for business, right?"

The man thinks for a moment.
"One hundred dollar."

"What?" Jim sneers.

"Dat's da price. Take it or leave it."

"How about the cans?"

"Twenty dolla each." He bristles confidently, patting the bat head in his meaty left palm.

Ray stumbles behind the counter but remains hidden.

"Whos dat?" The shopkeep searches nervously over the empty shelves.

"My friend."

"So thar are two of yas?" The man shivers. The bat dangles loosely from his right hand just inches above the floor.

"I have a gun!" Ray yells forcefully, shielding his body from view.

"Take what ya want then leave me alone. Go." The storekeeper motions keenly.

The two scramble out onto the sidewalk and sprint down the street where they had parked.

"Boy, yar sure are some piece of work." Ray shakes his head while they sit inside the car.

"What?"

"While ya were having fun with the owner, I found

some of these."

He pulls a hand full of packaged meat sticks from his pockets. Four bottles of unopened water rattle in his arms.

"We have a feast!" Ray smiles. He hands Jim a few rods and a bottle before digging in. The chip bag is ripped opened and the two begin to gorge.

Wrappers litter the front seat of their car while they sit comfortably gazing with satisfaction through the windshield.

"It'll be dark soon," Ray remarks.

"We have to find a place to sleep. I don't want to stay in here," Jim declares.

"The street lights should be on by now. Guess we bedda get to find'n a place soon. It'll be pitch black out there."

Ray steps out and opens the trunk.
"What are you doing?" Jim asks.

"Get'n some protection."

He pulls a tire iron from behind the spare. "I wanna be holding a bat this time." An old duffel bag serves to conceal their stash. The remaining water bottles and packaged meats are stowed for safe keeping. Yet each openly grabs a couple of rations.

After locking the car, they cross the street and eye a small mattress store. Gratuitous smiles abound.

"It's locked," Jim stammers. He pulls on the framed glass door.

"Don't fret. We'll just break it then lower the steel security door afterwards," Ray passively insists.

"But the alarm?"

"What? Even if it worked, who's gonna come?"

Ray shatters the glass, allowing easy ingress. He pulls down the accordion gate to safely seal them in. On the ceiling, small shards of fading light trickle through an overhead skylight.

"I found some blankets," Jim asserts. He pulls them from a shelf. Like musical chairs, they each test various mattresses before settling on a perfect chaise at opposite ends of the showroom.

"Pleasant dreams," Jim offers in the nearly dark void.

"Same to ya. Sleep tight and don't wake me till the sun shines directly overhead."

Chapter 7: The Escape

Daylight beams through the skylight, but it does little to wake the comfortable duo resting on sinuous ecstasy. It has been a while since either of them had a good sleep.

Jim wakes first. He sits up, dangling his legs over the bedside like a school boy on an upper bunk bed. A spontaneous yawn further revives him.

He stretches and looks around. For a brief moment, fear grips him. "Where am I?" he whispers before reality fills the void.

He glances at Ray snoring. With each deep breath, a round mountain moves rhythmically atop the mattress.

Sunshine has yet to align with the overhead shaft. Jim stumbles to the back of the store where offices reside. As he approaches, darkness abates. Daylight penetrates through vaulted windows, caged in wrought iron bars bolted from the outside.

Jim notices a small office where a backpack sits on top of a paper strewn desk. A quick check of the area reveals an unopened can of tuna and a box of dry crackers. Jim stuffs them into his newly acquired sack before leaving the room.

In the hallway, a heavy steel back door sports a simple bolt lock. Jim unlatches it and ventures beyond the threshold.   Warm rising sun beats down upon him while eager eyes scan the sky.

With a satisfied grin, Jim takes a deep breath. The air is clean and vibrant. There are no planes or sudden noises cluttering the environment. Only pure unadulterated sounds fill the air.

A static billboard etched on the side of a building depicts a family sitting for dinner. Jim glares at it until his eyes wilt with guilt. His children and wife bleed into his consciousness until all other visions are pushed aside.

"Daddy." Alisha smiles while sitting on an outdoor bench. Warm air surrounds them in a quiet corner during a family reunion.

"Why is Grandpa so happy?" she asks.

"He is 99 years old today."

"But why is that so special?"

"His father and those before him never made it this far. We all suffered from a genetic disorder. To see my Dad pain free and full of life is astounding."

"Will you live as long as him?" Her eyes bulge with concern.

"I sure hope so. My DNA has been mapped and cleaned years ago before we had you."

"Jim?" A voice growls from behind, pulling him

away from the reunion and back to reality. Ray stands with a frown. "I wondered where ya went. Catch'n some fresh air, eh?"

"I want to go home." He turns with tear filled eyes.

"I hear ya. It's a beautiful day for a hike, don't ya think?"

Jim nods as the two secure the back door.
"I found some more food," Jim exhibits, showing the contents of the bag. "Crackers and tuna fish. Yum."

In the showroom, Ray gathers his things before lifting the security gate. Brilliant daylight floods every crevice when the gate is lifted.

"We better close it," Jim remarks while straddling the entrance.

"Why?"

"In case other poor souls need a place to sleep."

"Yar right," Ray grins. "Let's return the favor."

A quick stroll down the street finds their automobile securely waiting. "We'll get as close as we can with the car before bailing out," Ray offers before entering the driver's seat.

Soon, they speed down the street toward despondent traffic. "That's about it," Ray remarks after coming to a stop. The long line of cars stretch beyond the horizon, like women queuing for a restroom at a public event.

The two crest a small incline. Gleaming before them stands a steel blue bridge standing magnificently across Spuyten Duyvil Creek. The girder fixed arch structure is nearly a third of a mile long with two levels stacked atop each other. The bottom is reserved for inbound navigation while the top holds abandoned cars endeavoring to leave. Few protrusions at this topmost level would suggest a bridge. It resembles a parking lot.

"These cars are empty," Jim indicates. He peers inside a dormant vehicle. "Did they just get up and leave?"

"I would. Ya can't back up or go forward. So what'cha gonna do?"

The bridge entrance is in sight, only a mile away. Ray takes the lead with a heightened stride a few yards ahead of Jim.

"Help..." a weak voice strains a few cars behind them. "Help..." it says again softly.

"Where is it coming from?" Jim ponders.

"It's probably someone sick. There is not'n we can do. Let's go."

"We just can't leave."

"Why not? It will only infect us," he replies coarsely.

"We don't know that for sure."

"So why take the chance. Let's go," Ray insists.

"Hello. Where are you?" Jim answers, ignoring the risk.

Ray rolls his eyes contemptuously.
"Hey. I'm going ahead. Ya can do what ya want." He turns, and walks casually up the blocked highway with a lackluster stride.

"Hello?" Jim spews. "Hello."

"Help me..." a dire voice whispers back.

Laying face up in a back seat of a large car rests a pair of young eyes. A pubescent girl stares blankly while propping her head against a backdoor armrest. Her thick red coat acts as a blanket. A partially opened window allows a horrific stench of body odor to leach out.

"Hello," Jim affirms. "Do you need help?" His eyes languish for even asking such a question. Anyone can use help in times like this he ponders.

The girl gingerly lifts herself up. Covered beneath the coat is a sweatshirt emboldened with the words 'Haldane Volleyball' along with an image of a blue and white horned sneering devil.

Her hazel eyes are swollen from stress with splashes of smudged mascara. Her dirty blonde hair frizzes haphazardly around her long youthful face. She approaches the partly opened window.

"I want to go home," the young girl timidly musters.

"Where is the driver?"

"Who are you?" she asks, cautiously backing away from the window.

"I am Jim. I'm trying to get home to Poughkeepsie."

Her eyes gleam, inching close to the door as if a magic word was spoken.

"I'm from around there in Cold Springs. My Dad left and went for help but never came back. I went to look for him, but came back to wait here. Is everyone sick?" her watery eyes brood.

"Are you?"

"No. I don't think so. I'm just tired." Then she emits, "I think I'm hungry too."

Jim plucks a wrapped beef jerky stick from his pocket.

"Here, this will help."

She eagerly grabs it through the open

window. The tight wrapper is a challenge to open. The teen tries with all her strength but cannot remove the impenetrable wrapper. Her weak hands are numb with stress.

"Let me open it for you."

Reluctantly, she passes it back to him.

"So, what's your name?" Jim inquires while fiddling with the wrapper.

"Emily," she whispers.

"Here, the top is open just peel..." But before he can fully explain, she snatches it through the window and engulfs the entire stick with little more than a single chew.

Her eyes close with a   brimming smile.
"Well," says Jim, "I'm on my way north to meet up with my family. You are welcome to tag along."

The car door pops open. Her weak legs quiver like a new born colt, straddling the door and automobile. The stench of body odor hovers around her like an invisible cloud of sewage.

Jim's nostrils flare, culminating in a tight, sour guise, but he recovers, staring into her scared eyes.

"I'm afraid to leave," she says agilely. "Suppose Dad comes back?"

"If he does, a note can explain why you left. But it is up to you."

In the distance, Ray has not gone too far ahead. In fact, he has stopped at the mouth of the bridge, resting on a car roof about a quarter mile away.

Jim waves to him, prompting Ray to sprint back, but Emily does not notice the gesture. She is deep in thought, contemplating whether to leave a note or not.

"I've decided," she boldly emits. "I already wrote this note yesterday. What do you think?"

"Well, it says you are going home and to meet you there. Then you signed it. That will work."

She prods it away from him and places the scrap on the driver's seat. She plucks a small pink knapsack from the back where she had laid. "I had to eat my lipstick," she admits sorrowfully.

Her expression changes.
"You won't hurt me will you?" Emily folds her hands defensively.

"That is the furthest thing from my mind. I just want to get home to my little girl and boy."

"But you've just said you thought about it, right?" she huffs.

"That was just a figure of speech. I won't do anything to hurt you, I promise."

"How old are your kids?"

"Alisha is thirteen and Tommy is ten."

"I have a younger brother too," her arms unfold then dangle by her side. "He is eight."

"How old are you?"

"Fifteen." Her gaze passes over his shoulders. "Who's that?" she reams, eyeing Ray running toward them.

"My friend. His home is just over the bridge. We met while escaping the city."

Ray huffs with exhaustion. He stops a few car lengths away and stares at Emily while resting against a fender.

"Is it safe?" he pants.

"Emily is not sick, just tired and hungry."

"Oh," Ray sighs with distrust. "I thought ya were calling me over for something else. That's why I come a running."

"I noticed you didn't cross the bridge. Were you waiting for me?"

"Two is better than one," he dances with a doleful grin.

"You care about me don't you?"

"Don't get like that. I ain't saying not'n anymore. So are we ready to go?"

"I think so. We will have a guest accompanying us."
Ray eyes her with disdain.

"She probably won't make it past a few cars before collapsing."

"Don't bet on it," she fires back. "I'm going all the way home to Cold Springs."

Ray grins.
"We have a fighter here. I ain't saying ya don't have spirit kid, but ya sure don't look healthy enough to make it that far, at least not for a while. I live just over the bridge. Ya can rest there before going north."

Ray turns and walks ahead. Jim follows, but he glances back to find Emily looking over her shoulder at the car she had once called home.

"Are you coming?" Jim gently prods.

"Yes," she replies before picking up speed and forging forward with her small pink backpack flung over her shoulder.

"What's that God awful smell?" asks Ray as a light breeze pushes from behind like an avalanche. Emily's poignant aroma bathes the area with a dose of impenetrable musk.

"It's me." The epicenter is revealed as she sniffs her clothes. "I reek." Though still shy, she attempts to portray a relaxed demeanor. Her awkward grin does little to spur conversation.

"Don't worry about it," Jim remarks, keeping his eyes focused ahead at the approaching bridge. "You can wash up at Ray's house, right?"

"Yeah," Ray grunts without a backward glance. He picks up pace and passes the toll plaza. Those indomitable booths that pop up just everywhere, feasting on our hard earned money for those who have no choice but to pass through.

Jim has closed the gap between Emily. "How are you doing?" he asks with a glance.

"Fine," she replies. Her pink and white sneakers barely leave the ground with each step, but she perseveres, trekking forward with constant momentum.

Everyone nearly comes together halfway across the span.

"Let's take a breather," Ray insists. He stops at mid mark. A sip of bottled water prompts Jim to do the same.

Emily's eyes beam with curiosity but not a word breaches her lips. Instead, she fumbles around in her knapsack. A lipstick container shows in her hand.

"This is my last piece," she whispers, garnishing Jim's attention.

"Do you want a drink?" he offers.

"Yes, please."

Jim smiles while handing over his bottle. She takes a few sips before reluctantly handing it back.

"I have a lot of those around the house," Ray asserts. "The sooner we get there the better. I'm good to go."

The group meanders between stalled cars on the narrow sidewalks. Soon they emerge in the Bronx. Ray smiles with satisfaction on entering his territory.

"Home," he breathes confidently, then walks toward the right through a clump of sparse trees and into a parking lot. He keeps going for nearly a quarter mile more.

Chapter 8: Shake Down

"How much longer?" Jim asks.

"It always seems closer when ya not walking," Ray remarks. They press on, meandering through neighborhoods and businesses, then down desolate streets. Every now and again, pedestrians dart in and out of buildings in the distance.

Nearly a mile later, after following roads and going through parking lots, they come to West 225th street, passing beneath a train trestle.

"So you live on the other side of the tracks," Jim grins playfully.

"Yah, something like that. But I work hard to live in this area. It ain't easy."

They pass over the Major Deegan Express Way, prompting Emily to cry out.

"I'm not sure I can keep going."

She stops and leans against a building. "My feet are sore." Her legs wobble moments before collapsing onto the sidewalk.

Jim and Ray rush to her.
"Here take a sip." Ray puts his bottle to her lips. She takes a few gulps, then some more before finishing the entire bottle.

"I'm just a thousand feet ahead," Ray explains. "Ya can wait here with her. I'll come back with a car or something."

Jim nods, offering his water bottle to her.

Ray goes down the street alone, veering towards the right. He steps onto Heath Avenue.

To the right are multifamily homes stacked together like sardines in a can. Nimble feet glide up a four step ramp to his front door. It unlocks with ease.

"Hello!" he yells, but not a sound replies. "Kisha?" he continues to spew. Intrepidly, Ray searches each room, but his house is empty. He sighs remorsefully, then suddenly, a voice from outside calls to him.

"Ray," says an elderly man standing below the steps. His bulky neighbor from across the street smiles. Not a bald spot is present. His face is clean shaven, exposing deep craters and pits on his lightly colored skin.

"I am so happy to see that you made it home Ray."

"Mr. Alverez, have ya seen her?"

"You mean Kisha? There hasn't been much going on around here lately. This whole street has been quiet the past few days. It's the strangest thing. No one has come or gone since now."

Ray bows his head sorrowfully. He glances up the street to where his friends are waiting.

"Well at least we have each other," says Alverez. "You look tired. If you're hungry I have some food."

"I brought two others with me. They're waiting down the street."

"Do you need my car?"

"Yes."

"And I'm free to help, too." He smiles boldly. "Ray, you can call me Hector you know."

"I was raised to respect my elders."

"Nonsense. How many years have I told you that my first name is not taboo? Besides, Mr. Alverez is my dear departed father. I'm Hector."

Ray smiles as the two manually open Hector's garage door. Inside sits a gleaming vintage car decked out in bright chrome and emerald paint. "I only take it out for show you know, but today is a special day I suppose, a very special day since we're going to help some friends. It has been years since this thing served a useful purpose, other than giving me awards."

Hector pops open the hood and checks vital engine fluids. "This mechanical beast requires a lot of care."

"How long has the power been out on our street?"

"Well, it comes and goes," says Hector. "It was on for a while until about six hours ago. But we still have water pressure, praise be."

Hector closes the hood and pulls out a set of antiquated metal keys before sitting on the plush white leather interior. The combustion engine roars to life with a turn of the ignition. There are few such automobiles still allowed to exist. The vintage age car is exempt from current laws dictating specific engine types.

On the lonely streets, Jim and Emily sit patiently against a sidewalk store where she had collapsed.

"How do you feel?" asks Jim, nursing her with the last few remaining drops of water.

"Better, but my feet still hurt."

"Hey!" a voice shouts from across the street. A group of two men and one woman stop mid stride. They gawk at the two sidewalk-bound pedestrians before dashing across the large empty intersection.

Jim vaults from the ground. Emily tries to get up but manages to get only half to her feet before lowering back down again.

"Yes?" Jim asserts defensively.

"So whada we have here? A father and daughter? Whada sight," a man in his thirties offers slyly. Built like a rock, he towers over everyone. A younger man of about twenty stands to his right. The girl stands in the back, behind the two in an oversized red sweat suit. Big loop earrings suggest her age is midway between her two escorts.

"Where ya from?" the younger male asks.

"Cold Springs," Emily offers.

"Where's dat?" the younger man asks.

"Dats far upstate somewhere," the girl interjects.

"What chu all do'n down here?" The rock built man asks.

"Trying to get home safely," Jim tensely explains. "Please. Can't you see she's hurt?"

"You think we here for sump tin else? Na, it ain't like dat. Why do ya always think it's like dat?"

"I'd be afraid too if ya'll came up in my face," says the girl. "Shit, we musta scared the crap out of ya."

Ray and Hector turn the corner and pull up alongside the group in their vintage automobile. The car rests on the wrong side of the road like an emerald jewel.

"Hey Nate," Ray struts while getting out of the passenger seat. "Ya cause'n trouble again?"

The rock wags.

"Na, not me. I'm just here to help."

"Ya, you got that right. Help me bring the girl into the car."

Like honor students, the two young men respectfully place Emily in the back seat of the wide classic car.

"Nat and Nadine. What a sight," says Ray. "Hey have any of ya seen my little girl."

"She ain't with chu?" asks Nadine with a concerned guise.

"I can't find her anywhere," Ray admits.

"It's crazy out here," Nate offers. "Everyone is sick. They say it's a virus let lose at the North Pole. Santa gots his revenge."

"Where did you hear that?" Jim inquires.

"It was all over da place. Up in the arctic some bug came through da ice, then the wind spread it around or some tin."

"It ain't right," the younger man chimes in. "We have nut'n now."

"My feet hurt," Emily cries, trying to steer the conversation.

"Let's get her to your place." Jim motions.

"What's go'n to happen to all us?" Nate asks.

"Why don't cha go home to ya mama." Ray motions.

"My mama is gone." Nate lowers his eyes sorrowfully. "I just gots my bro and sis with me and that's all."

"I'm sorry. She was a fine woman. Stop by tomorrow and we'll talk," says Ray as he climbs into the front seat of the vintage car. In the back, Jim cradles Emily's head atop his leg. "The three of yas stay out of trouble," says Ray before the car barrels down the street.

"Roll down the windows," Ray signals, squinting distressingly at the malodorous stench coming from the back seat.

"What is that?" asks Hector, sniffing the air like a cat.

"You don't want to know." Ray smiles as the car rolls to a stop at his house. The old man holds open the car door while the two gingerly extract Emily. Perched between them, she is escorted above the ground towards the front door. Her legs dangle inches above the surface.

Hector dutifully opens the ingress and allows them to pass. "I'll come by later," he says before happily leaving.

Ray guides his two guests to the bathroom where a small window illuminates the tiled room. "Please take a shower," Ray insists, staring at Emily with a crinkled nose. "And toss those things away. Kisha's clothes should fit ya," he says before closing the door behind her.

"It's been a long day," Jim affirms sitting in the kitchen with Ray drinking a warm bottle of water.

"If I knew it was that far, I would have told ya. But I never walked it before. Sorry."

"That's okay. The important thing is that we made it here and have a safe place to sleep for the night."

Ray nods while gulping his drink.

Chapter 9: Caesura

Emily cracks the bathroom entrance.

"Where are the clothes?" she yells out, water still beading from her clean hair.

"Just look down in front of the door," Ray yells back from the kitchen.

"Oh, yah, I see them." She swiftly reseals the entryway.

"So ya really planning on going all the way north with her?"

"I must get home," Jim insists.

"Ya know she'll just slow you down. I'm not say'n she's a bad omen or anything, but who knows what ya'll find along the way. In times like these, some men are drawn to her like a mosquito. She can be a magnet to depravity."

"So what are you saying?"

Ray thinks for a moment.
"Ya both can stay here until things get back to normal. Yah, but I know. What is normal when there are millions, maybe billions of people gone."

"You are welcomed to come with us up north instead of staying here all alone, I can use an extra hand."

"I'll wait for my daughter. Besides, I have Alverez and the Johnson kids to keep me company."

"So you're really not coming with us?"

"There is nothing for me where ya go'n. This is my life, my soul belongs here."

"I can imagine that this was a vibrant place filled with life, but not anymore," Jim submits, glancing out from the kitchen window.

"Ya can say that again." Ray grins.

"Today, that long walk from the bridge made me realize that this is big. We barely saw a half dozen people along that whole route and you're telling me you're going to stay here?"

Ray's eyes water.
"The same drive ya have to find your family is how I feel for my daughter. I can't leave. I just can't."

Their attention diverts as Emily stands delicately at the kitchen entryway. Her once dirty hair and odorous fumes have been transformed into stunning beauty. Her clean glowing face beams with life.

The newly acquired wardrobe fits loosely around her supple body. A pink cashmere sweater flows to her knees where a pair of dark brown pants continues downward to her feet. Brown, ankle high boots round out the ensemble. Eyes ignite as she strolls into the kitchen.

"Kisha would be proud," smiles Ray. "You fit in them there clothes just fine, but those boots have to go."

"I like them," Emily beams.

"No. They ain't no good for trek'n up north. I'll fetch ya some sneakers before da-morrow."

"It's getting dark. Do you have any lights?" Jim asks.

Ray pulls open a drawer and plucks a handful of long stemmed candles. He places three in separate holders before setting them ablaze atop the table.

Suddenly, a knock on the door interrupts their lighting ceremony. Ray goes to investigate. Standing in fading daylight at the front door is Hector Alverez carrying a large sealed box that covers most of his chest, right up to his chin.

"That must be heavy," says Ray, taking it promptly from him.

"I brought dinner for everyone."

Ray strolls into the kitchen and deposits the box on the table. With the cardboard flaps opened, delicious aroma saturates the air. Flickering candlelight illuminates the room beyond mere light. A sense of hospitality surrounds the four.

"I used to have my own restaurant," says Hector to the smiling newcomers. "Ray ate there just about every day before I retired. I'm Hector, Hector Alverez." He smiles proudly before vigorously shaking their hands.

"I'm Jim and this is Emily."

"Are you two related?" he politely asks.

"No." Jim smiles. "We found each other while escaping Manhattan."

"Is it that bad down there?" Hector asks with bated breath.

"Yes," says Ray. "It's quiet and nasty at the same time."

"Well," Hector submits. "Just for a little while why don't we forget about everything outside these walls and have a friendly meal together. They'll be enough time for talking later. Here, dig in."

Watering mouths dine on spicy rice, pork and other delectables until stomachs are filled.

"It's been days since I felt satisfied," smiles Jim with deep contentment.

"Me too," adds Emily.

"That was a great meal. Thank you," Ray praises.

"It is such a weird and sudden thing this virus,"

Hector bristles. His eyes turn from a cheerful grin to a cold stern gaze. "More than two thirds of the world population is sick or dying. Do you know what that means? Two thirds? That's billions of people."

"What is this thing that caught everyone off guard? Was it actually buried beneath the arctic?" Jim quires.

"That's what they say," Hector explains. "It was dormant for eons, sitting there waiting to breathe warm air. We set it free with our arrogance."

"How come not everyone is sick?" Ray inquires.

"Ah, that's the mystery," Hector reveals. "Some are immune. We're part of a small group of less than one eighth of a percent unaffected by this virus. Some are carriers while others are in the beginning stages of death."

"So that means we are the potential cure," Emily iterates.

"You would think so," Hector responds.

The four sit silently around clean licked plates and flickering candles.

"With most people gone, what will become of the world?" Emily sighs.

"We will survive," Hector denotes with an upbeat smile. "It won't be easy, but human spirit will always endure."

"How can you be so confident about that?" Jim asks.

"When I lost my Maria those six years ago, I thought it was the end for me. She was my partner and friend. We did everything together, even opened a restaurant. If it wasn't for her I would have been in jail or something worse. After her death I moped around for almost a year. It was hard and took lotsa work but I persevered. And so will human life."

"Thank you. Thank you both for taking care of us." Jim smiles.

"It ain't nothing," says Ray. "If we can't be civil to each other, then all is lost."

"You've seen it here," adds Hector. "In this small little room, humanity persevered."

"We are leaving tomorrow." Jim reveals.

"Leaving?" says Hector with confusion. "Leaving for where?"

"Home. I need to find my wife and kids."

"Like my Mom and brother are waiting for me too," Emily adds.

Hector nods in recognition.
"Of course. I understand devotion. You can take

my car if you want."

"No offense," Ray replies, "but ya might wanna take a more modern car. That mint stallion stalled a few times on the way up the street."

"It's a finicky beast," Hector admits. "It still needs tweaking... but he's right you know. A modern automobile would be more to your liking. I know where you can find one. I'll show it to you in the morning."

"My house ain't big," Ray presents. "Emily can sleep in Kisha's room. I'll take the couch while Jim can have my bed."

"There's no need for that. I'll take the couch," Jim insists.

"No. I want to wait up for Kisha. You take the bed and I'll stay down here."

Jim relents.
"Well goodnight, and thank you for a great meal."

Hector smiles.
"That's the least I can do for weary travelers. I'm just glad I could help."

In the still of the night, a soft cry lingers on the wind. Jim wakes to a sound emanating from inside the house. He strolls to the living room and finds Ray slumped over on the couch. A single candle flickers atop the coffee table.

"Ray," says Jim softly. "What's wrong?"

He looks up with sore eyes.
"Everything. Where is Kisha? My baby girl, where is she?"

Jim kneels before him.
"You'll find her."

Ray holds out his clenched hand to reveal a small black handgun.

"Take it," Ray insists. "Ya might need this to get out of trouble. Hide it somewhere other than ya pocket."

Ray looks up with tearful eyes before placing the cold steel into Jim's outstretched hands. "But you might need this yourself."

"Believe me, it is better if ya take it then having it laying around the house. I might get desperate enough to use it," he gulps. "Promise me that wherever ya are, remember tonights dinner and how it was shared."

"It was a wonderful meal filled with great company and friendship."

"Yes. Remember that feeling wherever ya go. It will be an example of how humanity should behave."

"You're special, you know that Ray."

"Don't get sappy on me again."

"Why don't you come with us?"

"I can't. Who will take care of Hector?" He sighs.
"I'm sorry if my crying woke ya. Get some sleep.
You'll have a long day ahead of ya tomorrow."

Chapter 10: Farewell

Early morning light wakens Ray from his unsettled sleep. He peers through the window blinds onto a desolate street that usually buzzes at this hour.

In the kitchen, Ray musters up three cups of instant coffee warmed over a stack of dwindling candles.

Jim arrives first in the kitchen. His bleary eyes reek of sporadic sleep. Ray hands him a steamy cup.

"Thank you," Jim barely offers after a few sips. "This is coffee? Hot coffee?" his excited eyes declare.

"Yes." says Ray, eager to look beyond this apparent feat of magic.

"How?"

"Never ya mind."

While Jim ponders, Emily strolls in with a restful face. A frilly white nightgown laced with silk hangs over her tall slender body.

"Good morning!" she smiles blissfully, her cheeks rosy. "When I woke up, it took me a while to figure out where I was." Her smile fades. "Then it all came back to me."

"Coffee?" Ray motions.

"Yes, thanks." she beams.

"Ya found the sneakers I see."

"Yes. They fit and look great and have the same pink laces that my old stinky ones had." She smiles.

The three sip their morning meal while listening to utter silence seeping in from the neighborhood.

Just past eight thirty, they dig into a box of dried cornflakes.

"I would offer you some milk," says Ray, "but it's gone bad already." They each take handfuls of dry cereal from the box.

A knock at the front door sends Ray scurrying through the livingroom, leaving Jim and Emily alone.

"It looks like you got some sleep," smiles Jim.

"It wasn't easy," she sighs. "Images rushed into my head after I closed my eyes," she recants. "What calmed me was last night's dinner. Like seeing everyone happy made me content. I was able to fall asleep then."

"You did better than me. I tossed and turned all night. I think I got about a couple of hours of rest at most."

"Do you think we'll make it home today? I mean to my home since it comes before yours?"

"If we get a car, we should make it there in no time."
Emily smiles then takes a sip of her coffee.

"Morning everyone," Hector grins brightly on entering the kitchen. "Breakfast?" He places a small box on the table. It brims with freshly cooked eggs and meaty sausages.

"How did ya manage this?" Ray salivates.

"Didn't you smell the grill? I don't want them going bad. So why not cook them up I said. You can take the leftovers on your trip."

Smiles abound as the sumptuous meal is eagerly consumed. A sizable portion remains.

"You have a long journey ahead of you," Hector smiles. "I'd say there is over seventy miles of road." He calculates while doling out leftovers into plastic zipper bags.

"That's not too bad of a haul," Jim submits. "We should be able to make it there in under two hours."

"I doubt it," Ray wags. "That assumes smooth sailing. Heck, what we've seen should've set ya straight. I'm sure yar have to take the back roads since the highways are clogged."

"I beg to differ. Stick to the highway if possible," Hector argues. "That way you're less likely to attracted unwanted attention like you would on those side streets."

"Just remember, ya can always come back here," Ray offers.

"Yes," Hector asserts. "You're welcomed anytime."

The four sit back with satisfied smiles, but time pushes Hector to the door. "I'll be right back."

Jim sips the remainder of his coffee before rising to his feet. The two travelers gather their bags then head outside.

"I think he found a car for ya," Ray submits.

In the street sits a small blue gem poised for use. Hector exits the driver's seat with an eager grin.

"What do you think?"

"Where did ya find it?" Ray asks.

"I have my sources, but I didn't steal it. It belonged to a friend of mine. He won't be needing it anymore. Hop in," he insists.

Emily turns to Ray and wraps her arms around his thick neck.

"Thank you for everything." A tear rolls down her cheek. "Tell Kisha she has good taste in clothes."

"I will." He sighs before eyeing Jim. "Now ya take care of her. She's count'n on ya."

Her hug slowly breaks as Emily runs towards Hector with the same offer. He accepts with a buoyant smile.

Meanwhile, Ray holds out his hand toward his ex-traveling partner.

"Thank you," says Jim with a tight grip. "I wish I could let you know if I made it there safely. Are the phones working?"

"Na, I checked last night. Everything is dead. Ya just take care. Kindred souls will eventually find themselves together in this life or the next."

Chapter 11: Journey

A small white plastic crucifix dangles just below the rearview mirror. But the most poignant accessory permeates the interior with the artificial scent of sweet flowers.

The dashboard display pops to life. Jim checks the navigation system, it activates instantly.

Emily sits snugly in the passenger seat eyeing the road ahead. They wave goodbye as Jim slowly accelerates the automobile down vacant local streets.

"I plan on heading north and across the Tappan Zee Bridge," Jim explains.

"Why? When my Dad and I came down, we took the Taconic parkway all the way. Besides," she argues, "there could be a lot of traffic on the bridge."

"The bridge is the most efferent way. Besides, the nav system tells us that route is the best. I'm not going to argue with it since I usually come into the city by train."

"There is a better route," she insists. "First we have to get on the Saw Mill Parkway which will eventually go to the Taconic heading north."

They both ponder their predicament, eyeing the wall of traffic coming into view. It stretches beyond their eyes for miles ahead.

"Turn down that street." Emily abruptly motions.

"How do you know?"

"I just feel it."

Jim smiles."Oh really."

"Trust me," she pleads.

Jim obliges by turning onto the sparsely lined venue where few automobiles dare to venture.

"Now what?" he says dismissively.

"Keep going straight but eventually you'll have to make a right."

"Why?"

"That will keep us going north."

Through winding streets and narrow avenues, the car migrates slowly north. A pathway filled with trash emits cautious trepidation.

Bang!

"What was that?" Jim squeals.

"I think something hit the back of the car," she answers in shock.

Jim slows down to take a look, but his sudden change of speed prompts a group of six pedestrians to appear in the rearview mirror.

"Don't stop!" Emily yells.

Jim speeds onward without looking back. "That was close," he sighs. The road widens but Jim grows frustrated. Nearly thirty minutes elapse since the encounter and yet, they have not gotten far. "This can't be right. I keep turning where you tell me but we are not making progress."

"Look at the map," she affirms, pointing at the navigation system. "Every turn is getting us closer to the parkway."

Jim wags with disdain, but continues following her directions. "There." She smiles smugly, pointing to a sign 'Saw Mill River Parkway, 1 mile.'

Jim gulps remorsefully.
"Sorry if I snapped at you back there," he offers. Nearly ninety minutes have elapsed since they had left Ray and Hector. "How did you know we were going to end up here?"

"Like I just felt it." She smiles.

Though traffic persists, Jim dodges between, the stalled cars using the roadway shoulders. "This one looks bad," he comments at the dormant cars ahead. "I'm taking this exit."

Moments later they are back on the parkway. Over

two hours have passed since leaving the
Bronx. They have barely made it out of the city
trying to dodge immobile traffic.

Up ahead a sign reads '287 Tappan Zee
Bridge'. "I'm going to take your suggestion and not
take that route," Jim affirms while speeding past
the sign.

Her delight is quite evident.
"Thank you." She beams with tight dimples. "It
will be a lot better than crossing a bridge."

"Does the radio work?" she asks. Emily activates
the controls, but searching the spectrum reveals
static.

The sun has begun its decline after cresting nearly
an hour ago.

"Do you think we'll make it before dark?" she asks.

"I don't know," says Jim, focusing on the road
ahead. Time melts the miles.

"You're married, right?" Emily asks.

"Yes."

"You don't talk about your wife much."

"That's none of your business."

"I was just trying to start a conversation. Sorry."
She glowers.

They continue for twenty minutes before coming to an exit marked Taconic.

"There." Emily points.

"I see it."

Jim takes the long ramp and merges onto the parkway. The route is mostly clear except for some stalled cars straddling the shoulder.

"We fight sometimes."

"What?" says Emily.

"My wife and I. We sometimes get into terrible fights."

"Is that why you don't want to talk about her much?"

"We are staying together for the kids."

"So you don't love her anymore?"

"I still do," he muses. "She drives me crazy sometimes."

"My parents fight once in a while too, they love each other though. I can see it. They make up after a fight with hugs and kisses."

"I suppose." Jim stares straight ahead, showing mild interest. "Karen always ignores me after a fight," he adds nonchalantly.

"Do you ever try saying you're sorry?"

"You just don't understand." He glares at her. "How could you, you're just a kid."

"That's not fair. I'm fifteen and I know more than you think. Saying you're sorry can be hard to do but it works. I know it does."

Jim stews without a word, directing his attention ahead. The road shows clear, offering no obstructions. He nervously cruises along at nearly sixty five miles per hour, scanning the horizon. "You can go faster if you want," says Emily. "I'm sure we won't get a ticket."

"This is as fast as I want to go," Jim vents.

Moments later, Emily spots an automobile pulling onto the highway from an entrance ramp. "We have company," she announces, eyeing a white van to her right. The industrial model consists of rusted metal and decaying paint. Its fenders show signs of moderate decay. Most modern cars are made of composite materials, yet some later models crafted with metals remain in use.

A small folding ladder is fastened on top of the speeding van. Except for the windshield and front doors, there are no other windows.

The white van plows through the yield sign at the ramp and passes on the right. It pushes ahead, beyond six car lengths before gliding ahead of Jim in the middle lane.

Brake lights instantly illuminate ahead, causing Jim to squeal his tires. A flick of the steering wheel pulls the car into the left lane.

Jim passes the van while attempting to catch a glimpse of the driver. The closed window is tinted, offering no view of the occupant.

"I can't see in!" Emily exclaims as they speed by the static hunk of metal sitting in the middle of a three lane highway. "Go faster!" she ebbs in a frighten tone.

Jim complies by maneuvering around a tight turn with increasing speed. Soon the fleeting van vanishes over a hill.

A second glance through the rearview mirror reveals a rapidly approaching vehicle.
"We're being followed," Jim calmly offers.

"Is it the van?" Emily sighs.

"I think so."

"Well, don't let it catch us!" she exclaims.

"I'm getting off at this exit."

"No, remember what Hector said."

"I have no choice. I cannot out run him."

Jim speeds through the ramp and onto a side street where a clump of stores reside. In the center of the strip mall stands a large grocery store. Jim whips around the corner, speeding to the rear loading docks.

He parks between two derelict tractor trailers stationed about fifty feet apart.

"We should be safe here for a while," Jim predicts. His eyes nervously scan the rearview mirror.

"I hope so." Emily breathes apprehensively.

Tense minutes slip by without sighting the van. "How long should we wait?" Jim asks. His hands tightly grasps the steering wheel.

"At least an hour." She exhales.

"An hour? Why?"

"They can be waiting for us," she insists.

"Alright," Jim smirks. "I'm hungry, how about you?"

"I was until being chased by the van. I guess I'm hungry, too."

"Why don't we take a look around the store? There is bound to be food inside."

"But Hector made us a meal." She pulls the plastic bag from her knapsack. It oozes with condensation, the eggs and sausages are runny. "I guess we can look around." She frowns at the slime filled bag.

"Let's put these things in the trunk in case we find a lot of food," says Jim. After relocating their meager belongings, they spot a closed entrance door into the grocery store.

"It's not locked." Jim glees. Upon opening the door, a pungent odor of rotting food stops their ingress.

"That stinks!" Emily recoils, but Jim presses onward into the darkness. They wade through the stockroom of empty crates and box skids scattered haphazardly on the floor.

A crow bar stands vertically near a small forklift. Jim's foot kicks it, sending it crashing to the ground. A hollow ping echoes through the stockroom.

Ahead of them is another door that leaks faded natural light at the bottom. Jim slowly pushes it open to reveal the main store. Bright outside light blazes through the storefront windows at the far end, blanketing the dark gloomy aisles with natural illumination. However, shadows remain as the light diminishes toward the back.

"It stinks less in here," Jim whispers, straining to read the aisle signs. "I'm looking for peanuts or dried meat."

Jim turns left, peering down each vertical aisle like a ravenous predator. On the floor, discarded food wrappers and empty boxes cast shadows, but some of the flotsam is animated. Mice scurry across the aisles and into darkness causing Jim to momentarily recoil.

"Did you see that?" he whispers, turning toward Emily. But she is not there. Instead, different edibles had catch her attention in another aisle.

A glorious sight captivates Jim. He has found the snack alley. Some items remain, lingering on shelves like orphans waiting for adoption. A few cans of peanuts, some chips and a handful of dried meat products lay waiting. Jim snatches all he can and deposits them into an empty cardboard delivery box.

Down the beverage aisle, drinking water has all but vanished, leaving only a few bottles of unbranded soda. A pair of three liter bottles fill his tiny box, but he hauls it proudly atop his right shoulder like a caterer to a picnic.

On a mission to fill the car with food, Jim navigates through the stockroom to emerge outside from a different rear exit. He freezes at the door, eyeing a white windowless van parked directly in front of his car.

"No," he whispers frightfully. Fearing discovery, Jim slowly reenters the stockroom quivering with anxiety as he lays the box on a counter.

"They must be inside the store," he reasons, peering through the doorway, eager to catch a glimpse of the infiltrators. The shadowy aisles reveal nothing.

He sneaks into the store, clinging to the darkened corners in search of Emily. Using only sight to identify friend from foe, Jim discreetly glances toward the horizon but nothing, not a sound pierces the silent void.

His mind races with vivid thoughts that Emily has already been snatched and taken outside. Or worse yet, they had left with her. Jim frantically locates a stockroom door, eager to find out if the van is still outside.

"Stay away!" Emily yells in the distance.
Jim's ears perk. He runs through the aisles like an Olympic sprinter. Though his strides are bold, he manages to emit only faint sounds.

The large store windows bathe the front in brilliant sunlight, exposing a quartet of grungy men. Each grins deviously at their find.

"Come on now," says one, hunched over like an ape ready to attack. "We won't hurt cha."

Emily stands her ground with a shopping cart poised for the checkout lines. She managed not to get trapped within the lane by only a few short feet.

The men close in, trying to block her escape. One stands at the end of her intended lane while two advance adjacently. The other creeps closer with his hands held out just above his ears.

"Just take it easy Missy," he says condescendingly. The looming man stands about six feet tall with a slender build. A short stubble beard caresses his long bony face. Beneath a denim jacket and jeans is a thirty year old with crazed eyes.

"Don't touch me!" Emily screams, but the group of four continues to encroach. The others are of mixed ages. Two straddling the checkout lines are between late teens and mid-twenties. The lane blocker is much older than all of them. A man in his late forties. He stands as a stocky rock, shaped like an upside down incandescent light bulb. His stomach protrudes beyond his tight blue windbreaker.

His hands firmly grasp the rails between the escape route. Backlit from the blaring sun, his face remains obscured, casting an ominous shadow down the short narrow checkout lane.

Emily swiftly spins the cart towards the denim man but holds on to the handle.

"Whoa, we have a feisty one here boys." He grins insidiously.

"Don't come any closer or I'll hurl this at you."

"I'm so afraid," he mocks.

"What do you want from me?" Emily shouts.

"Only what you can give us," smiles the Denim man. "We have enough food, water and shelter, so what else do you think we need?"

The two young men suddenly lunge at her. The cart barely moves as Emily is taken by surprise. Her legs flail while her upper body is restrained by the two assailants.

"There now. That wasn't so bad," the Denim man chuckles. "Take her back to the van," he commands.

"Why?" says the twenty year old. "We can do it right here."

"She smells nice," says the teen as his mouth suckles her soft pink ear. Emily's legs continue flailing, kicking the air in front of her. The boys manage to keep her from escaping.

"The store stinks," says Denim man. He edges closer, allowing light to show his seasoned face. "Besides, there were two of them in that car. I want to know where the other one went."

"Willy," yells the Denim man into the air. "Did you find him yet?" A fifth raider has yet to answer from the shadows.

"Willy? Where are you? Damn that kid. How hard

can it be?"

Jim quietly steps back, down the aisle hoping not
to be seen or heard. The fifth bully is barely twelve
years old. His dark leather jacket falls below his
knees as he quietly sneaks around corners in
search of Jim.

"Stop calling me Willy," whispers the boy, exposing
his location. The air is thick with anxiety but the
seasoned mind has an advantage over the
boy. Jim clings to the corners while Willy stands
at the mouth of the aisle seeking his prey. He
moves on to the next, unable to differentiate Jim
from a display rack midway down the corridor.

Jim passes him a few lanes down in the dark and
sneaks into the stockroom undetected. Lying near
a forklift, he spots the long metal bar he had
kicked earlier. He grasps it quickly and dashes
outside.

Chapter 12: Miscreants

"Let me go." Despite her strong determination, Emily's legs tire. She buckles under her own weight. The two boys prop her up while their hands become frisky.

"Willy?" yells the Denim man staring towards the back wall.

From out of the last aisle, the boy emerges with a flustered guise. "I can't find him." He sighs with exasperation. "Dad, I looked down every hall."

"You must have missed him," Denim man asserts. He turns toward the boys holding Emily. "Keep your hands off that until later. Take it back to the van and tie it up."

"No!" she screams. "No! Jim help me! Please help me now!"

"Ken, Willy, let's find this bastard."

The three spread out and pace through each aisle with rhythmic precision. Denim man rounds the corner and waits for the others.

"Come on now," he whispers. "Pass me up and go down the next two," he commands before taking the third lane in secession.

"Where are you Jim? We got her," Denim man cries sarcastically. "If you want to see your little girl again, yell now. Otherwise, we're leaving with her."

The boys carrying Emily breach the back door and emerge outside. Her limp body offers little resistance while a bruise grows above her left temple. She is unconscious. Knocked cold by a single blow, the once pristine blouse is torn between her breasts, yet the bra remains intact.

"I'll hold on to her while you get the van ready." The older boy sends the teen away while he rests against the sliding van door. He stands behind the girl, holding her by the waist

"No way. Kirk told us not to touch her yet."

"Yeah, I know." The twenty year old rips away Emily's remaining upper garment. His hands gravitate to push the bra away, exposing two pink mounds of tight young flesh.

"Wow!" says the teen, facing the glorious nymph head on. His eyes are transfixed on the mesmerizing orbs, hanging perfectly like ripe apples dangling from a tree.

Suddenly, the van door rolls open with a clean jerk. The older boy falls inside. Jim raps him once on the head with the steel pipe rending the twenty year old unconscious.

Jim leaps from the van, brandishing the small pistol Ray had given him. He aims it squarely at the teen. His trigger finger flinches, firing off a loud shot. The teen tumbles instantly to the ground.

"What?" Jim whispers dully. His eyes blink before realizing what has just happened. Rather than gawk at the boy lying in a pool of blood, Jim turns and flings Emily over his shoulder expeditiously. One hand pulls open his car door. He throws her into the back seat and seals her in.

With dexterous speed, Jim jumps behind the steering wheel and pops the car into drive, pushing the van ahead a few inches with squealing tires. He escapes the quandary, as Kirk and Willy bolt from the stockroom door.

Jim fires the handgun aimlessly from his window, scattering the miscreants. He speeds off, beyond the lot, toward the parkway. The northbound on ramp is clear as he careens up the freeway.

Frantic sounds emanate from the back seat. Emily punches the door before realizing where she is.

"It's okay Emily. You're safe now," Jim asserts before easing off the throttle.

"Where's my shirt?" she cries coarsely.

"Those two kids took it off before I had a chance to stop them."

"I called for you but you didn't come. I thought you left me!" she spouts venomously.

"I wouldn't do that. It was one against five. So I had to plan this if we were both going to escape. The deception worked. I hid in their van then attacked the two boys when they came close."

"What did they do to me?" She squirms indecisively, covering her bare chest with toothpick like arms.

"They knocked you out then fondled you."

Her eyes water.
"I feel dirty."

"I stopped them before it went too far."

"Suppose they come after us again?" she whimpers, glancing at the rear window.

"Not in that van." He smiles. "While I was waiting inside, I pull all the wires out from under their dashboard. That thing isn't going anywhere."

"Are we driving through the night?" she asks in a daze.

"No. I don't want others seeing our headlights. I'm going to put a good twenty miles between them before finding a place to sleep."

"Did you get any food?" she asks.

"I had a nice box of sodas and dried meats, but when I saw the van, I had to drop it and find you."

She blushes.
"Thank you. You saved me."

"I would not leave you."

"I just wasn't sure. You could have just left and
went home to your family."

"I'm sorry if I snapped at you when you talked
about my wife. I didn't mean anything by it."

She sighs as if all is forgiven.
"I guess those wet eggs and sausage will have to do
for dinner."

"We'll see. Maybe there's a better place up ahead."
Jim stares optimistically through the windshield.

Chapter 13: Espy

The sun hovers near the horizon, signaling Jim to find a place for the night. He steers the car to exit US6, where they pass beneath a powerless traffic light. Heading right on route 6, a static mall sign announces its presence.

Jim follows with keen interest. After a few more derelict traffic control indicators, they emerge into a mostly vacant parking lot. A few cars dot the expansive asphalt which usually accommodates hundreds of automobiles.

"I have a bad feeling about this," says Emily, popping her head between the drivers seat. Her bare shoulders sink below the headrests. "There must be people for those cars."

"Not necessarily. They could be abandoned."

"I want to go now," she declares.

"Alright," Jim capitulates. "Let's drive around a little."

Down a few streets from the mall are smaller outlets. Strip malls and boutiques crowd the landscape, vying for commercial attention, but each show signs of possible inhabitants.

Automobiles dot most of the shops, sending Jim further down the road to appease Emily's apprehension. "How about a house," she says, eyeing a secluded dwelling from the road.

Jim pulls deep into the wooded driveway. It opens into a circular pathway surrounded by an inactive water pedestal.

The house stands majestically, bedecked in stone and dark wood. Large glass windows expose the dormant house as a modern piece of architectural art.

"This might be fine," says Emily staring wearily at the large facade.

"It's getting dark and we can't keep driving all night."

She bites her bottom lip.
"Alright. Like you'll protect me if anything happens, right?"

"Of course."

Jim pulls the car off of the driveway and around back. The wheels sink into the neatly manicured lawn. He pops open his door and steps out beneath the dwindling twilight.

"Are you coming?" he whispers, looking back at her.

"I have no shirt, remember?" she berates.

Jim takes off his coat and hands it to her through the back door.

"Turn away," she demands while grabbing the vestments.

Jim collects his gun and crow bar before advancing beyond the car. At his feet are small octagon wooden decks cascading like stepped lily pads, right up to a set of sliding glass doors atop a steep slope.

Jim traverses them until he is standing at the precipice, staring through the glass doors into the dark abode. Shadows of tables and chairs expose the lair. The door is locked but he refrains from smashing the glass.

His trusty bar becomes the key of choice. The gun rests in his pocket while he grasps both hands around the cold steel claw. The teeth are wedged between the lock facing the door jam.

A few quick tugs send a large snap through the air. Splinters fly as the jam gives way, releasing the door from its moorings.

Jim cautiously enters the void.
"Jackpot," he whispers as the kitchen shines around him. The wood grain refrigerator conceals its identity. He gravitates to the cupboards. Glassware greets his eagerness. He quickly opens other cabinets to behold bottled water and juice boxes.

Emily's silhouette stands in the doorway holding two knapsacks. Her eyes adjust to the darkness.

She finds the kitchen table and plops herself down in a chair with a thump.

"Here," says Jim, depositing two glass plates, forks and water on the table. "You start eating. I'll look around before it gets too dark."

"No," Emily whispers. "We'll do it together. Then we'll eat," she insists.

The living room is sparsely decorated suggesting a minimalistic approach to furniture. Each room is explored exposing sumptuous beds, all devoid of use. Clean sheets and pristine towels speak of a lavish living. It is almost as if they had walked into a five star hotel.

"That's my room!" Emily declares, pointing to a lush king sized bed. She spots a flashlight behind an armoire and snatches it. Dynamic picture frames lay dormant around flanking night tables.

On the dresser is one small paper picture. Two smiling adults are surrounded by two children; a teen boy and younger girl.

"Are you coming?" Jim asks before entering another room. Emily dashes out like a frightened child to grab Jim's hand.

Five bedrooms are explored, each with its own character. It is clearly evident that a young child had once occupied the next room. Pictures of clowns and comic book characters line the walls.

Back in the kitchen, a set of matches and candles are plucked from Jim's backpack, thanks to Hector's foresight. Under the soft glow, they dine on their morning leftovers. "This is so beautiful," says Emily gazing around the spacious kitchen.

She spots the concealed refrigerator. Jim notices her gaze.

"Whatever you do, don't open it."

"Why?"

"Remember the grocery store? There is probably rotting food inside."

"Oh," she nods in recognition. "So, maybe tomorrow we'll get all the way home?"

"That's the plan. Your house comes before mine, but if we don't get there tomorrow, we'll keep trying until we do." Jim smiles dully from across the table.

"I'm afraid," she stresses. "Afraid of what I won't find when I get there." She grimaces. "What then? What will happen to me?" A single tear trickles down her face. "What if I find no one at home?"

Jim gulps but continues eating.

"Like I can stay with you and your family, right?" her voice cracks.

"Of course."

"And if your family is not there either?"

"Then we have each other," Jim laments.

"I miss my Mom, Dad and my pest of a brother."
She grins before her eyes sag. "I wish I could see
their faces and touch their skin."

"You don't know their fate yet. Let's hold off
speculating until we get there."

"But my Dad. There's no way he can make it
home, right? Be honest with me." She sniffles.

"Well, there's always a chance. He can keep
walking north."

"I said be honest with me." Her voice stings.

Jim bows his head.
"There is nothing any of us can do, but I will get
you home. I promise."

After dinner, Jim extinguishes all but one of the
candles. He palms it with respect. Emily ignites
her flashlight as they parade up a flight of
stairs. Five bedrooms leach off of a majestic
hallway, looking down onto the airy first level living
room.

"I wonder if the shower works," says Emily. She
turns the sink faucet in the bathroom to a stream
of flowing water. "You gotta take one too," she
insists gleefully.

"After you," Jim agrees.

Inside her newly adopted room, Emily rummages through the extensive closet while Jim explores his lodging. It obviously belonged to the eldest boy. Models of ancient airplanes hang by fishing wire dangle from the ceiling.

He gazes out the window. Nothing, not even a twinkle of starlight pierces the darkness to differentiate the sky from the ground.

Meanwhile, blouses and pants drape over Emily's thin arms as if on a shopping frenzy, until she spots a sumptuous flannel nightgown. Her eyes beam with excitement before dashing from the room.

The coat that Jim had just given her falls to the floor inside the bathroom. The hand-me-down clothes from Kisha haphazardly fall outside the tub. The flashlight is set with care, blazing from the sink, shining directly through the sliding glass shower doors.

Standing nude inside the stall, she ponders how to turn the on spigot.

"What the hell?" she groans, trying to comprehend the single lever protruding from the wall.

By trial and error, the water begins to flow. A push of another button diverts the fluid through various nozzles around the tub. A litany of warm jets embedded in the stone slab walls inundate her. A satisfying smile beams from Emily's angelic face.

A bar of soap is quickly put to work. It lathers effortlessly, emulsifying her white silky skin. She washes the suds with thin fingers that glide over her soft body. Wet clean hair drapes onto her shoulders like overcooked angel hair pasta.

She begins to hum a tune, but it doesn't last long. It is quickly doused by the intrusion of cold water replacing the hot. Instantly, she turns off the faucet.

After a quick dry from a plush towel, she adorns the one piece pull over nightgown. It's a bit long but she pulls it up with her hands to keep from tripping.

"Jim?" she echoes in the hall. "It's your turn."

He emerges from his room with a candle in hand. "I'm looking forward to a good shower," he smiles.

"Um. Well I think I might have used up most of the hot water. Sorry." She grins.

"That's okay. It'll be a quick shower." He sighs.

"Where are your clean clothes?" She eyes his empty hand. "Oh don't worry, I'll find you something. Just go in and get clean."

"So you're going to pick out my clothes?"

"Just get in there. You stink." She pushes him through the bathroom threshold.

With the candle set near the sink, Jim steps into the moist shower. The protruding lever mocks his intellect, but he persists.

"How do you turn this thing on?" he yells. But before a response finds his ears, the liquid begins to flow.

The tepid water blasts his weary body. He endures the dwindling warmth until only cold fluid pelts his skin. A shiver prompts him to extinguish the spray.

After drying, he peers through the partially opened door. Lying on the floor beyond the door is a stack of neatly folded clothes.

A pair of maroon pajamas lay atop fresh day attire. He snatches the bundle and closes the door promptly. Moments later Jim emerges wearing the loose fitting night wear. Clenched in one hand are the new and old garments. The other carries the melting candle.

"Emily?" he sounds. Jim stands near the master bedroom waiting for her response. An eye peers in, flooding the void with his dim flame. She lays beneath the covers of the massive bed, fast asleep.

The large mattress accentuates her diminutive stature; like a baby lost in a sea of sheets.

"Sweet dreams," he whispers before closing the door gently.

Chapter 14: Rude Awakening

Jim's melting candle nears the end of its life. With less than an inch of wax remaining, the flame sputters, casting eerie shadows on his bedroom walls. Planes tied high above resemble demon puppets held by translucent fishing lines. They dangle in midair with menacing grins.

He is oblivious to the dancing specters. The rhythmic snore rattles the room during the darkest hour of night. He turns over without a care, temporarily silencing his explosive wheezing.

Down the hall, Emily's warm breath does little to heat the cooling room. She instinctively bends into a fetal position beneath the sheets.

Deep thoughts regress from the ordeal in the grocery store. Being subjugated multiplies her fears. Though her innocence has never been breached, images of rape flood her subconscious.

Emily screams out loud but her cry goes unnoticed. She is dragged helplessly into a dark room where a speck of light bleeds warm midday sun from the ceiling. It pools like a spotlight encompassing her entire form in the boundless hallow cavity.

The clothes disintegrate, exposing her delicate figure splayed to the tepid radiance. With wide eyes, she searches the dark void for her captor. There in the corner, a shadowy mass lingers just beyond her perception. It breathes heavily without movement as it watches the newly acquired victim.

"Who are you?" she spews defiantly, but there is only silence. "Answer me!" she screams. Though her body is not physically restrained, she cannot move.

Seemingly helpless, Emily declares her strength. "You let me go or they'll be hell to pay."

Out of the darkness, a male voice laughs mockingly.
"It is my will to do with you as I please!" it roars nefariously.

"Show me your face you coward!" she demands.

The dream dissolves where it had originated, back in the master bedroom. Emily's eyes flutter open to gaze upon Jim. He smiles, sitting at the side of the bed. His sputtering candle illuminates the darkness.

"You had a nightmare," he whispers. "Are you alright?"

"I think so," she gulps.

"Do you remember what it was about?"

Her brow strains.
"I was dragged into a dark place and stripped nude."

"You had it rough yesterday, but you're safe now. Go back to sleep."

She sighs before a smile graces her once somber face.

Jim recedes to the door, carrying his shimmering light with him. It disappears into the hallway, leaving her room utterly dark.

Moments pass before she grabs the flashlight laying face down on the adjacent nightstand. With a click of a button, it washes the room with blearing light.

Emily sits up in bed grasping the torch in both hands while pointing it haphazardly around the room. Thoughts linger, forcing her to shine the light on every possible shadow.

The dream has caused irreparable damage to her nocturnal habits.

"Jim?" she bleats fearfully, but he doesn't answer. "Jim!" she persists.

"Yes," he replies sleepily from the confines of his bed.

"Were you just here?" she asks.

"No why? I've been sleeping since I got out of the shower."

"I'm afraid. Can I come and stay with you?"

Footsteps echo from down the hallway as Jim sprints to the master bedroom. He rounds the corner just in time for his sputtering candle to spit its last flame. Emily's flashlight rescues him from the darkness.

"What's the matter?" he says groggily.

"I had a nightmare. Then I woke up and thought you were sitting on the bed talking to me. So that wasn't you but just a dream too?"

He scratches his head wearily. "You must have been dreaming because I never left my room."

"I had two dreams then. The first was a nightmare. There was a hidden figure that stripped off my clothes."

"It was probably a very scary dream, but it was only a dream."

"Yesterday at the store, was that a dream or did it really happen? Was I attacked?"

"You were detained."

"They took my shirt off and had their way with me, right?" her lips quiver.

"I rescued you before anything could happen," he asserts.

"Just like the second part of my dream. You came into this room and told me everything will be alright." She pouts. "Can you stay here with me?"

"My bed is pretty comfortable," he sighs. "But I suppose I can stay in that chair next to the window."

"The bed is big enough for us both."

"What? No," Jim bemoans. "I can't do that. The idea of me sleeping next to you is not right."

"Why? Wouldn't you do that for your daughter?"

"Yes but... You're..."

"I'm what?" she glares, anticipating a sly remark.

"Never mind. Promise me you'll go to sleep if I stay."

"I promise," she delights.

Jim timidly rolls down the covers and slides in. His body gravitates toward his side of the bed, leaving most of the space for Emily so not to touch her.

Her dimples tighten elatedly before nestling deep inside the covers. "Thank you," she whispers. "I feel safe now."

"Go to sleep."

Emily extinguishes the flashlight laying lengthwise on the nightstand. With the light off, the room blinks into utter darkness.

Chapter 15: Lost Innocence

The sunny morning light exposes the majestic master bedroom, all aglow with antiques and finery, but the most cherished elements remain asleep in the king sized bed.

Emily wakes first, peering across her pillow at the back of Jim's head. His whole body titters on the edge of the mattress with one leg out of the covers. Any slight movement would cause him to tumble onto the hardwood floor.

Emily yawns, then stretches before sitting up. A deep breath awakens her, culminating in a content smile. She glances toward Jim before getting out of bed.

Her new clothes are neatly folded on a nearby table. She snatches them on her way to the bathroom. Inside, Emily dresses then heads to the kitchen.

The bright eatery instills her with courage to open the refrigerator. Inside, the dim interior exposes a perfunctory odor unlike that of the grocery store.

Only slight fumes of decaying organic matter flow from the cooler. Fresh fruits line the bottom crisper. She plucks an apple and begins to eat, staring out the double French doors from which they had entered.

Beyond the sequential decks are dense woods filled

with green pine trees. It will not be long before spring fills the forest with additional foliage.

A loud twig snaps close by. It forces Emily to stop eating and peer deep into the thicket. Her eyes search for any discernible movement. Then suddenly, a bunch of trees sway while others surrounding it remain dormant.

In the center of confusion emerges a triplet of deers. Two fawns follow their mother on a journey for food. They nibble on blades of old grass left from last season. They are oblivious to the enormity of humanity's plunging status. Consequently, they and other wildlife will flourish without impediment.

Emily smiles before returning to her apple.

"Good morning," Jim declares in a gravelly voice upon entering the kitchen. He carries his coat and backpack over his shoulders.

"Morning. I found apples," she declares with a bubbly smile. Her brimming knapsack bares evidence of her find. "They were in the fridge."

"You opened it up?"

"It wasn't too bad in there."

Jim looks for himself. Amidst a litany of decaying foods, he spots bottles of unopened energy drinks hiding against the back wall. In the freezer, perfectly preserved vegetables and nearly frozen fish wait for the taking.

"The clothes look good on you," she boasts.

"They feel good. Thank you for making a fine selection." His head leaves the refrigerator.

Jim's backpack bulges with supplies as the refrigerator is cleared of all edible nourishment. "We should get going," he asserts.

They hop down the constructed lily pads resiliently. In the car, Emily sits in front, pawing through her knapsack.

Down the road, Jim speeds to the parkway on ramp, heading northbound. Miles disintegrate along their path.

Soon, at the precipice of a sharp left turn, an exit sign brandishing the words 'Peekskill Hollow Road' blares before them. They pass it by just before a sweeping incline nearly circular in appearance begins its ascent. The long tight turn forces Jim to slow down.

"You don't drive this route much, do you?" Emily asks.

"As I said, I take the train."

"So you have never been down this way?" she leers.

"Not for a long time."

"Well," she says smugly, "in about five miles we need to exit at 301."

Jim nods while coming out of the hairpin turn. The parkway straightens for a few miles before another sharp angle approaches. This time a flashing warning light powered by the sun suggests forty miles per hour instead of normal highway speeds.

"We're close," Emily declares. "Just after this, take a right."

The small tight turn uncoils before the exit.

The ramp is short and stout. It comes to a stop sign in just a few yards from the speeding parkway.

"Make a right," says Emily, pointing down a paved single lane road.

The scenic route weaves through Fahnewstock State Park offering majestic wilderness views. To the right, a large waterway appears after a steep descent. The southernmost point of Canopus Lake passes alongside Route 301.

Like the Taconic Parkway, this route offers a challenging adventure for a novice driver. "Slow down!" Emily emits as they come to a ninety degree right turn. The road continues snaking through residential areas until an active traffic sign signifies an intersection.

This familiar panel constantly flashes advertisements by means of solar power. Its intended interaction with waiting cars is no longer relevant, but it continues cycling images. Pizzas parade on the display alongside the red stop symbol.

Upon the sole approaching car, the indicator depicts an animated green circle. "Just go straight," says Emily, confident of her navigation abilities. "My home is not far from here."

After a few yards, she interjects, "Turn here." They continue passing small homes, each with multiple cars in their driveways. Yet no life is visible along the thoroughfare.

"There." She smiles with delight after directing Jim onto another road. "That's my house." She points ahead on the right. In the short driveway is a parked automobile.

Jim pulls alongside the mailbox. Before the car comes to a complete stop, Emily bolts. "Hey wait!" he yells to deaf ears. She sprints up the walkway and through the front door, vanishing into the modest sized home.

Jim tucks the handgun between his belly and shirt to ensure that it does not find his pant pocket as Hector instructed. The metal bar rest gently in his hand.

He steps out, staring at the house with a cautious

glare before trekking up the walkway.

At the main door, muted sobs fill the void. In the living room, Emily kneels near the sofa. There on the couch is body of a mature woman face up. Her mouth is wide, frozen in the agony of death.

"Mama?" she cries. "Mama no."

"I'm so sorry." Jim sighs but nothing stops her clamor.

Jim kneels behind Emily, resting his hand gently on her shoulder. "What's your brother's name?"

"Kevin," she manages to emit between tear-filled moans.

"Let's see if we can find him."

Jim gently picks Emily up by her shoulders until she stands on her own. Her moist sore eyes blaze with misery. Her youthful vigor has all but vanished.

In the living room, a windup wall clock chimes, indicating the hour. Jim is startled at first while Emily remains still, transfixed on her mother's corpse.

Jim takes the lead and searches the bottom floor of the two story raised ranch. Emily follows behind with a lackluster gaze.

They ascend the steps and peer into the first of 3

bedrooms at the top level.

"That's mine," she evokes, pointing to her pink and white chamber. Next, the parent's room shows an ordinary unmade bed.

Kevin's room is pristine with no ruffled bedding or stray toys littering the floor. "How old is he?" Jim asks, perplexed at the immaculacy.

"Eight." Her eyes wrench. "I bet he's gone too." Tears copiously cascade down sore cheeks prompting Jim to tightly pull her against his chest. Her arms fold in front of her as Jim bestows a firm and caring hug.

"My family is all gone," she bawls defiantly. "My fears have come true."

Jim repels his own emotions.
"I know how you feel. I must also face that inevitability."

She looks up, resting her moist chin on his stately chest.

"What will happen to us?"

"Nothing if we stay here. We must go."

"Go where?" Her eyes swell.

"To my home."

"You want me to leave my family?" She baulks.

"There is no one left Emily."

"You can go but I'm staying right here."

"To do what?"

"This is my home and I'm not leaving," she asserts.

Emily pushes away his embrace and dashes to her room. Pink pastels and brilliant whites lavishly appoint her chamber. Small stuffed furry animals sit neatly on shelves and night tables. Each epitome of love smiles with overt affection, testing Emily's fragile innocence.

She lays face down on the bed with her head pressed against the pillow.

Jim peers into the teenage room.
"Don't you want to know if my family is alright? I thought we were a team Emily."

Her drenched face tilts towards him, staring into his eyes.
"Don't you understand? This is my house and I just can't leave it all behind."

"So you want me to go without you?"
She turns away, sobbing deep into the pillow.

"How about we bury your mother," he says tenderly. "You stay here until I call for you." Her face remains firmly implanted in the soft pillow.

Jim languishes down the steps. He searches the garage for digging tools. It has been a long time since this space had held a car.

Rakes, shovels and lawn equipment have taken up permanent residence inside the one car garage. However, near the corner on a free standing rack is an assortment of shovels and a pickaxe.

Jim selects the sturdiest looking ladle along with a lone pick. The long handles rest on each shoulder as he scopes out a possible gravesite along the property. The backyard seems a suitable place he muses.

A small fenced area delimits a seasonal garden. Despite being winter, the cultivated soil can be easily excavated. The pickaxe makes the first pass, squaring off the intended site to accommodate a tomb. He dredges around the outline, burrowing nearly a foot deep into the airy soil. His hands blister but he continues while sweat trickles from his brow.

The deeper the pit, the harder it is to dig. After almost two feet down, the soil is frozen like hard cement, impeding further mining.

Jim throws the shovel down in disgust and ponders the trench, hoping that it will be just enough to secure a body.

Inside, Jim winces distressingly, lamenting over the dead woman lying face up on the couch. Her eyes are closed but the face exhibits great pain.

Searching the room, he spots a large blanket draped over a plush chair. He grabs it feverishly and spreads it in front of the couch just below the corpse. Jim inhales deeply, holding his breath while rolling the stiff body onto the blanket. It hits the floor with a slight thud.

"Sorry Madam," he whispers with shallow breath as the wall clock gongs the hour. Jim grabs the comforter and pulls it through the house like a sled. The corpse rides through doorways and down a short flight of steps until it emerges outside into the backyard.

The textile sled is pulled over dingy grass and into the freshly dug pit where it lays face up, depositing cold death upon its dirty fibers. Jim's aching hands grasp the shovel. He bemoans his next task while gazing at the lifelessness before him.

This innocuous piece of flesh once epitomized the essential part a typical family. Instead, it now symbolizes the disintegration of that unity. Both mother and father have vanished, leaving a scared girl alone for the first time without her progenitors.

Endeavoring to look away, Jim scoops the loose soil over the corpse until it is completely covered. A slight mound bulges from the earth signifying the burial site. A nearby twig is pushed into the ground as a makeshift headstone. The marker stands just a foot above the dune.

"Emily?" Jim calls up toward the top floor window. "It is time to pray over your mother."

Footsteps stumble down the second story stairs then skim across the room, until Emily emerges outside. She stands motionless just beyond the doorway.

"It's time," Jim says gingerly.

Emily saunters over with a cold expression. She peers down at the protruding mound. "Is that... Is that her?"

"Yes. Your mother has found a peaceful resting place."

"You put her in the garden?"

"Yes. Is that alright?"

"I suppose so. She loved that garden."

Her knees wobble. Then Emily crumbles down to the soil.

"Mama?" she grieves. "I'm so sorry I wasn't here for you. I lost you."

Jim stands behind Emily with his hands cupped below his waist.

"Pray Emily. Pray that your mother is in a peaceful place. I'm sure she worried about you," he offers relevantly.

Emily rises alongside Jim, bowing her head silently. They stand together, scrutinizing the fresh brown earth.

"Let's go inside," Jim utters.

"No, not yet," she sniffles. Her eyes glaze. "It feels like a part of me has been ripped out. The wound may heal, but the loss can't be repaired. Oh Mama, your memory is my keepsake with which I'll never part. God has you in His keeping and I have you in my heart. In life I loved you dearly. In death I love you still. In my heart you hold a place, no one can ever fill. It breaks my heart to lose you, but you didn't go alone. For part of me went with you, the day God took you home."

She stiffens her resolve.
"I remember that from school."

"It is a lovely poem."

"There's more but I don't remember it. I never thought about such things until now."

"Your mother would be proud of you Emily. She raised a strong confident woman."

Jim grabs the pickaxe and shovel. He props it up outside against the house near the doorway.

In the living room, Jim slumps into a comfortable chair, but Emily walks over to the windup clock. It protrudes from the wall about six inches and emits a constant tick.

Below the large Roman numeral face is a golden pendulum. It swings rhythmically, keeping the time accurate, but it requires extra mechanical energy to maintain momentum.

Emily plucks a small metal key hanging near the clock and inserts it into a groove. After a few turns, the key is placed back on its hook.

She eyes the vacant couch.
"I wonder what her last thoughts were."

"Probably of you and your Dad."

Her chin sinks.
"I suppose you want to leave now."

"I'm tired. Besides, it's getting late and I don't want to arrive home at dusk." Jim sighs. "Maybe we should spend the night here?"

"That would be wonderful." She grins mutedly. "I can sleep in my own bed."

"I thought you would like that. Where would I sleep?"

"I'll fix up my parent's room. For dinner, my Mom kept a lot of can foods in case of an emergency."

"I think this would qualify as an emergency."

"Let's go see." She forces a smiles.

The kitchen exemplifies non contemporary living. The cozy scullery is surrounded by shades of yellow. Thin veiled curtains lay against wallpaper depicting corncobs and wheat.

Yellow and white tile floors support old wooden chairs around a gleaming formica table in this uncommon galley. A modest stove, microwave and refrigerator invoke modern appliances.

Emily smiles proudly while opening the pantry door. The walk-in closet has three sides, all filled with long shelves. Cans and dried packages line the mantles with brimming food.

"There is tuna fish, beans, vegetables, fruits. What do you want?" She beams while examining the plethora of labels.

"Surprise me," Jim submits.

Emily deliberates her choices. Then like an art critic, she pushes cans aside until the intended target is within her grasp. A few more are plucked to the forefront. "Go wash up while I prepare dinner," she asserts. "There is a bathroom near the front door."

He readily complies. The unlit washroom extrudes a mysterious odor forcing Jim to enter intrepidly. He continues inward, allowing his eyes to adjust to the darkness. In the corner, near the toilet by a small stall shower is a static shadowy mass.

The hairs on the back of Jim's neck straighten. "Hello?" Jim whispers while slowly advancing toward the figure.

Suddenly, the image of a small boy materializes in the darkness. Jim recoils in fear, but instead of running, he kneels down to find a lifeless shell slumped near the toilet.

The huddled child had an agonizing death. Dried blood has crusted around his nose and mouth as he sits near the opened toilet seat. His ears are partially decomposing despite being dead for just a couple of days.

Jim winces, knowing that the dead child is not much older than his own flesh and blood. The morbid sight is more startling then seeing the comatose mother, for this could be the fate of his own boy.

Jim's eagerness to keep Emily from knowing this calamity manifests into a frenzied dash. He plucks the body up from the floor like a porcelain doll. The stiff corpse is swiftly transported into the garage where it finds a temporary grave behind paint buckets and trash bags.

Jim scurries back to the gloomy washroom. A turn of the facet sends only trickles of water into the sink. He quickly lathers a bar of soap, just in time before the dribbling water subsides.

Shaken by the ordeal, Jim air dries his hands then

strolls back into the kitchen trying to conceal his distress.

"You'll like what I made," Emily asserts. In the center of the table sits a large serving dish brimming with assorted offerings. She scoops some into awaiting bowls.

"Not bad," says Jim after taking the first sample. Emily smiles while consuming her own concoction.

It is not long before the serving dish empties, leaving not a drop of food.

"Just leave the dishes in the sink, I'll clean them later," Emily offers.

"There is no water left."

"What?"

"I barely had enough to wash my hands in the bathroom."

"Where did you go? I called but you didn't answer."

"Um, I didn't want to use the toilet so I went outside to relieve myself. Then I came back to wash my hands."

Satisfied by the answer, she changes the subject. "When are we leaving tomorrow?"

"After an early breakfast," Jim suggests.

"Then before we go can we try to find my brother?"

"I suppose." He glares while idly twiddling his folk.

"Well it's kinda early but I want to get a good night's sleep. I can't wait to rest in my own bed." Emily sighs.

"Does your bedroom window face the backyard?"

"Yes," she frowns. "I'll try not to stare at the grave. It hurts so much when I think about it. My mom was very special to me."

"Mothers usually are. Mine lives in Iowa, or should I say lived. Who knows after all this if she is still alive."

"Keep a hopeful heart." She smiles. "I expect to find my brother one day."

"And if you don't?"

"As long as I have hope, I will be happy."

Jim nods.
"Hope is a powerful thing."

"Good night Jim."

"Before you go, I need some lighting."

"Oh," she smiles bashfully. "There are candles in the kitchen drawer and some flashlights in the garage."

"I'll go get the flashlights." Jim asserts.

"You don't know where they are."

"I'll find them. Just give me a hint."

Emily grins perplexingly.
"Okay. They're near my Dad's tool rack."

The last word sends Jim sprinting into the garage. He eyes the dim void with great curiosity. His exhaustive search continues for a few minutes. Soon Emily stands in the doorway.

"Did you find them yet?" she asks.

"Almost," he replies nervously.

"What does that mean? Here, let me show you."

The glow of her candle washes the garage with warmth as she enters through the adjoining doorway.

"Wait, I found them." Jim sighs. In a collection of cabinet drawers, a set of long black flashlights are shown by Emily's candle.

"I told you I would find them." He smiles, standing in front of her, protecting the garage like a watchdog. He escorts her out hurriedly.

With the garage sealed, they congregate inside the

living room.

"Here," offers Emily, handing Jim a lighter and a new unused candle set in a holder. "Since the flashlight batteries may be very old."

Jim hands her a flashlight.
"Good night Jim." She smiles before ascending the staircase.

Chapter 16: Morbid Reunion

Beneath a dark overcast sky, night overtakes day. The clock has gonged twice since Emily had gone up stairs. She is fast asleep in her comfortable childhood bed.

Jim sits silently in the dark living room. The plush chair soothes his body, yet his mind races.

The most imminent thought is of the corpse sitting in the garage. Kevin should be buried near his mother, Jim ponders. He laments about keeping Kevin's death from Emily as to not shatter her fragile hopes of finding him.

"I must bury the child," he murmurs.

With steadfast determination, Jim exits through the back door carrying the lit candle. His back pocket corrals the flashlight.

Outside, the glowing flame is set on a patio table as a beacon. The pickaxe and shovel lay ready, standing upright against the house. He advances toward the grave site, lugging the tools in one hand, and the flashlight beaming in the other.

He spots the protruding mound inside the fenced garden and quickly extinguishes the flashlight. At the outer edge of the cultivated soil, Jim digs. Instead of a wide trench, a hole is excavated and stretches to a depth of two feet until he hits frozen soil.

The flashlight sparks to life for only an instant to illuminate the hole.

"It has to be deeper," he sighs, measuring the pit by the shovels handle. The flashlight is extinguished again.

The long night continues as the dwindling candle melts. Jim leans against the shovel wearily to critique his work. Hardly noticeable from the main mound is a small indentation. Beneath the soil sits a buried boy alongside his mother.

Jim gathers his tools and treks towards the dwindling candle. He snatches it from the table and heads inside.

The flickering stub illuminates the downstairs bathroom where the dead boy had been found. It is no longer a place of dread but a simple washroom. He ponders for a moment, gravitating towards the toilet. With eager expectation, Jim opens the ceramic lid of the water tank. It is full with clean liquid.

Instantly he drops his clothes. They scatter haphazardly near the sink. Inside the small shower stall is an abundance of grooming elixirs. Bottled body wash, shampoos and sponges fill every crevice.

A bar of soap rests atop an innocuous cellos pad. He grabs it then reaches from the opened swinging glass door and into the toilet tank. A sponge bath ensues until the dreadful day washes away.

With a refreshing gleam, Jim dries off before dousing the diminutive candle. Leaving his dirty clothes on the bathroom floor, he creeps up the stairs naked. The flashlight blazes before him, leading the way into the master bedroom.

As promised, the sheets have been changed and tightly pulled across the bed. Jim grins pleasantly as he plunges beneath the covers.

Chapter 17: Peregrinators

"Jim? How long are you going to sleep?" Emily blares, standing in the doorway wearing new day clothes.

He opens one eye to the blinding sun blazing spaciously through the windows.

"What time is it?" he sputters, staying low in the bed as not to reveal his bare body.

"Almost ten and your breakfast is waiting."

"When did you get up?"

"About eight, but I slept great. I feel so refreshed."

Jim peers beneath the covers.
"I'm going to need clean clothes."

"I noticed. I went down this morning and saw the mess you left in the bathroom. It took me a while to clean all that up. There was water everywhere. Where did you get it from?"

"The toilet."

"That's disgusting," she baulks.

"No, not from the bowl but the clean water tank."

Her eyes squint perplexingly.
"So you think this is a hotel?" she contends with

folded arms. "This is still my home and should be treated with respect. You left an awful mess."

"You are right of course. I would treat my own home with reverence. Forgive me."

"You're forgiven." she smiles smugly. "Now about those clean clothes. That closet is where my Dad keeps his stuff. I'll be down stairs packing food." The door swings shut.

Emily descends the stairs. In the kitchen, an array of packaged foods lay on every counter top. Breads and dried items are placed inside cloth grocery bags.

Emily pools the tins into a large black duffel bag. She lifts the heavy luggage beyond the front door and into her mother's parked car. The trunk is filled with non-perishable foods. Emily has been at this task for some time.

"Done," she huffs with relief, staring at the loaded car. "You're mine now."

Back in the house, Emily stands in the quiet living room as the clock gongs. Her eyes gravitate to a paper picture resting in a frame on a wall shelf.

She grasps it reverently, gazing at a family portrait. It was taken just last year at an amusement park. Gleaming parents flank the two smiling siblings with a backdrop of the world's tallest roller coaster, or so the overhead park sign proclaims.

"Hey guys," she whispers while stroking her right index finger across the entire photograph. A budding smile quickly turns to gloom.

She clutches the frame against her chest, trying to hold back tears. Her eyes widen in a zombie like state while moving slowly to the backyard door. Like a magnet drawing metal, she is pulled outside with an inscrutable gaze.

Her march terminates at the garden gate where she awakes from the stupor. Emily peers down at the fresh knoll.

"Mama," she whispers on the verge of crying. "Are Dad and Kevin with you or should I keep looking for them?"

A stray breeze spreads a pile of dead leaves over the gravesite. Undeterred, Emily remains transfixed. "Should I stay with Jim or go my own way?"

Be it spiritual intervention or a gut reaction, words form in her mind. "Go with him," she hums as if the words came from somewhere else.

Emily nods.
"Thank you Mama. I kinda like him."

"Emily!" Jim bellows from the backdoor. "Let me know when you are ready."

"I'll be there shortly." She turns.

"Take your time."

"Well Mama, this is it. I'm leaving soon. Please watch over me like you did when you were alive. Like I may not have always agreed with you but I know you tried to keep me safe. I will always love you." She blows a kiss toward the mound.

Her shoulders quiver while surveying her yard for the last time. "Bye Mama." She frowns before entering the house.

"Is everything alright?" Jim asks.

"Yes," she offers somberly in the kitchen.

"What's that in your hand?"

"My family."

"Can I see?"

Emily surrenders the frame.
"You have a wonderful family."

"Not anymore," she sighs mournfully.

"They'll always be your family. Nothing will change that. Keep remembering all the good times you had with them, for they are your strength."

"I packed the car with clothes and food. We're taking my Mom's car."

"Oh, okay."

"Like as soon as you're done eating we can go."

"Thank you for preparing breakfast." He smiles, handing back the picture.

"It ain't much. Just some canned fruits and junk."

"I like them. Thank you."

"Jim," she says dolefully. "Will your family accept me?"

"I know you must be feeling lonely right now, but I can assure you, whoever is left in my house will welcome you as I have."

She nods with a passive smile.
"I'll be outside."

"I won't be long."

"Remember to wash your plate and clean up," she insists before strolling past the living room and out the front door.

Jim eyes his last fork of sweet oranges floating in heavy syrup. He smiles when eating the last morsel.

The empty waterless sink makes for ingenious adaptation. Jim finds a towel and wipes his utensils clean. He snatches his backpack lying by the kitchen door and heads into the driveway.

"Ready?" he asks rhetorically while jumping into the driver's seat. She nods mutely.

They maneuver onto the main route, heading northbound. The road snakes through the countryside. Their path is devoid of derelict cars. Yet there is considerable debris littering the venue.

Tree branches and man made garbage rumble beneath the speeding wheels, but they persist northward. Desolate intersections materialize after long stretches of nothingness.

"Just about ten more miles," Jim spontaneously declares. Emily stares out her window with disinterest, watching houses and trees blur by.

A moment of reflection casts her eyes at the picture still clutched in her hand. The somber gaze quickly blossoms to a smile.

The debris filled road is tingled with leaves and fallen branches, but one obstruction quickly materializes across the byway.

Jim jams on the brakes, sending the tires screeching for a few hundred feet. The car comes to an abrupt stop inches from a large tree lying across their path.

The two sit awestruck, staring beyond the windshield from the motionless car.

"That was close," Jim admits. "I almost didn't see

it in time."

"You were going too fast," Emily snaps.
Jim gets out and walks to a large tree trunk
straddling the road.

"It looks like it has been chopped down by either a
large beaver or a hand axe. No wait. I see human
boot prints. It was deliberately brought down,"
says Jim while pointing to fresh muddy foot
tracks.

Emily leans against the car fender gazing at the
thick trunk. It blocks their path with stark
determination. "There is no way we're going to get
across this," she utters. Her eyes widen with
awareness. "We're being watched."

Jim scans the dormant woods, laden with layers of
dead fall foliage. A couple of homes sprout in the
distance like intrusive weeds. A momentary glint
reflects off the distant window.

Then sounds of barking dogs emanate from one
house. A fury of activity sends voices through the
air, shattering the encompassing silence.

"We have to get out of here!" Jim exclaims. The
two scurry back inside the car. Jim throws it in
reverse, making a u-turn just in time to spot a
group of rifle toting men running from the house
toward him, but they are left in the dust.

"It's the long way around but we can get back on
the highway again," Emily emits.

"Agreed," he endorses. "I remember what Hector had told us about staying off the side streets so not to attract attention."

"Like he was right." Emily grins.

They navigate back, passing close to Emily's house before emerging on to route 301. After retracing their path through six miles of hilly terrain, they meet the parkway and head north up the Taconic.

"It's a good twenty miles from here." Jim contemplates. "We'll get off at route 55 then head west. If all goes well, it should take less than an hour."

Clouds have overtaken the brilliant sun, casting the surface into lonely gray. The sky darkens farther until an errant snowflake hits the windshield. A few more cascade down, dotting the view.

"Like is that snow?" Emily squints.

"I think so," he groans before turning on the wipers.

The precipitation has increased from a minor nuisance to a full two inches of fresh powder, but there are no plows or speeding cars to help whisk away the accumulation. The drive becomes hazardous. The momentum has slowed from sixty five miles per hour to a mere thirty as Jim continues with silent determination.

They trek north until coming upon their exit. "Almost there," Jim sighs, gripping the steering wheel with fervor, gliding around the ramp. His knuckles clench with stress before turning onto the route. "About three more miles."

"It's after three o'clock already," Emily notes. "It'll be dark soon."

"We'll make it," Jim insists. His eyes bulge with anxiety, focusing beyond the windshield at the treacherous tree lined artery.

Nearly eight inches of fresh powder blanket the street, making it hard to discern features. Only tall road signs delimit the pathway along the route. Dwellings line most of the street but they are set back from the main thoroughfare.

Jim reduces his speed to a crawl. They roll down the byway at just under ten miles per hour, while snow pushes against the tires.

"How much further?" Emily bites her upper lip, fearing imminent disaster. "Why don't we just get out and walk?"

"Through this?"

"It's better than sliding off the road. It can't be much further, right?"

Jim ignores her comment and continues pushing onward until the car slows on its own. The wheels spin on the tempest. The snow is so deep that it slides up and over the hood.

Jim puts the car in reverse, but it does little to extricate them from mounting pressure.

"We are wedged in and there is nothing else I can do. We'll have to leave everything," Jim assets. "We can come back later when the snow clears."

"I'm not leaving my bag behind," she contends, clutching her knapsack. Jim agrees and grabs his from the back seat. He pushes open his door, but the snow fights back. It takes considerable force to clear the exit. Emily does the same as the snow continues to fall.

Jim forges ahead through three foot drifts. His legs barely breach the powdery boundary. His trek is nothing compared to Emily's struggle. Her short legs force her to lag behind. With the bag slung around her neck, she languishes in the drifts.

"Wait!" She yells only a few hundred feet from the car. "I can't do this."

Jim has a considerable lead, but he backtracks along the same deep footprints to meet up with her.

"What's wrong?" he asks from just a few steps away in the buffeting snow.

"It's too deep for me. How much further?"

Jim looks up and realizes his home is farther down the road than anticipated.

"Alright," he sighs. "We can bunk in one of these homes instead."

Together, they walk up snow covered steps to a modest looking home parallel to the street. The front door is locked, but Jim is not deterred. A swift kick from his shoe sends the door flying inward.

Fresh wood splinters lay inside on a dark red carpet.
"Hello!" he bellows while pulling Emily with him.

Chapter 18: Calm Before The Storm

The cold still air appears as eupneic vapors lingering like disembodied spirits. To the left is a small living room with cluttered furniture. Jim folds Emily onto a paisley colored couch. "Stay here!" he demands. "I'll check things out." She nods with shivering exhaustion.

The single story home boasts no wasted space. Every nook and cranny is filled with clutter. Old books and outdated paper magazines are stuffed haphazardly on shelves and nearly every horizontal surface.

The exhaustive search reveals no semblance of human life, dead or alive. Jim makes his way back through the kitchen, but he stops at the back door. It opens onto a small enclosed porch with stacks of firewood neatly arranged.

"Emily. Wake up." He signals while entering the living room with an armful of firewood.

"I'm awake," she replies groggily as if she had just dozed off, but her eyes quickly close again. She lays motionless on the couch.

Jim kneels by the living room fireplace allowing Emily to snore.

Inside the hearth is a steel grate designed to hold logs in place.

Jim claims some of the papers piled around the house and spreads a few sheets loosely inside the hearth.

Small sticks of wood lay atop the paper, followed by larger logs. He searches frantically around the mantel until a set of long matches manifest from behind an old oil lamp.

They spark to life, igniting the paper. Soon the wood catches, sending flames shooting up the open flue.

Later, Emily wakens to the fiery warmth glistening from the fireplace. Its brilliant glow shines radiantly on every nearby surface. Luminosity fades not far from the hearth as she absorbs the surroundings.

Jim is slumped over the opposite end of the couch, snoring in deep slumber, but his senses are quickly stirred. "How do you feel?" he asks when seeing Emily stir beneath a heavy comforter.

"Better. Where are we?" she asks, glancing down at her protruding bare feet.

"I removed your socks and sneakers since they were wet. They're warming next to the fire."

"Oh," she replies timidly, accepting his word.

"We are about two miles from my house. It looks like we're going to spend the night here."

"Are we alone? I mean did you find anyone?"

"I think an old lady used to live here. She would be out in the yard gardening when I would pass by. The hospital probably has her now."

"I'm sorry about not making it all the way to your home."

"It's not your fault. I doubt that I could have lasted much longer out there myself."

Emily rummages through her knapsack to retrieve a morsel of food. A clear zip lock bag of raisins dangle from her fingertips. "Want some?" she asks daintily.

"That's okay. I already ate some of my rations while you were sleeping."

"How are the bedrooms?"

"It's too cold to sleep away from the fire. You can have the couch. I'll use that chair," he motions. "Besides, I have to keep the fire going all night."

"You know how to do that? I mean tend a fire?" She squints while eating her dinner.

"Of course I do. I have one of my own."

"I'm sorry, I didn't mean anything. It's just that you seem out of place when it comes to manual labor."

He grins.
"You might not believe me but I grew up on a farm in Iowa. Every day I had chores."

"Tell me some of them," she gushes, anticipating a good story.

"Have you ever cleaned mud traps? It's a nasty job."

"I had to clean out the garage once." She grins playfully.

Jim stares into the buoyant flames dancing in the fireplace.

"There is always so much work to do around a large farm," he reminisces. "I kept working there until I was in high school. By then, the land couldn't support life. Dad had to relinquish the reins since it was almost impossible to make things grow. In the end it was better for him since I was heading off to college."

"Do you have any siblings?"

"I had two younger brothers." His eyes sag.

"I don't think this is going to be a good story," she advises. "You don't have to tell me anymore if you don't want to."

"Well, needless to say, by the time I entered college, I was the only child left."

"I'm sorry to hear that," she glowers. Her thoughts wander. "Do you think I will ever find my brother?"

Jim pulls his gaze from the fireplace and stares deeply at Emily.

"It's very unlikely."

"I think so too but I don't want to accept it. If I do, then all hope is lost."

"You are a part of my family now."

"I know." She smiles. "I appreciate that."

With the bag of raisins almost depleted, Emily places the leftovers back inside her knapsack. "How bad is the snow?"

"An hour ago it was beyond three feet. I could barely find our car."

"There is nothing we can do now except relax and wait for daylight?"

"I suppose." Jim sighs. "Tomorrow I will return home."

"Of course we will," she affirms.

"I can go on my own to make sure it's safe."

"What? You want to leave me here?"

"Just for a while. I will come back once I know what is waiting for..."

"You're not leaving me. We're going to do this together," she presses.

"Alright," Jim nods. "but we'll have to find a better way to get through the snow. Maybe a sled?"

"Then that's what we'll do," she asserts, settling back into the covers with a defiant shrug. Jim wraps her feet with fatherly care.

A tall plush reclining chair stands next to the fire. Jim adjusts it somewhat before nestling in. The footrest mechanically opens to offer a passable bed.

"You'll be cold without a blanket," says Emily.

"I'll be fine," he dismisses.

Chapter 19: Proximal Excitement

A bright sunny day beams through the thinly veiled windows, prompting Emily to wake. She peers into the fireplace where new logs crackle with seductive warmth.

"Jim?" she whispers to his vacant chair. "Where are you?" Her voice strengthens and spills from the room, but the air is silent beyond her plea. She gets up and spies through the front window with budding discontent. "You better have not left without me," she seethes.

Suddenly, heavy footsteps pound the stairs until a door flies open. Jim emerges from the basement carrying wood planking.

"Did you miss me?" He smiles buoyantly.

"Where were you?"

"I found a pair of snowshoes," he presents. "Then I made another set out of boards."

"Like I thought you left me," she pouts.

His eagerness quickly fades.
"Left you? I made a promise."

"I lost everyone I had ever known," she sighs. "Like I can't bear the thought of being left all alone. When I didn't hear your voice, it scared me."

"Rest assured that my promise was genuine."

"When do we leave?" she bounces back.

"I left some food for you in the kitchen. When you're done, just come outside. I'll be testing the snowshoes." Jim pulls open the front door while Emily recedes into the kitchen.

A wall of snow nearly four feet tall blankets the landscape like a majestic river. Their abandoned car is just a small abutment above the level flow. The glaring sun reflects off the freshly formed powder, causing a blinding glare.

Jim kneels at the stoop to adorn the newly fashioned wooden planks. Loops of string pierce through the boards to form laces, which he eagerly ties around his current shoes.

He steps tentatively beyond the doorway and into the snow with his right foot first, sinking only an inch through the tundra. With guarded optimism, Jim walks into the street and peers back at the house. Water drips from the eaves while a warm breeze flows around him.

"It's above freezing," he sighs before returning inside.

After stowing the shoes on the steps, he enters the kitchen.

"How is it out there?"

"Very warm. I'd say the snow has no fighting chance in this fifty degree weather."

"Did you find my car?"

"It's buried beneath heavy snow. We'll have to come back for that later."

"Like I have clothes in there," she insists.

"Those doors are not going to open with all that snow around."

"My clothes are in the trunk," she persists.

"Do you really want to walk two miles with large bags?"

"I'm not leaving without my clothes."

"Alright," Jim signs in disgust. "I'll see if I can get the trunk opened. You just get ready and wait for me at the front door."

Emily continues eating while Jim disappears beyond the living room. Her eyes gravitate toward the cereal box sitting on the table. A carton of soy milk lay open as she pours another serving into the bowl.

"12 essential vitamins" blare across the top of the cardboard box. She stares at the words intensely until the statement blurs. The room brightens and voices of her family clamor around her homebound breakfast table.

"Honey, pass me the cereal," her mother asks. "Honey? Emily, pass me the cereal."

"Sorry Mama, I was daydreaming."

"You mean morning dreaming," her brother playfully interrupts.

"Is there anything wrong?" her mother asks.

"I love you. I love you all," she wheezes.

"We love you too," her father injects, looking up from his pliable digital paper. "What's wrong Emily?" he notices her placid face.

"I wish I can tell you for real."

"Tells us what? We are all right here," her father presses.

"No you're not. You're just in my head."

"If you can hear and see us then we're more than just a figment of your imagination," her mother explains.

"I've seen you Mama, you're dead."

"Our personalities will always be a part of you. Tell us how you feel dear."

Emily laments, knowing that her mind is conjuring them.

"I miss being here with you guys for breakfast on a busy weekday. I didn't understand it then, but I do now. Those mornings were a piece of heaven before the four of us were sent out into the world. Mama, you were always so strong."

"Just like you," she smiles.

"Dad, you were so smart about things."

"Just like you," he reciprocates.

"Kevin, your eyes are filled with wonder about everything." Emily gleams.

The words on the cereal box refocus, drawing her consciousness back into the cool kitchen. She looks around bewildered at the lonely room where reality has taken hold.

The empty bowl is carried to the sink and cleaned under trickling water. The cereal and milk are stowed in a cupboard while the table is wiped down.

"Thank you for the use of your home," she utters before putting on her coat. With the knapsack slung over her shoulder, she heads outside into the blinding sun.

Jim looks up from the car where he has opened the trunk.

"Hey, do you need everything in here?"

"Like just the two blue bags for now," she yells.

Jim fetches them and seals the trunk. Riding high above the snow, he places the bundles near Emily's feet.

"Put these on," he explains, handing her the prefabricated snowshoes. They strap tightly around her sneakers.

"Let's go." Jim smiles, clutching one blue bag along with his personal backpack. Emily does the same as Jim leads the way down the left side of the snowy sidewalk.

The air is crisp and clean under blue sun drenched skies. The sounds of human endeavors have vanished while songbirds vibrantly fill the void. They fly from street poles in flocks, anticipating the two travelers trek.

A mile into the journey, the houses increase in size. Quaint cottages give way to oversized new homes that sprawl their boundaries. Each estate has large attached garages exemplifying heightened stature.

Jim pulls ahead with each step, eagerly scanning the horizon for his abode.

"I see it!" He squints down the long street with only a half mile to go. His eyes water with anticipation. He begins to sprint leaving Emily behind, burdened by her knapsack and large blue duffel.

Jim scampers up his driveway then veers off toward the front door. It is bedecked in elegant frosted glass and gold trim. Surprisingly, the door is already unlocked. It swings inward without touching the handle.

Chapter 20: Realization

"Hello? Daddy's home!" he expounds, scanning tenuously for life. "Tommy? Alisha?" he continues to inquire.

The constant ping of snow dripping into the rain gutters outside is the only sound that pierces the silence.

Jim enters the airy living room. Modern gadgets blend seamlessly into the decor. A plush couch is aimed at what appears to be a blank wall. The large screen is applied like wall paper over sheetrock.

In the corner is a brick fireplace enclosed by folding glass doors. Old ash collects beneath a cast iron log holder.

Jim anxiously climbs the stair rungs to the second level.

"Hello!" he yells, peering into his shared bedroom. The king sized bed has not been used. The sheets are tight.

His daughter's pink room is also clean and devoid of life, yet a strange odor lingers as he approaches his son's room.

A mound is nestled beneath the sheets. Jim approaches cautiously.

"Tommy?"

The boy's nose barely breaches the snug covers. Jim slowly pulls them back to reveal his dead son. The skin is cold and clammy, exhibiting a pale white completion, but a peaceful smile brims from the dead face.

"No! Please no!" Jim whimpers with agonizing grief. "Tommy. I'm so sorry," he cries while stumbling out of the room and down the stairs gagging.

He enters the dining room where a tall wooden table majestically rises to chest level. Eight lofty chairs surround the rectangle, all crafted from natural wood.

He passes through a large door and into an island kitchen. The expansive area holds four low chairs around a traditional white formica table. Unlike the dining room, this set had seen a lot of use.

Sitting atop its gleaming surface is a loaf of wrapped bread, sealed by a twist tie. An empty peanut butter jar stands alongside. The lid is removed to accommodate a protruding knife extending from its rim.

"Alisha's favorite snack," he whispers remorsefully. A red light blinks on a nearby wall. Jim approaches, then touches the flashing square.

His daughter's distressed face fills the vertical surface.

"Mom, Dad I hope one of you gets this message" she laments tearfully in the video. The sun has just risen in the prerecorded message, casting a streak of fresh rays across her drawn face. Below her neck dangles a unique medallion supported by a tiny gold chain.

The heart shaped silver locket is inlaid with gold vines surrounding a golden cross. Inside the talisman is a cherished picture of her family, given to her at the age of ten.

"Tommy is sick," Alisha exclaims towards the camera. "I don't know what do to. I tried the Wilson's next door but no one answered. I think everyone is getting sick."

She gulps, palming the pendant between her tiny fingers. It springs open to reveal her strength. On the back, her name is inscribed accompanying a birth date.

She stares at the image with watery eyes. "I'm okay, so far. Daddy where are you?"

The message was recorded over seven days ago as depicted by the date stamp on the bottom of the image. The current battery indicator shows only about five percent of energy remaining. Alisha stops the recording. Two days later it resumes.

Her face is drawn with a somber gaze as if she has not slept. The afternoon sun barely penetrates the room casting shadows on her young delicate face.

On the table in the background sits the loaf of bread and peanut butter jar.

"I'm all alone now," she offers frigidly, sitting at the table. Behind that calm exterior, a raging torrent of emotion builds inside her. "Tommy is dead and I don't know what's going to happen to me."

She crumbles on the table with elbows spread apart, covering her face in utter distress. Jim touches the wall with his fingers, attempting to console her.

Alisha cries deeply. She wails for a minute until an external sound grabs her attention.

"I hear something," she whispers. "Someone is outside."

Suddenly a loud bang reverberates inside the living room. A group of military clad figures rush into the kitchen brandishing rifles. Each is laden with heavy backpacks and paraphernalia dangling from their bodies.

All of their skin is covered in flexible black clothing. Even their faces are shielded by night vision equipment and breathing respirators.

"She's just a kid!" yells one of the clad men.

"Take her," another commands.

Numb with fear, Alisha shrieks.
"Leave me alone!"

She is led beyond the kitchen camera. The fury that had invaded tranquility quickly subsides filling the vacuum with eerily stillness. Sensing no activity, the camera turns itself off.

"Jim, that's horrible," Emily whispers behind him from the kitchen doorway.

"They took her," he replies, slumping into the chair.

Rage, fear, anxiety, joy and disgust race instantly across his mind in a vicious blur.

"She's alive," he mutters. "But they can be anywhere by now."

Emily sits next to him.
"I bet they took my brother too."

"Your brother is dead," he bluntly exposes to quell his own emotions.

"What? You don't know that for sure."

"Yes I do. I buried him next to your mother late that night. That's why I couldn't wake up early the next day."

"You're lying!" her nostrils flare.

"I found his body in the bathroom before moving it to the garage."

Her incredulous gaze turns stormy.
"Like how could you! Why didn't you tell me?!"

"It was not a pretty sight. You should remember him as he was, not what he became."

"Like I can't believe this! So that's it? Everyone in my family is really gone?"

Both stew silently in their sorrow, sitting in the bright sunny kitchen of Jim's home. Suddenly, an external sound jolts them to attention. Outside, a snowplow rumbles down the road.

The two rush toward the living room windows. Out in the street a truck streaks by, violently pushing the snow aside.

"It's military," Jim whispers at the passing dull green behemoth.

"Maybe we can follow them in our own car." she injects.

"They probably hit it on their way down."

"How could you know that?"

"I'm just saying it is possible."

"We would have heard something."

Jim nods.
"You're right. I'm just guessing. I'll be back down in a few minutes. I have something to do upstairs

first."

"Do you want me to come with you?"

"No, I'll be fine. Just wait here."

"I'm sorry about blowing up at you about Kevin," she laments.

"I should have told you sooner but I wanted to spare you the unpleasantness."

"I know." She grins.

"I'll be right back," says Jim, dashing toward the bedroom with an eager stride. He gathers clothes from his room into a large rolling suitcase along with other personal items.

In Alisha's room, Jim plucks a paper picture of his daughter from a wall bound frame and stuffs it into his pant pocket. "I'll find you," he breathes tearfully. "No matter what, I'll find you if it takes me a lifetime."

The air tingles as he enters Tommy's room. "My poor little man. I'll never see you grow up."

He grabs a blanket and drapes it over the entire bed, covering Tommy's head.

"Sleep in peace my son." Jim limps toward the foyer carrying his large suitcase. "I'm ready," he sighs. "Let's see if the car is still in one piece."

The warm outside air has reduced some of the snow, but only the plowed area is suitable for walking without snowshoes. The two hop inside the freshly dug pathway, lugging their belongings the way they had come.

With each step, they scan the horizon for their street bound car.

"I see the roof," says Emily as they advance. The snow has melted, exposing the shiny extrusions. Roof, hood, and trunk gleam under the midday sun.

The plow has maneuvered around the car, allowing it to remain intact. Upon reaching the vehicle, they push away the remaining snow to open the doors. Their suitcase and bags are flung into the back seat as the two stand poised on opposite sides of the car.

The newly etched artery stretches like a ribbon in both directions, exposing wet blacktop in some spots. "This is it Emily," says Jim stoically standing by the driver's door. "We can either stay here or go into the unknown." He peers over the roof toward her.

She stares into the distance and in the direction where the snowplow had gone. "Our futures are down that way. I don't want to live in the past anymore."

"Agreed." Jim smiles before entering the car. He pushes through a snowy rift just as the tires grab the plowed pavement.

Keeping the car at a slow but steady pace, Jim glances over at this house as they pass by. "Into the unknown," he whispers with a sense of intrepidness.

Chapter 21: Pursuance

They pass freshly cleared intersections.
"This road leads into the heart of the city," Jim
directs.

A half mile along the road, large objects block a
cross street. Jim slows.

"Like, what are they?" Emily squints beyond the
windshield.

"Military," Jim blares.

Another nearby intersection becomes a hive of
activity. A lumbering tank rolls by with an
armored personnel carrier, passing two hundred
feet ahead.

"Do you think they saw us?" Emily trembles.

"I hope they did. That way I can find out what
happened to Alisha."

"Are you sure you want to do this?" Her voice
cracks.

"Didn't you agree not to live in the past?"

"I know." She nods subserviently.

"We can turn back if you want..."

"No, let's go forward," she insists, but her body

language says otherwise.

"Are you sure?"

"Yes," she snaps virulently.

Jim makes a sharp right and follows the matte green troop carrier. He slows the car to a crawl, matching the convoy speed. Suddenly the truck stops a few yards ahead. The back door swings open, instantly pouring six armored personnel out into the street.

They surround the car with long menacing guns. Two guards gravitate towards the back, aiming their weapons at the trunk.

The tank leading the way stops and moves to the side. Its massive turret quickly rotates around, pointing directly at the car. No insignia identifies their ranks. Only a small American flag is embedded on their upper arm sleeves.

"Get out!" yells one guardsman. It is hard to tell who gave the order since each is covered head to toe. They are reminiscent of those who had captured Alisha, offering physical uniformity to disguise individuality.

Jim and Emily comply by raising their hands high. "I'm looking for my little girl Alisha. Have you seen her? She lived a few houses down," Jim explains while standing outside the car.

The leader steps beyond his troops, prompting gun

barrels to lower. He walks up to Jim, staring though large camera mounted eyes. "You do not seem sick," the leader declares.

"We're fine," Emily expounds fearfully.

"We are not sick," Jim affirms. "I just want to find my daughter."

"I had a daughter too," the leader reveals, adding depth to the featureless soldier. His truculent appearance seems less intimidating.

"Have you seen Alisha?" Jim inquires further.

"Yes," the leader admits.

Jim's eyes swell with tearful joy.
"Oh please let her be safe."

The two soldiers standing behind the car inch closer. They peer inside to examine the interior.

"Open the trunk," one orders. Jim obeys under the leader's watchful eye.

"Is Alisha alright?" Jim asks.

"You can put your hands down." the leader gestures. "FEMA has her now."

"What?"

"The Federal Emergency Management Agency has your daughter now."

"Why did they take her?"

"I am not at liberty to discuss that."

"They're clean," says one of the solders after exploring their automobile. Another soldier pops up from the ground after inspecting the undercarriage. "All clear." He nods before accompanying his comrade stationed behind the car.

"Follow us if you want to see her," the leader instructs. The soldiers break position and reenter the truck swiftly. The three caravan procession is on the move.

The tank's turret remains pointed at the car as it rumbles askew. One cleat mashes the packed snow while the other pounds the cleared blacktop.

"You trust them?" Emily asks while eyeing the clanking tank.

"I have no choice if I want to see Alisha."

"They could be lying. Like maybe no one is in control anymore."

Jim offers no rebuttal despite her resonance of truth. Every aspect of their journey suggests social infrastructure has crumbled. Leaving only a few to fend for themselves.

Jim weighs his options. If these are rogue soldiers

he reasons, then one must hope that a shred of decency remains within them. Otherwise, we are walking into savagery.

"Stand near me when we get out of the car," he instructs.

"What good would that do?"

"In case they have other plans for us. I'm not going to give you up without a fight."

"Hello! Like they have guns and we have nothing. If you feel that way, why not just leave now. We can outrun them." But her words fade as they enter a canon of cement. Tall buildings rise from the natural landscape.

Derelict cars line the streets, yet a clear path has been forged down the center where the convoy leads. Hastily erected cement barriers topped with razor wire are manned by gun toting guards. Their heads turn and scrutinize the civilian car. A column of trucks rolls behind them blocking any perceived escape.

After a mile, the lead tank stops in front of a lofty stone and glass building. A few parked military vehicles litter the street.

The troop transport springs to life as the leader bolts from the back door. He approaches the car. Jim gets out immediately. Emily gravitates toward him and grasps his hand tightly.

"Come with me," the leader instructs. Jim and Emily take their most essential backpacks and follow the group inside.

The bevy of five weaves through the main lobby which has become a storage area. Large crates block the once expansive void. Sounds of others resonate off obstructions.

"Wait here," the leader demands before disappearing through a door. Two soldiers vault beyond to flank the closed entrance.

"I'm afraid," Emily whispers nervously, clutching his hand even tighter.

"Stay close," he whispers back.

Soon, the door opens revealing two people dressed in white bio suits. Each take their target by the arm, but Jim and Emily refuse to release their grip.

"Let go," says one of the white suited men.

"No," Jim asserts. "She's coming with me."

"You need to be processed individually."

"Processed!" Jim yells. "I came here under my own free will to find my daughter."

The group leader that had brought them here stands by the open doorway. He removes the systems surrounding his head to reveal an unshaven face. Dark hair and brown eyes depict a seasoned forty year old soldier. "They need to run tests," he says politely.

"Emily and I have been through a lot together. We battled gangs and miscreants. I'm not leaving her. Can't you see she's scared?"

The leader sighs.
"We're all scared."

"That may be true but we have no weapons, you do."

"I am just a squad sergeant. I have little power over such matters." He thinks for a moment. "You will see each other while the tests are performed. I promise."

The white clad men stand alongside their perspective patients. "Follow me," says one, but instead of forcibly leading them away, he points ahead.

Jim and Emily follow with tightly gripped hands, passing the sergeant.

"The exam is the least of your worries," he mutters

Chapter 22: Dissolution

A large auditorium is sectioned by thick transparent drapes forming rows of small compartments. Bright overhead lights illuminate the void. Behind the transplant veils are sorrowful faces lamenting their predicament. Each is confined and guarded by a few gun toting soldiers, two for every ten civilians.

Escorted into adjacent enclosures, Jim and Emily gaze across translucent barriers on top of plastic covered gurneys.

Each medic extracts a vial of blood from exposed arms. The flask is quickly placed inside a waiting machine, prompting instant analysis. The medics review the findings but offer no comment.

"Am I a carrier?" Jim nervously asks his handler. The medic takes little interest in him, instead, he waves a baton over Jim's body. The analysis is quick, resulting in a brief moment of intimacy. The medic takes Jim's right arm and exposes the underside for further scrutiny.

A large mechanical syringe is positioned just a few inches below the wrist. The thick shiny needle lies on his skin. "What are you doing?" Jim demands.

"Bio tagging," the muffled voice emits. Almost instantly, the unit hisses, sending a pellet sized tracking device underneath his skin. Jim recoils from the momentary prick. It is far more painful than blood extraction.

A commotion in Emily's cell garnishes interest. A soldier forcibly takes her from the room.

"What are you doing!" Jim exclaims, pounding on the thick plastic drapes. Another soldier quickly enters Jim's cubical. "Sit down, Sir," the voice stings.

"That's my daughter. Where are you taking her?"

"To a safer place."

"We didn't come here to be treated as criminals. Your sergeant promised us we would not be separated."

"I doubt that, Sir."

Fear rushes into Jim's eyes as he realizes all hope is about to be lost. "Emily!" he yells, trying to pass the soldier. Jim is restrained. In desperation, he attempts to rip down the plastic walls forcing a second soldier to intervene. "This is your last warning!" the new arrival blares.

Filled with adrenaline, Jim continues to paw at the drapes. A swift slap at his neck sends him tumbling toward the ground. His unconscious body is taken into a small dark room where he is lain on a soft cot.

Chapter 23: Bedevilment

"What a fine young specimen of womanhood!" says a guard to his comrade. Isolated in a small bright room, Emily is seated and handcuffed to a heavy oak table. Her eyes seethe with anger, gazing only at the ground.

The two guards stand near the closed door, watching the shivering pubescent from inside. She has heard the comment, but offers no outward response to their suggestive taunt.

"What a shame," says the other guard though his protective gear. "I can just taste her."

Suddenly the door opens. Another soldier storms in.

"Wait outside!" he demands. When they leave, his head gear is removed. The sergeant's seasoned face shows little emotion as he stands in front of the dark wood table.

Emily looks up.
"It's you!" she expounds through venomous eyes. "You promised we wouldn't be separated."

"You are a carrier," he explains while reaching down to unlock her restraints.

"Like what does that mean? I'm not sick."

"You may not exhibit the signs but you can infect

others." He dangles the unlocked cuffs in his gloved hands.

"Like how come you took off your helmet?" she leers, but the sergeant offers no response. "Is my Dad sick?" she asks.

"No."

"Then you are wrong. I've been with him for over a week. By your logic he should be sick or a carrier too."

"I don't know," he snaps in frustration. "He is not your father. The test proves that."

She nods listlessly. "He rescued me and treats me like I am his daughter."

"And what about your true parents."

"Gone." His eyes drop. Sorrow rushes in, evaporating the anger.

"Well I don't want to separate you from your adoptive father, but I have orders."

A knock on the door interrupts Emily's retort. "Come in," says the sergeant.

A guard enters followed closely by Jim, toting his backpack over one shoulder. Jim slowly recognizes Emily sitting on the ground. He dashes towards her and kneels, culminating in a reciprocal hug.

"Are you alright?" Jim asks, their foreheads tenderly meet.

"Yes," her teary eyes remit.

"Leave us," the sergeant demands toward the lone guard.   The two floor dwellers remain glued at the head.

"What will happen to us?" Jim asks, slowly turning his head towards the Sergeant.

"You will be sent to a lab for analysis."

"Analysis?" Jim balks.

"Your body may hold the cure."

"I must stay with Emily."

"What about your biological daughter? I inquired about her."

"You don't even know my name."

"We learned what was needed from DNA. Your daughter Alisha is undergoing testing out west."

"So I can see her?"

"I expedited your request to higher levels. They will do their best to reunite you, or so I am told."

"And Emily?"

"He knows I'm not your daughter," she reveals.

"Still, she's coming with me," Jim affirms.

"No. She's a Carrier."

"So what does that mean?" Jim blares.

"This pandemic was unleashed by our arrogance," the sergeant explains. "Found deep inside a frozen cliff a year ago, the spores still hang low in the atmosphere and spread like an invisible storm over the surface. It indiscriminately destroyed billions, including my family."

"I'm sorry to hear that sergeant," Jim offers, still bristling with anger.

"Olsen. My name is Nathan Olsen."

"My heart goes out to you, Sir," Jim continues in a softer tone. "I lost all but one of my family members and I need to find my biological little girl."

"I envy you," says Olsen. "You have something I don't, hope, hope of seeing your offspring."

"But at what price must I accept this hope? You want me to leave Emily behind? Her youth is like a magnet to immorality. Can you guarantee her protection?"

"Don't leave me," she pleads, grasping Jim's hand.

"You have no choice in this matter, Sir" says Olsen.

"We came here by choice."

"I have standing orders to roundup everyone for processing."

"There's a lot of land out there. You can't find everyone." Jim hints.

"So what are you saying sir?"

"Let us go."

Olsen sighs.
"Even if I could, your true daughter would be fatherless. Is that what you really want?"

Jim closes his eyes in agony.
"Tell me where she is."

"You will only be caught and processed again if you try to find her on your own."

"We'll take that chance."

"Unfortunately I cannot."

"What will happen to me?" Emily utters tearfully.

"You will remain here."

Jim stands.

"Let us go." His eyes burn with gravity. "No one is going to miss a sick girl."

"That's not true," Emily interrupts. "Those two soldiers waiting with me will. They want to do things to me. I heard them talking. I'm just a play thing to them."

"So it has come to that?" Jim blares sarcastically. "Hurting those you have sworn to protect?"

Olsen exhales with a remorseful gaze, but he opts not to answer. Instead, Emily seizes the moment. "Before Jim came in, I asked why you removed your helmet. Like aren't you afraid I'm gonna get you sick?"

"They don't pay me to think. I just follow orders."

"Even now?" Jim asserts. "Were you ordered to talk to us?"

Olsen glares slyly at the captives before a loud knock on the door breaks the silence.

"Enter," says Olsen just above a whisper.

"The inbound evac chopper will arrive in fifteen," the lone guard declares through his mask.

"Understood." Olsen replies with a heighten sense of urgency. "Leave." The room falls silent again.

"I beg you, please don't separate us," Jim petitions.

Olsen rubs his head stressfully. "I cannot in good conscience let you stroll out of here and back into the countryside. You will be caught." He sighs. "The transport is your best bet. You'll both get on it. What happens afterwards is out of my hands."

"Then I don't have to stay here." Emily grins.

"You can take your chances at the lab. Plead your case to Dr. Zeller. She has a sympathetic ear."

"Thank you." Jim smiles.

"Yes, thank you." Emily delights.

"It seems we share a common heritage." Olsen grins at Jim. "Records indicate you are from Numa, Iowa. I grew up not far from there in Unionville, Missouri."

"I know where that is." Jim beams.

"One day I hoped to return there and live out my retirement years in peace." Olsen attaches his breathing system. "That day may never come... Follow me," he declares. They pass the doorway where a pair of guards stands at attention. A silent instruction sends them away.

The three reach a narrow stairwell that stretches above them. Eight levels spiral upward toward the roof. Before they can ascend, soldiers speed down the landing. They stop in front of Olsen, speaking to him through closed circuit communications.

"Sir, I'll take the Carrier back to the pen."

"No. She goes with him on the transport."

"But she's a carrier!"

Another soldier rumbles down the stairs with an authoritative stride.

"Sergeant, let these two soldiers do their job," he orders silently. "I know what you are trying to do. It won't work this time. She must stay here. Step aside or you will be relieved."

The two guards brush by Olsen and grab their prey.
"What are you doing?" Jim shouts. He instantly pulls Emily toward him, but he is no match for the strength of the soldiers.

"Don't leave me!" Emily screams while being pulled out of the stairwell. "You promised you would never leave me!" She fumes with anger, glaring at both Jim and the Sergeant.

Jim musters just enough strength to push the guard away, but Olsen intervenes. "Trust me," he whispers "No harm will come to her. I promise on my family's memory."

Jim relents, letting the guards take her back inside.
"You bastards!" she bawls before being forcibly

pulled into the hallway like a cat being lead to a bath.

Chapter 24: Internment

Three elderly candidates stand quietly on the rooftop gazing toward the sunny horizon. Like heaven bound travelers waiting for the Elysium ferry, they stare serenely toward the western sky in silent dignity.

Two guards stand a few feet away, poised for trouble, but this group seems content with their fate. Two geriatric men flank an aging woman lined up shoulder to shoulder.

Jim is placed alongside one smiling man. "Welcome," says an old man. "I'm Max and this is my wife Mary." His leather face stretches with each word.

"You seem out of breath young man," smiles Mary with drooping jowls.

"They won't let me take my daughter."

"I'm sorry to hear that." Max shakes his head sympathetically. "These are trying times. Everyone has sacrificed too much."

"Is she young?" Mary asks.

"Yes, barely a teenager."

"What a shame," Mary sighs. "She must have been a Carrier."

"I guess the four of us are immune," says the second elderly man at the far end of the line. Though rotund in appearance, his thin eyes are lined by thick fleshy bags. A gray pepper stubble beard surrounds his olive face. Yet a full dark head of hair adorns his pointy head.

Jim notices a faint flutter in the air. He looks up to where a dark speck buzzes on the quiet horizon. The others hear nothing but gaze in his direction with a flock mentality.

"Here it comes," says Mary with an eager grin. "Our chariot of hope."

The object draws closer until a vibration echoes from the sky. The dull green helicopter descends on the roof. Its doors slide open, allowing an unobstructed view through the cabin. As it lands, a storm of dust washes across the speckled black tar roof.

Guards push the group toward the open door expeditiously. An airman inside is devoid of a protective breathing system. In fact, the entire crew is less protected then the ground soldiers. They do not need such defenses from the virulent strain. They are all immune.

The airman smiles at the four, causing reciprocating grins. "Don't be afraid," he declares while gingerly securing their seatbelts. "We're going to take good care of you. So sit back and relax, we have a three hour journey ahead."

The chopper rockets into the west with exponential speed. The rushing sound deadens conversation. Jim stares beyond the small side windows of the cabin onto blossoming rolling hills.

His thoughts gravitate to Emily's smiling face superimposed on the deep blue sky. His last image of her quickly fills his mind... a scared girl screams for her life while being dragged into the unknown.

His only solace is in the words Sergeant Olsen had whispered to him.

"I promise on my family's memory" speeds through his mind like an endless loop.

"He was lying," Jim deduces with an agonizing gulp. "It was an attempt to get me to leave without further commotion. I have done a bad thing. Emily, please forgive me."

He wilts against the soft headrest. The supple cushion calms him until his eyes close with exhaustion.

What seems like moments has become hours. Jim awakes amid a change in the ships velocity. The sound has become less oppressive. His fellow shipmates rise from their slumber, eyeing each other with confusion.

The helicopter hovers before descending over a vacant concrete parking lot. A two story cement building abuts the landing field.

The engine spins down while the airman unlatches the flight restraints. "We're here." He smiles. His voice is barely audible over the waning noise. His exuberance is evident as the cabin door slides open.

Outside, a group of four white suited escorts stand anxiously by the chopper. They are fully encased in pliable biosuits, startling the elderly arrivals.

One escort carries a small device, waving it over each bare arm. A small display reveals a plethora of information. Each guest is assigned to one of the ushers.

They are separated. Jim follows his guide into a small white room not far from the entrance. "Remove your clothes," the muffled voice declares. "You need to be decontaminated."

"But I'm not sick," Jim insists.

"Remove your clothes, Sir" the voice demands. "Then place them inside the bin."

Jim reluctantly complies by laying his trusty backpack inside first, covertly palming a paper photograph of his little girl. He peels away his layered garments until only his underwear remains.

"That too," the Guide demands pointing at his jockeys.
Jim deposits his underwear yet continues to

conceal the photograph. He returns to the circle, covering his manhood.

"Spread your legs and hold out your arms parallel to the floor," the escort instructs while demonstrating.

"Open your hands."
Jim opens his left while his right palms a photograph.

"Open your right hand," the Guide demands.

He unfolds his clenched fist, exposing the paper picture.

"Put that in the bin too before it gets defaced."

"This is the only memory I have," Jim pleads.

"It will be preserved, I promise."

Jim reluctantly complies then reenters the circle. Suddenly a vaporous haze fills the small white room followed by liquid jets cascading exfoliating fluid. It sprays from all directions onto both of them. "Stay still!" the escort instructs as Jim jumps back from the pressure.

A whirlwind of warm air quickly dries his body. "You can relax now," says the Guide "but don't move."

A small bench rises from the ground supported by a single pole. "Sit down. We need to clean your feet." A similar seat waits behind the Guide. They both sit and extend their legs forward, nearly touching each other.

"Spread your toes and stay still!" the Guide declares. The room fills again with a moist haze followed by a vigorous spray, soaking their feet and the rest of their bodies again.

After the drying process, the Guide stands. "Go through that door and you will find clean clothes. Then exit through the next door."

"But my backpack and picture. That is all I have of my family."

"It will be returned after cleansing."

In the next room, a white billowy garment waits. Jim plucks it from a wall hook. It fits perfectly, like a thin robe. As instructed, he exits through another door.

Waiting for him on the other side are two doctors in white lab coats. A studious young woman devoid of makeup cracks a small grin. Her eyes sag with exhaustion. She holds a thin glass display in her right hand.

Standing alongside her is an elderly man, sporting only a few strands of gray hair atop a mostly bald head. His stick-like figure and long shaved face depicts a lackluster gaze. His every move says, "Oh another specimen?" Yet he remains silent, eyeing Jim with disdain.

"What about my daughter?" Jim asserts. "Is she here?"

"We are aware of your interest in your biological offspring," says the female doctor. "You are slated for a battery of tests."

"I want to see her first," Jim insists.

"Not until the tests are completed."

"No, I want to see her right now."

"She is not here," the quiet male doctor admonishes, sending Jim into a wide-eyed rage.

"What do you mean she is not here! I had to leave behind a dear friend just so that I could find my daughter."

"Like you had a choice," the male doctor snickers.

"I don't need this. Where is Alisha?"

"Calm down!" says the female doctor. "Before we discuss Alisha, you need a full medical workup." She sighs. "Afterward someone will answer your questions. Let's get this started. How would you like us to address you?"

"Jim," he mutters, trying to regain his composure. "Just call me Jim."

"I'm Dr. Valarie Zeller and this is my associate Dr.

Herman Weiss."

Jim's eyes pique.
"I feel like I have lost everyone."

"I understand," says Valarie. "This has been a trying time for us all."

The group of three moves down a long bright hallway.

"What happens to Carriers?" Jim inquires.

"You're not a Carrier," says Herman.

"I left someone behind who was."

"We still haven't found a solution to this pathogen," she explains. "And Carriers still pose a threat."

"But who is left for them to infect?"

"Us." Valarie grins. "And everyone working to find a cure."

Etched in white letters on a gray door are the words 'BioLab3'. Two feet from the closed entryway is a small red x embedded on the floor. Valarie stands at attention on the mark until the single thick door rolls open. It lumbers to the left until it disappears into the wall.

Beyond the threshold looms a parallel hallway with long offshoots. They turn right and down a few more corridors before coming to a small lab indicated by the number 12. In the center of the bright white room is a clear acrylic table.

"Lay down," Herman instructs. Despite the hard look of the transparent surface, the top is pliable. Jim sinks a few inches into the clear malleable membrane. He lays face up, eyeing a multitude of unfamiliar devices dangling from the ceiling.

The two doctors scurry to wall mounted instruments. Valarie activates a touch screen. "Stay still please." She turns toward Jim. After a few screen taps, "close your eyes please."

The surrounding lights dim, casting the once brilliant room into a dull gray void. On the ceiling is a large rectangular glass structure comparable to the size of the exam table. It slowly lowers like a lumbering mechanical press.

Its dark flat surface comes to rest a few includes above Jim's nose. If it went any further, it could squish him like a bug.

"Keep your eyes closed," Valarie instructs.

Behind the surface is a long thick shaft supporting the massive structure. Reminiscent of an old style cathode ray tube, it even flickers like a mono colored television set.

Jim's body is quickly engulfed by a strong light

emitted from the tube; like a powerful camera flash. Then the unit slowly ascends back into the ceiling.

Images of Jim's internal organs appear three dimensionally around Valerie's touch screen. They float just inches beyond the glass surface. Her index finger pokes the revolving heart, which exposes the interior workings. Small arrows point to various parts, displaying alpha numerical information.

"That's a common trait," Herman offers while viewing the dynamic diagram. They mumble indistinguishably as Jim sits up.

Valarie notices his movement. "Well Jim, you finished the first round of physical tests but I need to ask you some questions." Her handheld glass display illuminates. She states his full name, age, and physical address as displayed on her screen.

"Correct," Jim replies with a dull gaze. His legs dangle over the table as he sits erect.

"Can I conclude that you are heterosexual?"

"Yes." Jim glares indignantly.

"When was the last time you saw your family?"

"I don't know," he falters. "What day is this?"

"April 23rd."

"I'm not sure, but it might have been over a week ago."

"Were you at work before all this happened?"

"Yes."

"Tell me more about the last day you left work," she rattles.

"The trains had stopped running from Grand Central. I couldn't get home."

"But you obviously did," she sternly remarks.

"I found others escaping Manhattan. So we teamed up. We stole a bus." His eyes water. "A gang brutally stopped us but we managed to flee. When we got to the bridge, we had no choice but to walk. There were miles of abandoned cars trying to escape. That's when we found Emily."

"Who?" asks Herman with passive interest.

"A child left to die in a closed car, the young Carrier I spoke about."

"Ah yes," says Valarie, eyeing her screen as the session is recorded.

"We saved her then went across the bridge." Jim continues to recant the entire story up until snow had blocked their path. Being able to share the experience invigorates him.

"And your wife?" asks Herman.

"No, I don't know where she is."

"Why do you think your daughter is still alive?" Valarie asks.

Jim squints.
"Why? You know why. I was told she was by Sergeant Olsen."

"What led you to search for her in the first place, before you met the officer?"

"She left a video message before being hauled away by soldiers. I saw them drag her from my kitchen."

Jim looks around with budding awareness.
"You haven't even inquired about Alisha, have you?"

"Please," Valarie presses. "We'll do what we can to reunite you."

"You're lying. I'm only here as a specimen!" he yells distressingly.

"Calm down!" Herman demands. "We will try our best to locate her. Until then, your cooperation is imperative."

"You must be hungry." Valarie smiles before turning to a wall-mounted intercom. "BioLab3, liaison report to room twelve."

"I must find her," Jim pleads.

"We understand," says Valarie. "During these trouble times, individual wants are overshadowed by social needs."

The only door to the room whisks open to reveal a tall slender man standing in a white robe and slippers. His shaven face exudes a youthful eagerness concealed in a fifty year old mind. He spots Jim wearing the same attire. "Welcome friend." He gleams like a priest to his flock.

"Jim, meet Dirk," Valarie presents. She clears a pathway to the door. Jim's stodgy gait ends with an outstretched hand. Dirk vigorously reciprocates with a tight grasp. "Let me show you the cafeteria."

Chapter 25: Natural Incipience

Once outside the room, Dirk smiles buoyantly. "Fresh food and water abound, my friend."

"What's going to happen to us?"

"We are treated like royalty here."

"You mean captives."

"Captives?" Dirk recoils. "No. You have it all wrong. They need us to find a cure."

"Can we leave anytime?"

"That is so selfish. Of course we cannot leave and squander away humanity's best hope for survival."

"I was doing quite well before being flown here. I just want to find my daughter. She was picked up and sent here a few days ago. Have you seen a young girl called Alisha?"

Dirk ponders for a moment. "Ah yes." His eyes gleam. "I recall quite vividly. She was scared to death at first."

"Where is she?!"

"I don't know."

"What do you mean you don't know? Aren't you the representative for us captives?"

"I am the liaison for this sector, yes." He squints condescendingly.

"Where did they take her?"

"Jim, can I call you Jim? You see, we are isolated from others. I don't know where most of those I met wander off. Many are taken to different facilities I suspect. I think this place is a clearing house of some sort."

They round a corner then emerge into a large cafeteria. Though lined with gregarious shiny tables, the room is all but empty except for a few fellow diners. At the back of the room are stacks of boxed meals waiting selection.

Dirk takes the reusable plastic container then hands another to Jim. Nearby is a table with prefilled plastic cups. The translucent beakers contain a dark glutinous beverage.

Their acquired possessions are relocated to an unoccupied table near the center of the room. Rows of bench-like chairs are permanently fixed to the floor.

"How long have you been here?" Jim asks while unpacking his meal.

"A few weeks I suppose."

"What are we expected to do all day?"

"We will be poked and prodded in an effort to reveal our secrets of immunity."

"So we are lab rats?"

Dirk leans closer.
"I've heard some strange rumors," he whispers cautiously. "Some are knocked unconscious with an induced coma. Others are mutilated in the name of science, but those are just rumors."

Jim gawks distressingly. But Dirk continues. "We are at their mercy," he concedes.

"Have you tried to escape?"

"Escape? Escape to what? There is nothing out there. At least we have food and shelter."

"So that's it? You surrender to this captivity? I don't know about you but I have a daughter to find."

"Keep it down," Dirk insists. "Don't create trouble."

"Oh then, I'm going to create trouble," he vows with a deep snarl. "If they think I'll remain docile, they have another thing coming."

Jim vaults, pointing his face defiantly toward the ceiling.

"Where is my daughter? Do you hear me? Where is she? Where is Alisha?"

Dirk lowers his head with embarrassment. "They heard you. Now sit down and finish your meal."

Jim glares at his compatriot. "I thought we could be friends but I guess I was wrong. Do you not see what we have become? We have nothing."

"Can't you just be glad that we are alive?" Dirk grumbles.

"Obviously you don't have family."

"Oh, is that what you think? Let me tell you a thing or two," his face twinges. "I had a wife, three kids and a grandchild too. I know how it is to lose your family and so does everyone here."

Jim's rage subsides. "But unlike you, my daughter is alive. You told me yourself she was here."

"Yes, I had seen her days ago but I cannot offer any more information." Dirk laments.

"But you just gave me hope."

"Indeed." Dirk smiles. The two sit silently staring at their empty meal boxes until Dirk stares deeply into Jim's eyes.

"You know," says Dirk, "humanity was long overdue for a cataclysmic event like this. The Spanish flu pandemic of 1918 killed millions, and now this, the deadliest one of all. Do you know that this disease is estimated to have infected about fifty percent of the population?"

"Who told you that?"

"The Doctors here did. They are on the forefront of analyzing this affliction. It is believed that the Arctic was at the equator eons ago where plants and animals once existed. Then the land masses abruptly shifted, sending the Arctic to where it is now, covering organic life with a thick layer of ice. This deadly strain was locked away until the glaziers melted, releasing the airborne spores to wreak havoc." He smiles, eyeing Jim with a sense of self satisfaction. "Obviously we are immune and represent hope for humanity."

"I don't care" Jim's eyes bulge. "I just want to find my daughter."

"It is getting late," Dirk indicates. "Let me show you to your private room."

Beyond the cafeteria and down numerous hallways, the duo emerges into a long corridor lined with evenly spaced doors.

Dirk searches for a demarcation. "Ah, there it is." He smiles, stopping at L3-754.

A diminutive room measuring ten square feet glows under dull lights. Inside and to the left is a small washroom denoted by an alcove. A stall shower, sink, and toilet molded from a single chunk of polymer.

"You should be comfortable here." Dirk smiles,

sitting on the edge of a pristine twin bed. Two pillows protrude below a billowy blanket. "If you need anything, just tap that red button above the headboard. I will do my best to answer promptly."

Dirk backs out to the entryway. "Have a good rest. I'll be here around eight in the morning." A quick click of the door seals Jim inside.

He folds his tired body onto the soft supple bed, staring up at the featureless white ceiling. Images from the day race through his mind. "Emily." His lips part, but only the slightest whisper escapes.

Her young angelic face bubbles to a smile as they ride northward away from Ray and Hector. Their small borrowed car speeds down the road.

"This will be a lot better than crossing a bridge," she says as they bypass the Tappan Zee exit.

"What have I done?" Jim winces atop the soft bed. "I put my trust in Sergeant Olsen. How could I do such a thing when trust is a fleeting commodity?"

He rubs his eyes. "I selfishly abandoned Emily when she looked to me for stability. Now I have neither her nor my precious Alisha."

His eyes roll beneath the lids until restless sleep overtakes him.

Chapter 26: Narcoleptic Ventures

Cries of pain saturate the cold sterile air while Jim
stands in one of four parallel lines. Behind him is
a string of naked men stretching beyond a distant
door down a bright corridor. A sea of hopelessness
lingers on blank faces of the wretched masses of
humanity queuing toward destiny.

Ahead of Jim are four lifeless souls waiting their
turn in line. Beyond the four is s contraption
working at peak efficiency. Large protruding
needles reposition their horizontal
angle. Supported by an opened mechanical
system, the apparatus administers the final
solution to life. The Death Machine pulls a person
into its beastly grip and kills them with rhythmic
precision.

One by one, men throw themselves onto the spike
under the watchful eyes of taunting guards.

"Don't hesitate you scum! Move!" they yell
insensitively to the dead souls marching resolutely
toward their fate.

Jim stands behind three men who in turn plunge
towards the spears. He watches fearfully as the
shiny metal spikes impale their victims. The death
machine quickly fills the cadavers with toxic
poisons to hasten their demise before a large
mechanical arm throws their warm bodies down a
chute.

From twenty feet away, Jim eyes the spears standing before him. He is now first in line.

"Move!" yells the guard standing behind the machine.

To the right of Jim are three other rows of men all flinging themselves to an unjustified death. He can see fear in their eyes yet they move toward their doom obediently.

A young man standing in the row next to him whispers, "Don't think about it. Just run up to the freaking thing and it'll all be over." The man speeds off and rams himself into the death machine letting out a diminutive sigh.

With the guard yelling to keep the line moving, Jim is resigned to this fate. He closes his eyes momentarily before mustering courage to face his demise.

He leaps forward a few steps, but suddenly, the room goes dark. Startled, the guards stand motionless in the shadowy hall. Faint light echoes from small outside windows.

Jim is invigorated by the momentary lapse of confusion. He vaults toward a nearby guard and easily wrestles the weapon away. Other condemned men quickly seize the moment and overtake the other guards creating a riot.

"Let's get out of here!" Jim yells, leading those in front of the killing lines.

Roaming dark halls, the dissipate men find other rooms besieged by darkness, each with lines of quiet men queuing to their deaths. Instead of breaking free, they stand with the guards waiting patiently for their fate.

Jim bursts in with his gang and quickly overcomes the constabulary. The roaming group grows as they smash through ground level windows leading outside. The nude men step beneath cool gray skies.

A steady stream of wretchedness flows quietly from the long broken windows onto the grassy grounds. Their dash for life seems uninspired. A slow stroll to nearby woods causes the group to momentarily falter.

"Keep going!" Jim yells. "Don't stop or we'll get caught!"

They heed his words and continue deep into the forest until only three men are within his sight. Breaching the budding foliage, a small cabin with a bellowing chimney announces its presence. The four converge around the small hovel.

"Should we announce our selves or just break in?" asks a tall lanky man.

"I'm not a criminal," Jim replies indignantly.

The three gather behind Jim before approaching the front door. His cold knuckles barely rap upon the ingress. It inches open by its own power.

"What do ya fellas want?" asks a gravelly voice from within the cabin.

"Clothing," utters one of the nude men.

"Friendship," Jim declares, prompting the door to gently crack wider.

The dark void quickly envelops Jim. He enters, peering into the darkness. Instantly a brilliant artificial light engulfs him. Disoriented, he feels his back against a soft bed. "Jim," says a soft female voice.

Dazed, his eyes open to his diminutive sterile room back at the laboratory. He lay motionless atop his appointed bed. Realizing it had all been a ghoulish dream. He is back in the confines of the room. A figure stands in the door way.

"Jim, we have more tests to run," says Valarie. She is supported by two guards standing behind her. Though dressed in typical uniforms, the soldiers sport no outward weapons. Instead, their steely demeanor exemplifies control and authority.

"Where is Dirk?" Jim slurs groggily.

"That is of no concern of yours. Please, we need to get started."

"And my daughter Alisha?"

"We are doing our best to locate her. In the meantime we need your cooperation."

Jim reluctantly rolls out of bed and follows Valarie and the two lagging guards.

Behind sliding doors is a dimly lit room. The cold air stings Jim's face, but he is not allowed to retreat. He is shown a sturdy table and asked to mount it as directed by one of the guards.

"Lay there," says Valarie. The guards blend into the darkness. Suddenly a bright flash glares over Jim's eyes. He squints in pain before being rendered unconscious by the blinding luminosity.

His eyes flutter open minutes later to find his limbs secured to the table. "What's this?" he yells crisply.

"The restraints are for your own safety," Valarie affirms.

Tubes and wires are affixed to his body like a porcupine, all attached to the ceiling. A press of a button robs him of consciousness. Days meld while Jim remains oblivious to his surroundings.

Eventually he is brought to full consciousness, but this time, Dr. Herman Weiss fiddles with wall mounted instruments.

"Where am I?" asks Jim, stiff with atrophy. The restraints and wires have all been removed.

"Ah, you're awake," Herman replies, gazing over his left shoulder. "You are going to get some solid foods before transport."

"Transport?"

"Yes. Another facility wants a specimen and you've been chosen."

"And my daughter?"

"Listen. Give it up. Very few find their loved ones. She is gone. Accept that fact and you will be more at ease, more accepting of your fate."

"Never!" Shaky arms lift his sore body from the table while legs dangle over the edge. A pair of new guards surrounds him.

"Give it up," Herman persists.

"How dare you! I came here under my own free will to find her. Where is she?"

"If you are going to be this much trouble, I will have to sedate you. Is this what you want?" asks Herman, glaring sternly at the specimen.

Jim bolts for the door, but his futile escape is easily repelled by the guards. He is thrown back toward the center of the room, hitting his thigh against the table. He winces, but the pain is nothing compared to the storm that swells inside him.

Rage wins over common sense. Jim leaps into massive waiting arms of the guards. They subdue his advance with a tight bear hug allowing Herman to inject a sedative.

Jim's knees buckle. The guards support his limp body. "Take him to L3-754." Herman waves dismissively.

Chapter 27: Unrequited Hope

Languishing in his diminutive room, Jim wakes from a drug induced slumber. His robe has been replaced by ordinary vestments, including socks and shoes. A drab brown shirt and matching pants adorn his thin frame.

Jim stumbles from bed and into the restroom with a placid gaze. He spots a tray of food lying on a nearby shelf. He opens it and gorges ravenously like a wild animal.

The corners of his lips fill with meal remnants, but he does nothing to clean his appearance. Instead he sits on the rumpled bed, staring blankly at the front door.

He has forgotten why he is here. Then it all comes rushing back. The reason for his incarceration flows like a broken dam, filling his thoughts with Alisha, Emily and his entire ordeal. For a brief moment, his mind was blank; offering glimpses into what humanity can become.

"I was a beast with no past or future," he mutters staring at his haggard face in the bathroom mirror. "Look at me. I'm nothing more than a grungy animal now."

"I need a miracle." His head sags sorrowfully toward the sink with bleeding fearful eyes, then something in his shirt pocket bulges.

Neatly inserted is the photo of Alisha. He pulls it out and stares lovingly at her before placing the photo back safely.

"How?" he whispers, trying to contemplate who could have done this. Speculation vanishes as the front door abruptly opens.

"It's time," a voice declares, dashing his hopes.

Jim steps alongside his bed to spot a group of four hefty guards dressed in black. They strategically place themselves around the room with swift accuracy.

"From this moment on you have two choices," says one of the men. "Either come with us peacefully or become a hostel transportee. Which will it be?"

"I just want my daughter."

"We are here to transport you. We know nothing else. You have five seconds to decide."

"Where are you taking me?"

"We are escorting you to an outbound helicopter. Beyond that we know nothing. You have two seconds left before we deem you hostile."

Jim's shoulders slump submissively. He saunters to the door. "I hope none of you have families. My daughter was taken to this facility and now no one knows where she is." He holds out his arms to be handcuffed.

"That won't be necessary, Sir," says the ringleader. He personally escorts Jim through the hallway, sandwiched between the other guards.

Though his face says otherwise, Jim's mind swirls with malicious thoughts of escape, but they remain just thoughts, for none of them can relieve the current situation. It is not long before Jim steps outside into brilliant sunshine.

A warm spring day wipes his mind clean of any pervasive thoughts. A deep breath of fresh air fills his lungs with optimism.

At a corner of an expansive concrete parking lot is a dormant green helicopter. The guards enter the chopper and strap Jim to the back seat with a locking bolt. "What's that for?" he glares at the clamp.

"In case you get frisky," says the ringleader. "Enjoy your trip." He grins before the gang of four vanishes into the building.

To his surprise, his black carrying bag sits alongside him. He glances over with a smile as a warm breeze races through the cabin like a venomous snake. A whiff of freshly cut grass casts his thoughts upon the past.

"Daddy?" Jim's youthful voice echoes from his porch seat. His father Tom sits alongside him on a warm summer afternoon.

"One day," says Tom, "you will inherit this entire farm."

"Really? I want to be just like you when I grow up."

Tom wags.
"Don't be like me son, you can do better."

"So you don't like being a farmer?" he inquires as if a bubble had burst.

"You can be so much more son."

"But you always tell me that farming is important."

"I know, I know. It is important but I'm just saying there are many things for you out there. Don't follow me. Find your own path in life."

The daydream fades as a dark speck in the azure sky catches Jim's eye. The beating sound finally follows the visual green beast descending a few yards away.

Windswept debris swirls around the landing site, forcing Jim to turn away, pulling tightly on the restraints. Soon, the beating rotors glide to a gentle stop.

Four soldiers armed with rifles speed from the cabin doors and take up strategic positions. A welcoming committee dressed in white biosuits bolt past Jim's dormant chopper.

The six white suits match up to each of the ragged captives that slowly emerge from the cabin. They are each dressed in drab military green garb. Thick fabric hangs loosely from their emotionless bodies.

Jim squints toward the new prisoners. He stares at one with particular interest. A young fair haired girl sluggishly totes a backpack over her shoulder.

His eyes are obscured by an approaching guard. A man steps into the helicopter. "Are you ready, Sir?" ask the upbeat man reeking of cigarettes. His leather face bares his addiction to nicotine.

"Let me go please."
"What? I can't do that. Just be happy that someone cares about you."

He plants himself in one of the cockpit seats as Jim eyes the parading arrivals. Their faces march closer; close enough for Jim to positively identify Emily. Their eyes meet, instantly transforming her drab gaze into an expressive smile.

"Emily!"
"Jim!" They yell across the field.

The armed guards glance with modest interest at the commotion before returning their focus toward the others.

She breaks from the pack and runs to Jim. Her ardent gallop forces her to nearly trip and fall inside the opened sliding door of Jim's helicopter.

Tears gush from their eyes. The backpack drops to the deck while her hands wrap joyously around Jim's head.

Jim's shackled hands preclude him from reciprocating. "I thought I would never see you again!" he cries between tears.

"Me too," she gushes.
The man sitting in the cockpit drifts slowly to the back. "You must be Emily," he says dully.

"You cannot separate us," she affirms, clutching Jim firmly to her chest.

"On the contrary, I have orders to take the both of you to another facility." He smiles while fiddling around with Jim's hand restraints. "There," he says with satisfaction after unlocking the cuffs. "Promise me that neither of you will run away. If you do, the guards will intervene."

"There is no need for me to run." Jim beams contently while embracing Emily tightly.

"Get ready, here comes the crew," says the man as he jumps back into the cockpit.

Three soldiers enter the chopper exhibiting no emotion. They strap themselves in and adorn headsets. One sits in back alongside Jim and Emily.

Soon the chopper is airborne, flying over the lush green land sprouting with new life. Patches of open plains speed by. These were once outdoor farms that had long been abandoned for newer methods of food production.

The morning sun glares from behind the chopper, indicating a westward path. They continue en route for fifteen minutes, flying just above ten thousand feet.

Suddenly, cabin sirens wail, sending everyone into panic. The crew speaks secretively through their headsets, ignoring their passengers.

Emily and Jim shiver with concern. Oblivious to the cause of their evident distress, the two begin to wonder.

"Maybe the pilot is sick," says Emily, pressing hard against Jim's ear.

The chopper begins to pitch downward with increasing velocity. Soon the entire ship spins on its axis descending spirally.

"I'm getting sick," Emily screams.

The tail rotates cyclonically, causing the entire group to vomit. That is the least of their worries as the ship reels out of control. The horizon approaches rapidly until the chopper hits the ground with a horrific bang.

The main rotors splinter in every direction, scraping the grassy ground. The tail boom buckles then snaps off from the main fuselage and the cabin continues to spin with centrifugal force until the engines die.

The remains of the once mighty helicopter come to rest with one side against the torn up ground. Except for a few lingering streams of colored smoke drifting into the air, the ship sits silently as a permanent part of the landscape.

Chapter 28: Entanglement

A single bloody hand breaches the shattered glass cabin door. It pulls itself up and through the opening until Jim's head emerges from the mangled wreckage.

Though dazed, survival instincts initiate. One leg dangles off the side of the chopper. Before descending to the ground, he looks back inside the cabin through the shattered glass.

His shoulders disappear for a brief moment. Slowly he reemerges with Emily's unconscious body. He jumps off then stumbles a few yards from the smoking rubble, before laying her on the ground.

"Emily!" he shrieks desperately. Bleeding scratches cross his sweat filled face. Though bruised, Emily's appearance seems angelic. She rests peacefully on the soft grass as Jim props her head up in his arms.

His left hand feels for a pulse but he detects nothing. "No please," he whispers in agony. His free hand gravitates to her neck for another reading. Unfamiliar with the technique, Jim feels around below her ear for a heartbeat.

"No, please no!" he yells with all his might, banishing his emotional pain in all directions. A tear rolls off his scraped cheeks and drips onto her delicate neck. She begins to stir. A short moan quells Jim's agony.

"Emily?" he whispers enthusiastically. Her eyelids part. "Are you alright?" he asks patiently.

"Am I alive?" her drowsy voice asks.

"Yes. Is anything broken?"

Her eyes focus beyond Jim's caring smile in an effort to conduct a self-diagnostic. "Nothing is broken," she replies. Emily attempts to stand with Jim's help.

"I'm okay," she remits, steadying herself on the grassy field. While looking around to assess the environment, she eyes the mangled chopper smoldering a few yards away. Jim wraps his arms tightly around her. "They didn't hurt you did they?"

"The crash?"

"No, Sergeant Olsen and the others."

"He kept me safe." She forces a budding smile.

"Why did they let you leave?"

"I'll tell you later. My head is spinning too much."

"Okay, Okay. Sorry. I thought about you so many times. I missed you so much."

She smiles.

"I missed you, too." Their embrace loosens as her eyes swiftly stiffen with horror.

"Where's my bag?" she snaps.

"It's still inside the helicopter."

"I need it," she reels.

"Okay, okay. I'll go back and get it."

"But you're hurt," she realizes.

"I'm fine." Before another word escapes, Jim jumps atop the wreckage and disappears into the ship.

Emily remains transfixed, gazing motionless at the quiet twisted mound. The smoldering smoke rising from the rubble causes her thoughts to stray. A blissful image from the past invades her thoughts.

It is late summer and all but a few people lay quietly on their beach towels soaking up the relaxing sounds of post season vacationers.

The hustle of summertime tourists have long gone, leaving the beach peaceful and quiet. "Emily," her mother beckons from a blanket laid out on a sand dune, "lunch time."

A game of catch with her father by the surging water fills both of them with joy. "Next year at this time, you'll have a little brother," says her father as he tosses the ball back to her.

"Daddy, will he like me?"

"Of course he will, he's your brother. You two will grow up together."

"Then I will look after him."

"That's right, you're the big sister."

"I will make sure he is always safe."

"I know you will Emily. You're my strong little girl."

"Daddy, will you ever die?"
He gulps, "One day I will."

"And Mommy too?"

"Don't you worry about that. We all have a long time together. Look," he says. "A flock of birds going south for the winter."

"But it's not cold."

"They feel things before we do. It will be getting cold soon no doubt."

Emily melts back into reality as a real flock of migrating birds head north, signifying Spring. She watches them glide high above the grassy plains toward the distant horizon.

An odd sight distracts her. Rising from the flat landscape is a black speck about five miles away. It moves closer, advancing smoothly.

Jim pops his head up from the chopper's door and slides down the side carrying two small backpacks.

"I got both of ours." He smiles, handing hers over. "The crew looks pretty beat up in there, at least those closer to the front. The guy sitting next to us might be alive."

"I think we have a bigger problem." She points to the ever growing dot on the horizon. "We should hide."

Jim stares for a moment at the moving mass, attempting to ascertain its composition, but his eyes are yet to discern the object.

"Come on!" Emily insists, tugging at his arm. "There are some trees we can hide behind." Emily points. She dashes toward the woods then squats behind a massive tree trunk until her body disappears in the tall grass. Jim does the same at another tree.

They peer from their camouflage at the approaching specter. It rumbles over the terrain with a thunderous roar until it materializes into a set of speeding open air trucks.

Their momentum decreases as they cautiously come upon the wreckage. Each vehicle has a set of three occupants excluding the driver. The soldiers are covered in green military fatigues. The drivers' remain seated while six others advance toward the smoldering ruins.

One parades a device at arm's length, scanning debris ahead.

"I have one life sign." He points at the fuselage.

Two men peer inside the smashed chopper. An older commander looks on, resting against the drab green fender of the transport truck. "It looks like our weapon found its mark. Let's salvage what we can and get out of here," he announces to the group.

One of the men enters the chopper and pulls an unconscious body onto the ground. "What do we do this one?" asks the soldier scanning the body.

The commander pulls a weapon and fires off one round indiscriminately at the unconscious man, leaving a large hole in his head. "Problem solved," says the commander with little remorse.

Unparsed, the others get to work on dismantling the chopper. Drills and torches cut mercilessly into the fuselage until little remains. Valuable scraps are stowed with rhythmical precision onto the trucks.

"Sir?" says the soldier waving his scanning. The commander whispers to him, prompting a blissful smile and a gentle nod.

The rapidly moving soldiers swarm like bees. Their exact count becomes blurred as they scurry between the disappearing wreckage and the trucks.

"Ah, record time," says the commander as the last piece is stowed. All the workers seem to have vanished into their preordained hives.

"Let's move out," the commander exalts, boarding his ride. Unlike their approach, the two transports split up and inch slowly in different directions, forming the top half of the letter T.

"Did you see that? He just shot him dead for no reason," Emily breathes. She stands against the tree, actively peering at the two moving trucks.

Jim sprouts and watches the transports fade into the distance.

"Lucky they didn't find us." Emily stares back beyond the tall grass.

"I know this land," Jim remarks. "I grew up in a place like this."

"A field?"

"A farm," Jim reprimands. "I wonder where we are." He gazes at the gray sky, listening to the sound of nothingness.

"Like what are we going to do?" Emily glares with frightened eyes.

Jim peers over his shoulder away from the wreckage and trucks. "Let's go that way."

"Where will that lead us?"

"Into that distant clump of trees and maybe we will come upon some shelter."

"That's so far. I'm not sure I can make it."

"Why? Are you hurt?"

"Nothing hurts, but I'm just tired."

"We have no choice. We can't stay here."

"I knew this was going to be a bad day when I woke up." Emily sighs.

"It can't be that bad. We found each other and lived to tell about it."

"Of course." She smiles, wrapping her arms around him.

Chapter 29: Veracity

A four mile walk lay before them. Tall grass parts with each step, yet they tread cautiously though the weeds. "Be careful," says Jim, recalling his youth. "There are things in here that you would rather not come in contact with. Just stomp hard with each step."

"I know all about that. I lived in the country too."
"That may be, but critters are bigger out here."

Jim walks a few yards ahead but is watchful of the gap between them.

"How are you doing?" he asks after thirty minutes of paced walking.

"Jim," she utters reluctantly. "There is something I have to tell you and you're not going to like it."

"There is nothing you can't tell me that I wouldn't like," he chuckles lightly.

"It's about Alisha."

Jim stops dead in his tracks then spins around with an ominous gaze. The two stand forty feet apart, facing each other between tall stagnant grass.

"What about Alisha?" his voice darkens.

"They ran experiments on her."

"Who told you that?" he snarls.

"Sergeant Olsen."

"They ran experiments on me, too," Jim reveals.

"But it's more than just that. Alisha is gone. She was euthanized for the sake of science."

Jim's eyes bulge with rage.
"No! That can't be!"

"He confirmed it. I'm sorry." She withdraws a few steps, anticipating a violent outburst.

"No!" Jim yells into the murky sky, like a howling wolf. His knees buckle. He falls into the tall grass with a powerful thump.

His head sinks. Tears gush painfully from his sore eyes like the sea at high tide. Convoluting in misery, Jim rocks back and forth with tightly clutched arms.

Emily steps closer in sympathy.
"At first I wasn't sure if I should tell you, but as we kept walking, I thought like it was the right thing to do." Her face wrinkles with a torrent of emotions until she succumbs to a watery eruption.

Just inches from Jim, she towers over him like a mother with a child. He remains transfixed in agony, staring despondently at the ground.

"I'm so sorry," she whimpers. "I wanted to meet her so badly."

Jim wakes from his stupor. He looks up with sore eyes.

"What did he tell you?"

"Don't make me, please."

"I must know. What else did he say?"

"All those experiments made her stiff with pain," she sniffles. "Eventually Immunes and Carriers alike are pushed to exhaustion until they can give no more."

"How does he know her fate?"

"Two days ago I was in the conference room when he received a message. Someone named Dr. Mudi worked personally on Alisha. Her death revealed a small piece of the puzzle, he said."

Jim ponders.
"They could be wrong. Just look at us. The Army will say that we died in a crash, but here we are alive and well." He rises from the ground like a tall statue of fortitude.

Emily looks at a small scar on her arm. "But they can track us with these things."

"The medical tags? No, they are only used to

retrieve data at close range like twenty or thirty feet."

"Jim," she says sorrowfully. "With my mom and brother both gone, I know I will never see my father again. I accept that fact. And you..."

"I know it sounds bleak but I must keep Alisha in my heart because if I don't, there is no reason for living."

"Everything that made me feel safe is gone too. I have only you now." She smiles ephemerally.

His arms melt around her with a clutching embrace. Behind Emily the tall wheat-like grass twitches. It moves independently from the environment.

"Something is following us," Jim whispers as their eyes meet. He grabs her right hand and tugs. "Run!"

They pick up speed and plow through the grass, peering over their shoulders in fear.

A man pops up from the brush coddling his rifle. Another rises abreast, just a few steps from the running pair, blocking their advance.

"What's your hurry?" a sultry voice declares, casually pointing his weapon at them. "You don't think we missed you back there at the crash site, did ya?"

The other man catches up from behind and aims his weapon squarely at the two with serious intent.

"Well," smiles the talkative sly soldier, "you two seem to be in a hurry all of a sudden. I guess you spotted us."

"We don't want any trouble," Jim expounds.

"Nor do we," smiles the soldier.

"Did you think we didn't notice you from our trucks? Well, you've been tracked and now it is time to surrender."

"We were just freed and now you want to capture us?" Jim decries.

"I heard your story back there. It is touching, it really is, but I have orders."

"You don't seem like typical soldiers to me," Jim deduces. "Picking the wreckage clean with no regard for fellow officers is a conduct violation."

"We are the Clancy Militia," he offers proudly. "We patrol these parts. Whatever flies over our territory or falls to the ground is ours."

"Please let us go," Emily begs.

"I see that you have a considerable offer for clemency," the man snickers.

"No," Jim affirms. "Leave her alone."

Unexpectedly, a single shot echoes from behind Emily. The stern soldier lowers his weapon then throws the firearm towards Jim.

"Take it and run," he declares. "Go quickly before they investigate the shot."

"Thank you." Jim smiles. "Where are we?"

"Milton Iowa. Stay on the left and follow the outskirts of the forest for eight miles until it clears. You'll be safe after that."

"Why are you helping us?" Emily presses.

"Don't ask questions. Go, now."

Jim picks up the gun and dashes through the field with Emily close behind. Just as they enter the edge of the forest, a large transport truck breaches the horizon. Before it meets up with the lone soldier, Jim and Emily melt beyond the green canopy and push on.

They skirt the outer boundaries of the forest until Jim can run no more. He stops against a tree. Emily looks back with a sweat filled pant just a few yards ahead. "I don't think we should stop for too long," she huffs.

"I just need a few minutes to catch my breath."

She doubles back and collapses against him. "What do we do once we reach the clearing?"

"I'm going home."

"Home?" She squints. "You already know what's there."

"No, home to where I was born. Once I get my bearings, I should be able to find it. I came from these parts."

Emily gulps.
"Then you accepted the future without Alisha?"

He tears up.
"My baby. I'm so sorry I wasn't there for you. Forgive me Alisha." His soaked head falls into Emily's arms.

Between tears of realization, Jim utters, "I have just one last hope from the past. The last time I spoke to my mother, she was at our family farm. My father had just passed in his sleep."

Emily consoles him.
"Then we will find your farm together." She rises from the ground and motions for Jim to follow.

The speed of their advance is not what it was, but they continue on until the forest opens into untilled fields. Not far beyond the edge of the forest is a farm. A small single story house sits alongside a large red barn.

"Is that yours?" Emily asks.

"No, but maybe there is food and water."

An old pickup truck is parked outside. It's faded red paint and round rusting fenders beckons to a past era when metal was used for construction. Unlike the body, the four tires have seen relatively little wear.

Jim looks inside the closed driver's side window. The torn bench seat is pockmarked with duct tape. Other areas show a haphazard approach to repair. Pieces of exposed foam cushions extrude from the dirty surface like a bubble in a thick algae filled pond.

Jim pulls the handle. The door pops open. "Maybe we should check inside the house first," Emily whispers. "Just in case."

They crest the porch, but any hopes of a silent approach are dashed by a creaky front porch board announcing their presence. Jim pushes open the dilapidated screen door. The dry hinges add further noise to the silent surroundings.

Jim tightly grasps the gun as he pierces the threshold. The hall is dark. Cheesy wood paneling absorbs most of the light. Some luminance seeps in just a few feet from perfectly preserved glass windows.

The single story building is no bigger than fifteen hundred square feet; barely enough for a family. The long hallway stretches from the main door to the back where it opens up to the left.

Emily clings close behind as Jim peers cautiously into the first room.

"What a mess," he breathes after eyeing a pile of clothes littering the floor.

A few steps down the hallway another ingress materializes. The tall sturdy door swings inward with a slight squeak. A stack of two bunk beds line the walls, filled with disheveled garments.

A scan of the remaining rooms reveals nothing but an empty house. At the end of the hallway to the left is an open kitchen. A small dark wood table is surrounded by a propane powered stove.

Unlike the rest of the domain, this area is awash with reflective light. Transparent green curtains tinge the room with an organic hue. Flower wallpaper lines the entire venue. A rustic double porcelain sink shows signs of mold.

The door of a diminutive refrigerator is fully opened. Except for the top shelf, the box is empty. Sitting on the upper rack is a lone glass jar of juice. It has long been orphaned, collecting a fine layer of dust for some time.

Jim plants himself on a chair and rests his arms on the old wooden table. Emily remains in the entry way. "I don't think we should stay here."

"Why?" Jim sighs without lifting his head.

"This will be the first place they'll look for us."

"He said if we went beyond the forest we would be fine."

"You're going to trust someone you just met?"

"He saved our lives."

"You don't know what his motives were."

"Alright," Jim laments, rolling his eyes toward Emily. "I'll try to get that truck going. If I can't, then what? Walking all night is unrealistic."

She sighs with a huff.
"We will have to hide for the night, maybe in the barn or something."

"A lot of these old houses have basements."

"Oh, so you think they won't know that too? The barn loft is probably the safest place since we can see who is coming."

"In the dark that is nearly impossible. A barn loft or basement makes no difference. If they want to find us they will."

"So what do you suggest?" she blares impatiently.

"Let's see what I can do with the truck, and then we'll think about the next course of action."

Emily frowns over his listless approach.

"We need to have a plan," she insists. "If that solider didn't let us go we would have been caught again."

Jim gets up with a weary gaze and spies the dark hallway leading to the porch.

"Let me see what I can do out there."

Chapter 30: Rudimentary Elements

Alone in the dilapidated kitchen, Emily folds her arm contemptuously, glancing at the white cabinets surrounding the room. Below the counter top are drawers and more cabinets.

With timid curiosity, she slides open a compartment near the sink. A row of forks and spoons lay neatly in a blue plastic tray. A manual can opener rests at the back of the drawer.

Another rolling compartment holds cutlery. She eyes the biggest knife, a long twelve inch blade resting in green goo. She wipes it off before grasping the black plastic handle in her small delicate hand. Her left index finger scrapes across the edge to ascertain its sharpness. "Nice," she whispers with a brief but poignant smile.

The knife is handled with great reverence, like a treasured talisman. Her eyes grow wide with anticipation. She points the sharp tip toward the center of the room, thrusting it into the air like a sword.

"You won't take me," she whispers angrily. The air fight intensifies as she begins to bob and weave on the dusty floor. Her eyes dilate. "Ah, did I hurt you?" she mouths mockingly, jabbing the knife at the imaginary group of attackers.

It is not until the knife accidentally hits the table that Emily awakens from her fantasy. The blade is embedded about a quarter inch into the dark wooden top. She yanks at the handle. Her strength sets it free.

Emily cradles the molded shank, imagining different scenarios, but one thought pushes away all others. It sparks to life like a blazing flame. She places both hands around the knife handle and points the sharp tip directly at her stomach. It rests on her tattered clothes.

Her eyes dance with memories. The images of her family emit through her retinas like an old glass tube television set. Her thoughts swell with emotion. Emily chases her little brother Kevin outside on a sun filled day.

He nestles a softball in his hands, attempting to run away with it, but Emily catches up and playfully tackles him to the ground.

"Mine." Kevin smiles, enjoying his sister's attention.

"Let's play with it together." She laughs while tickling his belly.

"Okay." Kevin hands her the ball. They back up a few yards in a sea of manicured grass.

"Catch it," she coaches before gently tossing the ball at him with an underhand throw. It misses the target and pops off of Kevin's wrist. Undaunted, he scrambles for it.

"Sorry." Kevin smiles before rolling the ball back to her.

"Kids!" their father yells. "The burgers are ready."

The beautiful secluded picnic area is awash with golden sun beneath lush green grass; a perfect setting for a lazy family outing.

Kevin catches the ball for the first time and clutches it tightly against his chest.

"You did it!" Emily praises, sending him on a buoyant stride.

"You're my best friend." He smiles as they head toward the picnic table together.

"You won't leave me like Fluffy did, will you?"

"Fluffy didn't want to leave you Kevin, he died."

"Will you die?"

"I'm your big sister and big sisters always take care of their little brothers."

"Do you mean it?"

"I'll always be there for you."

Her eyes flutter in the desolate kitchen with the sharp knife pressed against her
stomach. Emotions race with intensity as she looks down at the point crammed against her

clothes.

"I hate this life," she mutters gravely. The grocery store incident with Jim rushes past her thoughts, adding to her misery. "Everyone wants to hurt me for just one thing."

"Emily..." A whisper invades her consciousness, but it doesn't come from the environment. Instead, it rests gently in her thoughts like a warm winter blanket fresh from the dryer.

"I'm not going to listen," she utters. "You are just my subconscious talking, nothing more. I'm going to do this and you can't talk me out of it."

Her hands tremble as the point pierces the first layer of clothing. She presses harder until the tip bites over an inch into her flesh. She winces from the sting just above her belly button, but Emily is undaunted by the initial prick. She keeps the pressure steady.

Pain emanates from the focal point. Her eyes begin to water as the first tear of remorse trickles down her white elegant cheeks.

"Why am I still alive?" She sobs, placing the knife haphazardly on the table. It rolls over on its side, mocking her. She stares at it until her face shows like a mirror in the silvery blade.

"Why?" She laments tearfully, slumping in the chair. Emily pulls away layers of clothes at her stomach to reveal a small gash seeping with blood. A lick from her fingers smears the coagulating fluid, but does nothing to stop it. With each lick, the blood continues to flow.

Unfazed, Emily gets up and ignores the bleeding wound. She eyes the wall lined cabinets and opens each door to reveal empty cupboards.

In one, on a high shelf, sits a can of beets. She strains to reach the large oversized can until her efforts prove useless. Pulling a chair up against the drab counter top allays her quandary. She easily plucks the container from its seclusion.

She blows off a thin layer of dust from the lid then retains the use of a manual can opener. The tin top is easily retracted. Jabbing a fork into the first fleshy red beet sends her drab face into frenzied anticipation. The dripping vegetable meets her lip. Her eyes blaze in ecstasy, allowing the fragment to roll in her mouth.

"Emily," Jim calls from the hallway. He saunters into the kitchen with a confused gaze.

"That thing isn't going anywhere, but in the barn I found a couple of old peddle bikes."

Emily smiles while holding up the opened can. The fork head protrudes from the top. "Do you want some?"

"Beets? I hate beets."

"There is not much else to eat." She chomps down

on another morsel.

"Should I set the table?" Jim asks.

"Why?" She shrugs indifferently.

"Shouldn't we treat each meal as if we were living normally?"

She eyes him sarcastically.
"We're not living normally, you know that."

"But we can behave as such."

Emily frowns before handing him the half eaten can. He takes a few chunks, but leaves pieces rolling around in the bottom. With a sour face, Jim rests the container gently near the large kitchen knife.

"What's this for?" he asks with keen interest, spotting the red tip.

"I used it for beets until I found a fork," she misleads. "So when are we getting out of here?"

"As soon as you are ready."

"I'll be right there." She sighs, sending Jim out of the house to fetch the bikes.

Jim struts toward the tall red barn. Its exterior shows signs of decay around the old edifice. Wooden clapboards buckle, allowing shafts of light to penetrate the interior. At the main entrance, a single sliding door rumbles open with a strenuous push.

A collection of old hand tools lay near the doorway. Shovels, rakes and solid steel pipes balance against the wall.

However, instead of entering, Jim leans against the exterior barn wall eyeing the flat terrain. A deep breath of fresh country air fills his lungs with hope. "The land of my youth," he reflects pleasantly.

Suddenly a loud bang emanates from within the barn. He turns with fearful eyes and peers into to the void. Penetrating light illuminates the interior from open outside cracks. A shadow moves, sprinting swiftly across the dirt floor. It stops, then bolts furiously toward Jim at the open doorway.

"Stop or I'll shoot!" Jim expounds nervously, but the form continues to approach. It leaps, forcing Jim to fire off four rounds. The target is hit and falls to the ground with a thump. Though shaken, Jim cautiously walks over to the twitching mass. A grey and white coat of a thin coyote shows beneath his feet.

Emily bolts from the house with a strong stride. "I heard gunshots. What happened?"

"A dead coyote."

Their conversation is interrupted by a vicious

growl deep within the barn. Another shadow saunters across the floor toward the dead dog. It is his mate. Her shiny eyes gleam when hit by rays of exterior light. Her teeth gleam with ferocity at the two standing in the open doorway.

A quick sprint propels the animal toward Emily. Instantly, Jim fires one shot. It misses. He presses the trigger again but nothing happens. The gun is empty.

He flings the gun at the beast, stunning it momentarily, giving Jim just enough time to grab a shovel. He aims the spade atop the dazed dog's head with deadly intent. A quick blow smashes the skull. The bone crunching sound vibrates though the barn.

"How awful!" Emily screams, but her shock quickly fades.

"It's all over," Jim affirms. "I had dealings with their kind before. This time I am not the victim."

"What does that mean?"

"Never mind. Come." He presents like a master showman saying 'step this way'. "Let me show you the bikes."

Small slits of light shine along wide horizontal seams, large enough to push a finger through.

"So this is what an old barn is like?" Emily gushes at the dusty innards. "I've seen pictures of these but I've never been inside one until now."

"I grew up playing and working in places like this."

"Did you play with wolves too?"

"Coyotes do not make good pets," he corrects.

"Why did you leave your family and move east?"

"Prospects of a bright future drove me there, but I would always return home at least twice a year."

"For what?"

"No matter how hectic life became, I never missed a birthday for either of my parents."

Emily nods in recognition. "So you really lived in such a backward place?"

"Backward?" Jim glares bitterly. "We were at the forefront of agricultural technology."

Emily chuckles, staring deep into the barn. "Where are the bikes?" she inquires.

Jim points to a corner where a shaft of light cuts through a wall opening. It bathes the area with a golden glow. Two bikes rest against a vertical support post.

Each manual conveyance sports thick knobby tires and a center bar extending from just below the seat to the handle bars. The ancient contraptions show signs of extensive wear around metal fenders and tattered seats.

"I tested them out," says Jim. "They both ride well, but I'm not sure we should leave until the morning. Night will be coming soon and I don't want to be traveling in the dark."

"I don't want to be anywhere near this farm when night falls," Emily insists.

"Why?"

"I don't know why, I just feel it. We're not staying here. I'm not staying here. I'd rather be traveling in the darkness than sleep around this place."

Jim rubs his neck distressingly but remains calm. "Well," he sighs perplexingly. "We better get started."

Chapter 31: Provisional Hospice

A dirt road stretches into the distant horizon like a ribbon. The two bikers peddle beneath a silvery sky separated by only a few feet. Jim leads the parade with a slow and steady pace across the prairie fields. Their tires rumble on the coarse road laden with pebbles and organic debris.

"How are you doing back there?" Jim asks, peering over his right shoulder.

"Fine," Emily voices indifferently.

Miles bleed behind them until an obstruction rises ahead up from the bland plains.

"I think I see a house," Jim offers, pointing up the road. He stops and waits for Emily to catch up. She glides alongside him moments later with a dull gaze.

"It's getting late. We should investigate," Jim asserts. "I'll ride ahead and see what's inside. I'll call for you when it is safe."

"So you want me to hide? Where? This whole place is just one big open field," she flails sarcastically. Perspiration beads down her face.

"What's wrong? You seem upset," says Jim.

"Nothing is wrong." She sighs.

"Ever since we left that farm back there your mood has changed. Did something happen?"

"I'm fine." She grumbles as a bead of sweat rolls from her forehead.

"You look hot."

"It is hot out here," she insists. "Now where do you want me to hide?"

"You can lay flat alongside the road. That way you'll be hard to spot."

"Fine," she replies, placing the bike down in a huff.

"I'll wave my hands over my head to say all is fine."

"And if something is wrong?"

Jim caresses his chin.
"You'll know. And if I don't come out after a long while, then you should leave."

"Leave? You can't expect me to just ride away. Why don't we just bypass this place then?"

"I'm not going to spend the night outside. Besides, just look at the sky. It's getting dark and cloudy. Rain is coming. Please, stay here and I'll call to you soon."

Jim mounts the bike and rides speedily toward the house, gazing intensely at the specter ahead. His eyes widen as an old Victorian building materializes before him. The two story dwelling is meticulously maintained. A white picket fence surrounds the edifice while ornate carvings dance below soffits.

The pristine mailbox reads, 'Dr. Otis Miller, General Practitioner'. Jim places his bike against a post, adjacent to a low swinging gate. He pushes it in and saunters up the short pathway, gazing at the impressive structure.

The stately door greets him with a sense of awe. The impressive brass handle resembles an archer's bow. Decorative stained glass windows twinkle atop the door like a spread peacock. Long shimmering glass pillars flank the jamb.

Jim rises above two shallow steps to reach the porch. He touches the door handle to find it locked. Eagerly, he peers inside through the tall vertical glass column windows. Darkness fills most of the void with only ancillary light penetrating the interior.

"Hello?" says Jim in a timid voice. It is not until the third try that his words carry beyond the door. "Is there anyone in there?"

A heavy foot traverses a bevy of long steps. Jim backs away from the window. "I mean you no harm," he adds gently.

"What be your business?" an astute voice growls from behind the door.

"Shelter for the night."

"Are you sick?"

"I'm immune."

"Step back below the porch where I can see ya,"
the voice instructs. Jim backs down the steps until
he stands at the pathway.

The door opens with a bold inward swing. A stocky
man blazes in the archway with a full white beard
protruding below his chubby neck. Whiskers
bristle mawkishly like snow covered trees.

A clearing emanates around his eyes and nose but
his lips remain shielded by the overlapping forest.

A double barrel shotgun aims directly at Jim.
"Ya alone?"

"My daughter is waiting for the safety signal. How
should I respond?"

The man lowers his gun.
"It depends on you."

"We are just tired and hungry. By morning we'll be
on our way."

"Where cha headed?"

"Numa."

"Well, it won't be neighborly of me if I give cha the

boot. Folks must help each other in times like these. I was about to fix supper. Hail ya child." Jim steps beyond the fence while the bearded man disappears into the house.

Standing on the dirt road, Jim waves his arms over his head as planned, but no movement is detected on the horizon. "It's safe!" he yells, cupping his mouth. "Ah, she's probably sleeping or something." Jim mounts his bike and heads down the road. As he approaches, Emily is face up, lying motionless on her back.

"Emily?" he puffs before dismounting the conveyance. "Hey, are you sleeping?" He stares at her sweaty face. "Emily?" A gentle nudge does nothing to waken her, until an eye slowly opens.

"I feel sick," she mouths slowly.

"What happened?"

"It's my stomach." She pulls up her shirt to reveal a swollen red patch surrounding a small oozing hole.

"How did that happen?"

"I stuck myself with that knife back at the farm."

Jim stares at her sickly eyes with dismay. "Let's get you to that house."

Jim stands and cradles her in his trembling arms, trying to make headway towards the distant house.

"Stay with me Emily," he breathes frantically.

"I'm so tired," she slurs.

Jim's slow and cumbered steps get little traction. Despite immense fortitude, his pace falters. "Help!" he yells in desperation. His plea carries on the air and reaches his intended target like an arrow piercing an apple.

The bulky man steps from his porch with a gallant stride, waddling down the road carrying his rifle. Just as Jim's legs give out, the man braces their fall.

"I got her," he affirms, lowering both gently to the ground. Gasping for air, Jim reveals the calamity. He pulls up Emily's shirt to expose the festering sore.

"Sepsis," the man winces. "Let's get her inside." Jim staggers to his feet but maintains a firm grip on Emily. As before, her body is cradled against his chest.

"Do ya need help?"

"I got her," Jim gasps before cresting the porch.

Inside the doorway is a steel cage, like a small jail cell. Its dark iron bars stretch to the ceiling where it bends to form a secure roof. Two doors slide on tracks. One allows access from inside the house while the other is exposed behind the front door.

Beyond the cage is a clean house lined with rich throw carpets and ornaments of ancient times. Small treasures line dark wooden shelves mingling with a faint smell of formaldehyde.

"In here," the man directs, leading them into a medical examination room.

Jim lays Emily daintily on the paper lined table.

"How long has she been sick?" the man asks.

"I didn't know she was sick until now."

"Oh com'mon, ya can do better than that. Ya should have been honest and told me she was this way."

"She was sweating before I came knocking on your door, but that's all. Up until now she was fine."

"I see," the man acknowledges. "Chu can wait in the next room if ya want."

"I'm not letting her out of my sight."

"So be it."

The shirt and pants are cut away and completely removed, exposing her entire milky white body. Only a small pink undergarment censors her genitals. Military grade socks are also pulled. The man unassumingly lays a clean olive blanket across her shoulders and chest.

His skill is quite evident as the wound is cleaned with efficiency. Various chemicals are meticulously applied to the injury, culminating with a sterile dressing. "There now." The man sighs. "She needs a round of antibiotics. Lucky for ya I still have some."

A small device is pulled from a wall mounted rack in the company of other dangling medical contraptions. His seasoned hands position the long cylindrical instrument onto her bare arm. A quick click releases the desired dose of antibiotics.

"You are Dr. Otis Miller?"

"Yes, I be him. And who are you?"

"Jim, and this is Emily."

"Well, she sure got herself into a heap of trouble" he says before hooking her up to a bag of saline fluid. A small prick into her arm allows the liquid to flow, filling her with lifesaving sustenance. "If what ya told me is true," he says, "then this thing spreads fast. As fast as the Polar Doom."

"Polar Doom?"

"Yes. That's what many have come to call this there thing that cleansed most of humanity right out of existence."

"Will she be alright?"

"It's hard to tell at this stage." He stares at the

young maiden resting peacefully on his exam table. "All we can do now is let her rest." Otis gently lays a thick brown blanket over her entire body, exposing only her blissful head.

In the dining room, there are three sets of plates on a shiny oblong wooden table. "I always prepare a few extra settings in case company arrives."

"It was almost as if you were expecting us."

"Na. It ain't like that."

"Well two other settings are just, unusual. I'm from these parts and we always set just one extra plate."

"Well, this is my custom." He smiles nefariously.

Two big covered serving bowls vent tantalizing steam. When opened, the aroma of fresh cooked greens fills the entire house.

"I was the town doctor." He reminisces, doling out grand helpings onto Jim's plate. The second vat holds a white rice mixture. "Nowadays, I don't see much of anyone. So, how long have ya been trav'lin and from where?"

Jim strains to respond as tantalizing delights jockey for position in his mouth.

"That's okay," says Otis. "Enjoy."

A tear trickles down Jim's cheek.

"You have no idea how long it has been since a meal like this passed my lips. We've eaten out of cans and prepared foods most of the time."

"That's probably true for many survivors, I reckon. Suppose you tell me what it's like out there."

"You haven't left this area?"

"I'm not a trav'ler like ya'll. I've stayed put. Some would pass by my way and I'd treat them if need be. Others, well, just wanna take. I treated them too." He smiles slyly beneath his beard. "So, you're headed to Numa."

"Yes" Jim answers cautiously. "I hope to find my Ma."

"Chu have others in your family I reckon, like a wife and whatnot?"

"I lost them back east," he gulps. "It's just me and my little girl now, trying to find any remnants of family in this dying world."

"Well we all lost loved ones. Somehow I made it. And by the looks of it ya'll have too. I guess we share the same dang affliction of immunity. There were times I wish I were dead like them. It gets powerfully quiet around here. Too quiet. I was the town doctor and pretty busy at that. Folks from outlying areas would come and require my skills.

When the shoe dropped, many started showing up

with Polar Doom symptoms. They were camping out around my house. I couldn't do much for them. Then fewer and fewer came until there were none."

"What did you do with them? The bodies I mean."

"Well, that's a yarn in and of itself.   I took blood samples from each, try'n to catalog their history. Then the buzzards came. Well that was a mess. It took me a while but I done buried most of them out back."

"So you have been trying to find a cure too?"

"Ah," he laughs. "More like a reason than a cure right now. I reckon many docs who are left are do'n the same, but this thang is nasty. I've ain't seen anything like it."

"They say Emily is a Carrier."

"Oh really. And how bout chu?"

"I'm immune. At least that's what they told us when we were captured by the military."

"Captured? So you escaped?"

Jim back peddles.
"I've said too much already. Please."

Otis rubs the tip of his long beard.
"Well, ain't much for getting into peoples business. Ya'll can stay here until she is up to

trav'len."

"Thank you." Jim smiles reverently. "Do you have any idea when that might be?"

"Well, it's a tricky thing. A few more hours and she could have been dead."

Jim's eyes water.
"It is that serious?"

"Blood poisoning is very serious. If not treated with antibiotics quickly, it can and does lead to death. Now we just have to wait and pray that she gets better. There should be some improvement by morning."

"I don't know what I would do if I lost her."

"Well, it's out of our hands now." His eyes wander. "Tell me more about Emily. How old is she? Are there any genetic abnormalities that I need to be aware? That would go a long way in helping me treat her effectively."

"Fifteen," Jim breathes. "Otherwise she is strong and healthy."

"I see. Would ya mind if I took some tissue and blood samples from the both of you?"

"We've been poked and prodded already."

"You could be helping to find a cure. I ain't saying I'm a genius or nothing, but maybe those gov'ment scientists overlooked some'n. It's worth a chance, don't cha think?"

"Maybe later, when Emily gets better."

Chapter 32: Sanguine Flowers

Jim wakes by the first spark of morning light that shines through his window. The sparsely decorated room holds a twin bed and a single night table, but not much else.

A clean set of clothes lay at the foot of the bed. He quickly adorns them and heads downstairs.

Jim peers through the open door into the exam room, where Emily lay quietly atop the table. He glides in, standing alongside the slab, gazing down at his cherished friend.

"Emily," he whispers, watching the blanket slowly rise and fall with each breath she takes. His delicate fingers brush away a stray hair that had fallen over her eye.

"You're up early," says Otis as he rests against the door jam. "Her fever has gone down somewhat. Her prognosis is promising."

"Thank you."

"Don't thank me, but we're not out of the woods yet. I suppose ya'll be want'n some breakfast."

"I'm not really hungry now."

"Chu will be. I have chores for ya. I need some firewood cut and stacked."

"Of course," Jim proudly smiles. "I want to earn my keep."

"You come from good stock." Otis smiles. "Follow me."

He leads the way to a back door. Like the front, a large cage separates them from the outside.

"What is this for?" Jim asks.

"In case someone enters without my permission. Both gates slam shut if the lock is set, trapping a would-be intruder inside the cage like a rat."

"But you only have this on doors. How about your windows?"

"They have their own hidden systems." He grins.

They emerge onto a large deck in the backyard. "See those trees?" Otis points. "All three can come down. They need to be chopped and stacked in the corner near the other firewood. This is your chore during your stay here. In return I will feed and take care of ya'll."

"Agreed."

"Do ya know how to take down a tree Jim?"

"I helped my dad a few times."

"You best be taking your time with it. I don't want

anything crashing through the house. Ya'll find an axe and saw in that there tool shed. If cha need anything, holler. I'll be in my basement lab." He points to a ground level window.

Jim nods acceptingly."And the bikes?"
"Ah yes, the bikes. I gathered them for ya early this morning. They're under the deck for safekeeping."

"You got them before the sun came up?"

"People my age are up before the birds," he chuckles. "When ya feel'n a bit hungry, there are some morsels on the stove. Just find a clean bowl and take ya fill. I'll be much obliged if ya don't leave any leftovers."

Otis departs as Jim heads for the tool shed. Inside the dingy ten foot square wood structure are a litany of hand and power tools. Most of the electric ones seem moot without a power supply.

A handsaw and large axe lay ready for use, but a glance toward a chainsaw catches his fancy. The old petrol powered clunker is nearly as tall as Jim. A lumberjack's tool no doubt.

Jim handles the massive beast like a weight lifters bar. The fuel tank is desert dry. This does little to deter his intent to get it working. He muddles around the enclosure until spotting a small plastic fuel container.

"My Dad had one of these red things," he whispers

excitedly. His hopes are dashed as he lifts the empty keg. Not even a drop of fuel remains. Disappointed, he places the chainsaw back on its hanger.

A pair of work gloves are snatched from a bench and stuffed into his pockets. With the long handled axe balanced over his right shoulder and a handsaw in his left, Jim walks outside to the first tree.

He stares silently at the ten inch diameter trunk rocketing high above. Adorning the work gloves, Jim eyes the backside of the tree and visualizes where the first cut should be.

With eager voracity, he swings the axe at a forty-five degree downward angle. The blade bites deep into the viscous wood, vibrating the air with a loud knock. Subsequent blows leave a wide path of excavated wood. Like a skilled axe man, he stops a quarter of the way through and reverses the angle. Instead Jim chops from the bottom up, forming a v-shape cut into the trunk.

Soon, the stalk begins to lean. Cracks and snaps permeate the air. Jim backs away to watch the miracle of gravity.

The base gives way around the excavated area sending flying splinters running in every direction followed by a loud moan. Branches break high above as the entire tree comes crashes down with a loud whooshing bang.

Jim surveys the devastation with a satisfied grin. It has fallen exactly where he intended. Now the hard part begins, chopping and splitting the trunk into fireplace sized pieces.

In the basement of the Victorian house, Dr. Otis Miller fiddles with a liquid concoction bubbling in beakers hung above open flames.

Large glass specimen jars the size of industrial pickle containers line a shelf. Various human organs float in particle filled liquid. A liver, a kidney and other less discernable objects drift in their respective jars.

The container holding a heart is askew from the others. Its cap sits on a table signifying an active experiment.

Otis laments over a bubbling tube.
"I need her blood," he bemoans while eyeing the ceiling. A rustling in the corner catches his attention. He turns angrily at a living specimen, concealed in the darkness. "Quiet down" Otis blares. "Or I'll cut cha some more." It quickly complies, allowing Otis to regain his determination.

Armed with a medical bag, he ascends the basement steps clandestinely. Otis lurks cautiously around corners on the main floor, inching forward to the exam room.

He peers inside the quiet cavity lit brilliantly by the golden outside rays. On top of the exam tables lay the vernal vixen.

He pulls her arm out from beneath the covers where the saline feeding tube merges into her vein. The dripping elixir is temporally squelched to allow a waiting vial to fill with blood.

"There now," Otis whispers with a smile, glaring at a vial of dark rich fluid held up to the outside light. His gaze moves beyond the flask to find Jim laboring in the distance on a tree he has just sacrificed.

Otis focuses back into the room and down at Emily's delicate face. His pupils dilate then spark fiendishly, sending a delicious smile brimming from beneath his thick white beard.

With tantalizing curiosity, he rolls the blanket lengthwise to her right, exposing a side of her body. Her milky white leg extends through her underwear. He pulls it down to her knees to reveal a sparse patch of golden pubic hair.

His fingers fiendishly part the labia minora to divulge her femininity.

"A virgin, how novel," he whispers with delight. "Before yar time is done here, I'll have ya, said the spider to the fly."

A vicious tongue breaches his hairy lips and rolls up her unblemished thigh. "Sweeter than fresh summer corn." He smiles ghoulishly.

A snap of a tree branch outside quells his emotions, forcing a hasty retreat. He conceals the intrusion by rolling up her underwear before covering her entire body with the blanket. The elixir is set flowing once again, into her thirsty arm.

"There now child," he utters, patting her head gently as if nothing had happened. "There'll be time enough." He prances down the cellar steps, carrying the ruby vial.

In the silence of the exam room, Emily's eyes flutter open. They shift from side to side before her head follows, glancing around with nervous concern.

Her eyes focus through the window at Jim's deliberate motions. She stares, trying to comprehend the images. Her leg twitches then falls to the floor, off the side of the table.

She stands tenuously on her toes, balancing against the counter. It is not long before the blanket rolls down to her feet, exposing her bare upper body.

The blanket is quickly recaptured and strung tightly around her shoulders like a Roman goddess. Worry invades her face until it explodes into a frantic cry. "Jim! Jim!" she bellows, rattling the glass windows. Her plea catches everyone's attention.

Footsteps pound the basement steps. Otis reaches

the room first.

"Calm down now." He motions with his palms patting the air gently.

"Don't you touch me! Where's Jim?" she demands, clutching the blanket tighter. Creamy shoulders glisten against the dark covering.

Jim hears her cry and stumbles over a freshly chopped core. He pulls the axe from his latest whack and bolts from the worksite.

The back door flies open with a bang, followed by rapid heavy footsteps. Instantly he emerges in the doorway carrying the axe between his hands. "What happened?" he huffs with exhaustion, spotting Emily in distress.

Her emotions transition to instant joy. "I woke up and I was all alone."

"Don't be afraid, you're safe" Jim placates. He rushes in and places the axe on a counter. A tight hug flows between the two travelers. Otis watches cautiously from inside the doorway.

"Are you feeling better?" Jim inquires.

"I'm tired and my tummy stings. Like, what happened to me?"

"A slit in your stomach allowed for an infection to take hold," Otis injects. "Luckily ya were treated in time."

"How did you get that cut?" Jim asks while gingerly caressing her head.

"I'm so sorry," she cries bashfully, lowering her eyes. "I didn't know what I was doing. I was playing with the knife and then thought about killing myself. I wanted to kill myself. I miss my family," she utters gravely.

"I'm your father. Don't I count?" He stares poignantly into her tender eyes.

"I mean the rest of our family." She perks up, endeavoring to perpetuate the deception. "But I'm okay now. I don't want to kill myself anymore."

"You need rest," Jim affirms, pointing to the exam table.

Her head wobbles.
"I'm hungry and I need to find the bathroom, too."

"I can help with both." Otis gleams. "I use the outhouse during daylight. For now ya can find a washroom two doors down to the right. Just flush the toilet like ya normally would. I'll refill the basin afterward."

"I need clothes first," she insists.

"Let me see what I can find." Otis departs.

Emily's shoulders slump, allowing the taut blanket to dip below her breast line. "I don't trust him," she whispers sharply.

"He saved your life."

"I still don't trust him. Like are there others here?"

"No. Just us three."

Jim notices her sagging blanket, prompting Emily to examine her predicament. With a bashful grin, she pulls up the cover. "Where's my bag?" she demands staunchly.

"Over there with your mangled clothes."

"Thank God," she sighs. "Like my life is in there."

Otis thumps the floorboards leading to the room with heavy steps.

"They ain't pretty but they'll have to do," he says, carrying a large cardboard box filled with garments. He lays the container atop the exam table. "Take what ya like."

Emily notices the attached saline bag terminating into her left arm. "Like do I still need this?"

"Na. Not the bag, but I'd leave the conduit in ya arm for now. You'll need more antibiotics later. How do ya feel?"

"Tired," she replies guardedly.

"Ya need lota sleep," he comments while undoing

the clear lead tube. The injection port remains firmly attached to her arm. "The bathroom is two doors down at the right. Ya can't miss it."

Emily haphazardly plunges her free hand into the garment box while maintaining a tight grip on the blanket. A bushel of clothes are exhumed. She dashes from the room.

Chapter 33: Patch Work

"I heard ya whacking away at the tree out yonder. It came down cleanly," says Otis.

"I'm sectioning the main trunk. Do you want the twigs for kindling?"

"Sure, why not." His eyes glint with passive interest, contemplating other endeavors.

"So when do you think Emily will be ready to travel?"

"Er," says Otis with a wondering mind. "A few days, perhaps a week."

All eyes focus at the doorway where Emily sports a sour face. She has an apparent distaste for the long flowing dress that she choose in haste. Filled with numerous red flowers printed on a white canvas, the hem dangles above her bare ankles. Reluctantly she enters the room with a challenging guise.

"Nice dress," Jim teases impishly at the matronly garment.

But Otis remains transfixed at the shapely figure standing just inches away. "Lovely," he gushes, pointing to the exam table lustfully. "Now let's take a look at ya belly."

"In this?" she scolds. "I'm not lifting the dress up."

"I need to change the bandages," Otis insists.

She looks to Jim for support. "Let her get under some blankets before exposing her stomach."

"Okay," Otis sighs quickly, stepping back from the table with a preoccupied stare.

"Let's wait outside," Jim demands.

They wait patiently in the hallway for Emily's call. "I see how you look her," Jim comments. "It better not be infatuation or anything foul."

"I've done no such thing!" he cries indignantly. "Your perception is flawed, Sir. My hospitality toward the child is purely out of concern. I won't harm a hair on her head. To the contrary, I have great admiration for all my patients."

Jim nods softly. "Okay, I'll hold you to that."
"You have nothing to worry about."

"I'm ready!" Emily bellows from the exam room.

Hidden underneath layers of drab bedding atop the table, Emily's exposed stomach pokes through. One blanket covers her waist while another conceals her chest and shoulders.

Even her feet are hidden, poking up like mountains beneath the spread. She peers down past the digits toward the doorway.

Otis enters and races over. Emily's gauze-laden stomach rhythmically rises and falls in harmony with each rapid breath.

He slowly peels away the layers. With each successive film removed, the darker they become, filled with coagulated blood.

Dark blotchy skin surrounds a scar where the slit resides. With each touch on her delicate stomach, she winces. "It's still tender," Otis remarks while continuing to examine the warm wound.

He fetches a tube of penicillin ointment and swabs it over the entire wound. Clean gauze covers the area and is affixed with skin tape. "There," Otis submits with a satisfied grin. "Now it is time for ya next dose of antibiotics." He smiles at her.

Her arm is exposed, allowing the dormant tube to accept incoming fluid. A small amount flows through a syringe and into her veins.

"There," he smirks. "Now lemme find some food for ya. Stay here until we call." While passing through the entryway he motions to Jim. "Come, help me."

Just outside the kitchen, Otis pulls open a heavy squeaking door into an expansive pantry. The room is without windows allowing scant outdoor light to illuminate the void. Slowly their eyes adjust to the interior. The enormity of the room breathes before them.

Four extra wide old wooden shelves terminate at

the ceiling. Each rack is laden with cans, jars, and boxed dried goods. Otis plucks a few items and hands them to Jim. "Hold these," he instructs before disappearing into the back corners of the cavern.

Jim waits with laden arms at the precipice, trying to catch a glimpse of his progenitor, but the dark den emits no shadows. A shuffling of feet leaks sound into the hallway before falling silent again.

Without warning, Otis emerges with an armful of jars. "I reckon these should make us a nice meal." he glints, closing the squeaking door. It makes a solid sound as the strike plate latches with the door jam.

The kitchen comes alive with a flurry of activity. Otis spins to various cupboards pulling pots and pans from their moorings. They are haphazardly placed on a wood powered stove.

It sits as a massive metal icon to the past. Bedecked in heavy black steel, the rectangle behemoth stands on four sturdy decorative iron support legs. Large clean pots mingle on the three foot wide cook range. Two small front doors allow for baking while a larger door contains the fuel.

"Would ya be so kind as to fetch a cord of wood and some starters from outside?" Otis smiles passively. "Certainly," Jim replies, heading out expeditiously.

Pots and pans continue to collect atop the dormant

stove. Each is filled from the opened cans until no empty receptacles remain.   By the time the last pot is covered, Jim enters with arms full of twigs and small tree stumps.

"Those are from the seasoned pile, right?" Otis inquires.

"Yes, I know the difference."

"Wonderful, a true pioneer. Heck, it's hard to find our type given modern times." Not another word is spared.

Otis meticulously loads the stove. Arranged like a table spread, the twigs sit atop a blanket of old crumpled paper, followed by larger pieces of wood. A spark from an old lighter sets the paper aflame.

It takes a while before the stove heats up. It is nearly thirty minutes later until the pots boil. They send steam bellowing into the air. The tantalizing fragrance awakens Emily from her tentative slumber.

She sniffs the air before rising from the exam table. Her bare feet touch the ground, causing the dress to flutter effortlessly into its natural chiffonic position. "Jim?" She beckons from her doorway. Another cry sends heavy footsteps scampering toward her.

"I'm here," says Jim. Their eyes meet from around a corner.

She beams a sigh of relief. "I smell food."
"It's time to eat."

The kitchen table glistens with three sets of fine
china. The full ensemble consists of a bowl and
two concentric plates. Shiny forks, knives and
spoons lay with perfection around their respective
dishes.

In the center of the table are large pots, fresh from
the stove. They steam with salutary goodness.
"Just in time," Otis reveals before finding his
seat. Emily sits to his left while Jim to the
right. "Dig in," Otis insists, doling out ladles of
hearty soup filled with chunks of vegetables and
meat.

Emily grabs her spoon and plunges it deep into the
steamy bowl. The ravenous frenzy only stops
when droplets remain, prompting a smile for more.

"Take what cha like," Otis insists, pouring out
another ladle full. "So I know where you're
headed." He eyes Jim, eager for a conversation.
"You're not from these parts, but ya have roots
here."

"We've been on a long journey," Jim responds,
gracefully sipping his soup. "It all started in New
York. Now we're heading home to my mother, the
last vestments of our family."

"That's a long journey. Pray tell that cha feet didn't
carry ya all the way?"

"We had some help," Jim grins. "But it wasn't easy."

"I would say it wasn't. Travel'n all those miles without waypoint niceties is a sheer feat nowadays."

"How long has it been since this disease has started?" Jim asks.

"Er, let's see." Otis rubs the chin of his beard. "Just over three months since it hit these parts."

"It must be June now," Jim responds.

"Na, it's July 17th, my friend."

Emily's left hand cups her forehead. "What's wrong?" says Jim attentively.

"I'm tired and dizzy."

"Is it safe to assume that ya no longer hungry?"

"I'm full," she slurs.

"Well there is bedding up top," says Otis. "That'll be more comfortable then that there exam table, but it requires a good bit of steps to get there."

"Is there a bathroom near the room?" she probes.

"Of course, my dear."

Jim rises from the table, eager to assist. "Is her room next to mine?"

Otis hesitates.
"Close enough." He smiles beneath his beard.

Jim bends down alongside Emily, "Are you ready? I'll carry you."

"I'm so sorry," she quivers.

"Don't be."

Her left arm drapes around his neck as Jim firmly plucks her from the seat. Otis gets up and leads the way. The steep fifteen oak planks creak under his weight.

Jim begins his ascent, laboring bravely with each step. Emily's feet barely miss the wall as they crest the landing.

"Down here." Otis points to the left. Jim glances to his right at his room and spots other closed doorways. "Are any of those available?"

"Not right now. They're unfit," Otis contends.

Jim follows Otis into an immaculate room lined with dark wood panels. Antique lamps etched with glass ornamental shades lay atop night stands flanking a four post bed. The rails taper to a round wooden ball before reaching the ceiling.

Jim lays Emily on the soft full-sized bed. It is fitted with white and blue supple sheets. Her eyes slowly close.

"There," says Otis. "She'll be fine. The bathroom is at the foot of the steps." He motions. Emily nods gently before closing her eyes.

"Are ya finished with lunch my good man?"

"Not yet. I'll follow you down shortly."

"Fair enough. I'll meet ya in the kitchen," Otis remarks before softly closing the door.

"Will you be alright?" Jim smiles, sitting alongside her on the bed.

"How long will I be like this?"

"Maybe a week."

"Once I get better we can leave, right?"

"Yes."

"So it's up to me?"

"You have to get strong enough to ride a bike."

"I'm so sorry I did this." She sighs humbly. "If it wasn't for me, we could be home by now." A pause finds her eyes gaping at the bare ceiling. "I was defending myself against imaginary attackers, and then I saw my brother and remembered I had promised to keep him safe. I'm not really sure what happened after that but I felt the knife go in."

"Well, we all go through bouts of remorse. Alisha is still fresh in my mind, but killing myself is not the answer."

"When is it the answer?" she asks poignantly. "I mean I don't feel like it now, but there must be a time a place for everything, right?"

"We both lost those we held dear, but there is never a time or place to kill yourself. You never know who might need you."

"I need a father." Her eyes blink moistly.

"And I need a daughter," he replies with equal gravity. "As long as we realize that we both need each other, then suicide is a non-issue."

"And if you die in an accident and I'm left all alone with the wolves, is it okay then?"

"Are you asking me when it is okay to surrender? You are a strong woman Emily. Don't let anyone defeat you."

"So no matter how much misery they inflict on me, I am to endure it?"

"Who are they?"

"You know, those who always want to fuck me."

Jim's eyes fade. He understands her plight.
"Be prepared to fight back and use every means at
your disposal when your captors least expect it."

"I don't trust that man."

"I don't think he'll hurt you."

"Will you be outside?"

"Yes, I promised to chop some wood for him. It is
the least I can do since he is taking care of us."

"Be careful out there." She grimaces. She cannot
remain awake. Her eyes flutter closed with
exhaustion.

With a gentle click, he latches the door before
galloping down the stairs.

"Er, just in time!" Otis exclaims as Jim enters the
kitchen. "I'm going to the basement to continue my
work."

Held tightly between both hands is a bowl filled
with fresh food. "When you're done eating please
wash the remains and stack them on the drain
board. There's fresh water in the pot near the
sink. "

Jim nods. "What do you do down there in your
basement?"

"I'm studying Polar Doom." His eyes glisten with
excitement.

"Can I see your lab?"

"No," Otis balks. "It is filled with dangerous experiments. It is off limits for your own safety. Are you a scientist?"

"I guess you can classify me as a banker," Jim replies.

"Well, everyone has their calling. Mine came to me as a young child. Growing up I would see friends and family die of various calamities, some preventable. The last straw came after seeing my furry friend pass from Leishmaniasis. From then there on, Medicine became my passion. My thoughts turned to humans and that's why I became a doctor."

Jim smiles passively.
"Then I trust Emily is in good hands."

"She will make a full recovery."

Later that night, the group gathers around the kitchen table. Emily is more alert than she had been during lunch. Her eyes dance actively while listening to the banter.

"One day," says Otis twirling his fork, "I will run out of packaged food and be forced to live like our forefathers."

"You'll have to hunt," Emily surprisingly remarks.

"Indeed," Otis contends, staring at her as if her comment really matters. "And I'm no good at farming. But what happens when I run out of bullets?"

"Bow and arrow?" Jim hints.

"Perhaps. But I will tell ya this. Only the prepared and ruthless will survive."

"Being prepared is advantageous but ruthless?" Jim decries. "There is no need for that."

"Tell me." Otis pushes back in his seat with a sense of superiority. "If ya came to a large field filled with vegetables, would cha not fetch some?"

Jim hesitates.
"Possibly."

Otis snorts condescendingly.
"Suppose I didn't let cha into my house? What would ya have done then?"

"I would have pleaded to your sense of humanity."

"And if that failed? See, morals have a way of being subverted. They are acted upon when it is convenient." His voice deepens. "Ya'll have no idea of how many people came to this there door in search of humanity. I did my part to be neighborly. When they started to take advantage, well, we had some problems. The more ya give the more they take."

His eyes widen, bulging from beneath his thick beard. "Now I'm not directing this towards ya. I'm just saying that ruthlessness and morals is in the eye of the beholder. What would ya do to survive?"

"Whatever it takes," Emily voices.

"Thank you, my dear. See. She has the idea."

"We all know right from wrong," Jim preaches. "It is only to what degree we practice civility."

Chapter 34: Immaculate Violation

A strong breeze sways tall trees around the newly depreciated stalk, resting innocently on the ground. A new day dawns where Jim has chopped his last trunk. His laborious vivisection continues with dedication as he chops away usable chunks from the long arboriform.

Another cool gust buffets his face, forcing a momentary glance into the once sunny sky. A storm approaches, obscuring the vibrant rays into a murky haze until nothing but gray fills the wide empyrean.

A few hard drops plummet from the sky while an odor of dew permeates the air. Pings and pops echo off hollow objects as the speeding jets multiply from high above. Jim dashes from the area and takes refuge in the tool shed with the axe resting on his shoulders.

He sprints just in time before the sky opens, sending a deluge of rain smashing onto the surface. Water seeps under the doorway and runs into the shed with little regard for any impediments.

Jim waits patiently in the cold dark void listening to the tremulous sound hitting the thin roof. A crack of thunder vibrates the shed, sending wall mounted tools rattling from the shockwave.

One eye peers through the wall slats toward the

house.   Up on the second floor, a black mass slithers behind a pillar.

"That's odd," he whispers passively. A flood of emotion quickly takes hold of his thoughts. Troubled by the commotion, he panics, fearing for Emily's safety.

Jim ventures to the sheds doorway and pushes it open, bolting toward the house. His clothes saturate with the streaming deluge but it does nothing to stop his determination. Jim reaches the backdoor of the house in a huff of anger. It swings in, revealing the causeway cage leading inside.

Hostility subsides, allowing logic to dictate the next move.   Two gates at either end of the cage are opened, allowing ingress into the house.   But what if they close as he attempts to pass through, Jim ponders.

His mind wrestles with the conundrum until a spark of genius drives his actions.   He prances into the pouring rain to where the second tree had fallen.   A long branch sprouts from one side of the downed trunk.   His trusty axe chops away at the four inch thick husk.

The wet wood fights back, bouncing the blade away. It takes nearly double the hits to cut through the branch. The long newly cut stalk is balanced over his left shoulder while the axe handle is perched to his right.

Appearing at the house doorway, he props the branch between the ground and overhead gate nearest the front door. Feeling confident about this arrangement, Jim enters the expanse and lunges toward the inner gate.

Suddenly, the gate rushes down with a loud clang, latching at the bottom. He turns back toward his makeshift cog. It is under pressure, holding up the impending spring loaded gate. The wood clicks and pops, as Jim dashes from the cage with his trusty axe leading the way.

Out in the rain, he looks up at the two story edifice with disdain. "You will not keep me out," he murmurs, eyeing the first story windows. The double hung sashes seem unprotected, but Jim remembers the warning Otis had offered.

He peers into the dark void through rain spattered glass with caution. The dual pane crystal is no match for steel axe head. It smashes through. Almost instantly, a sharp sheet of steel plummets down like a wayward guillotine, trapping the axe blade at the bottom.

Jim pulls on the long wood handle, but it does not budge. The steel sheet is thick and is locked in position allowing for little movement. A small push upward seems to latch the bulkhead into the next locked position. There is just enough wiggle space to pry the axe head out. The sheet of steel remains locked, offering about an inch opening into the house.

Jim takes the axe and swings the back of the blade against the steel shade. It makes a loud clang but leaves barely a mark. His rage builds until a stroke of genius sends his budding anger toward a productive endeavor.

He swings the axe blade squarely at the side of the wood clapboard house, biting into the xyloid like a ravenous dog. Splinters fly everywhere. The chunks give way to an opening. He continues until a sizable hole is excised; just enough to squeeze through.

His wet shoe prints track the clean wood floors. It takes a moment before his eyes adjust to the darkness. He quickly discerns the upward staircase.

The axe precedes him as he climbs to the second floor, listening for any signs of malignancy. The air is still, exposing nothing but serenity.

Jim creeps up the steps like a crazed murderer, hunched over the axe. His mind drips with rage. He crests the second floor and turns left to Emily's room. The door at the far end is open. He stops and slowly peers around the corner inside.

Emily stands erect near the bed like a statue. She is dressed in a light green dress clenching a long knife in her right hand. The tip points downward, while droplets of fresh blood run from the edge. She stares blankly at the floor over a mound of convulsing flesh. Otis lay face down in an ever widening pool of gore.

She looks swiftly toward Jim. "He came at me," she explains, followed by a solemn gulp. Her light green dress has blotches of blood where Otis had grabbed her.

Jim motions for Emily to come by him. "Wait down stairs in the kitchen," he whispers sternly. She complies, carrying the knife firmly in her right hand.

When her footsteps are heard on the stairs, Jim rolls the body over to reveal multiple gashes to his chest, arms and face. He is still breathing. One eye pops open with awareness.

"Why?" Jim stares at the quivery mass with disgust, egging the old man on.

"I pity ya," Otis gasps. A deep rumbling cough expels more blood. "You will never feel safe when there are men like me wanting to taste her."

"Not all are like you," Jim balks.

But before another vulgarity breeches Otis' lips, his eyes roll up culminating with one last exhalation. The quivering mass moves no more.

Chapter 35 : Luminosity

Emily bristles with anxiety while the knife remains firmly in her right hand, ready to strike again. As her adrenaline wanes, a flood of emotions rush in, taking her by surprise.

The blood soaked blade begins to coagulate, forming a dull sheen across its face. "What have I done?" She trembles, but remembering the ordeal rekindles her strength.

Lying in bed under a dull sleep, her ears remain on duty. A crack of thunder energizes her resolve. She squints at the closed bedroom door. The handle twitches. With rehearsed dexterity, she grabs her trusty knife from the knapsack sitting below the nightstand.

The clean blade is covertly tucked away beneath the sheets. The door flies open as she pretends to sleep. Otis creeps in. He slowly closes the door behind him. In his right hand is a capped syringe filled with liquid. He kneels below the bed to her right, breathing softly as not to disturb her fictitious trance.

Her eyes open with a bold flutter. "What are you doing?" she vigorously voices.

Otis shakes with surprise. "Nothing my dear. It's just time for another dose of antibiotics."

"You always give them to me at night. Why now?"

"An extra dose will help speed ya along."

"Where's my father?"

"There is nothing to be afraid of my dear."

"I don't trust you."

"Me?" He chuckles while uncapping the syringe. "I only want to make ya better."

"No!" she insists, grabbing his arm forcefully.

Otis huffs. "It will make ya feel better."

"I feel fine already."

Otis easily deflects her protests. His large frame traps Emily. She is pinned down by his lumbering arms.

"I said no!" she screams. Her fingers fumble beneath the sheets, fishing for the hidden knife. She finds it and quickly palms the handle. The blade pierces the sheets and plunges into his soft belly.

"Get off of me!" she clamors, but the initial sting does nothing to deter him. She retracts the tip then drives it harder into his stomach from the side. This time, Otis cringes.

He backs off and eyes the shiny protrusion. "What's this?" He pitches while still kneeling on the floor. Blood expands beneath his shirt like a rippling pond.

"I told you to get off of me." She rolls off of the bed, clutching the blade firmly in her right hand. Rage builds in Otis. His eyes squint with discontent. He lunges across the bed, catching her dress in his bloody hands. Landing face up, he claws at her dress.

Obsession burns in his crazed eyes. "I had ya before and I'll have ya again," he pontificates.

"How dare you!" she balks.

"Last night I crept into your bed."

She seethes with disgust before plunging the knife completely into his stomach, exposing only the handle. But she is not done yet. Her fury drives the knife three more times in rapid succession, forcing him to roll off the bed.

Her eyes flicker, exploding her thoughts. No longer is she on the bed, but instead downstairs inside the exam room as Jim had instructed.

"Emily?" Jim whispers before entering. "Are you alright? Did he hurt you?"

She looks back at him, breaking her concentration. The knife falls from her hand and lands squarely on the exam table.

Soft eyes give way to a somber gaze. "Is he?"

"Yes, he's dead."

She runs toward Jim with watery eyes.
"I killed him?" Her arms wrap tightly around his neck.

"Yes. Did he try to attack you?"

"He wanted me," she snorts.

"Well," says Jim attentively. "I pulled his body downstairs and outside into the tool shed. Stay away from the windows and doors. They are booby trapped."

"How did you get in?"

"I bashed a hole into the wall. Nothing will stop me from rescuing you, but I see you had the situation well in hand."

"I told you I didn't trust him."

"You were prepared, instead of submitting to doom." He smiles compassionately.

Night falls as Jim pushes a large dresser in front of the makeshift entryway where he had broken through the wall. "That should keep out undesirables," he says as Emily nervously looks on.

"I can help," she insists.

"No need." He smiles, brushing his index finger under her chin. "You must still be upset."

"I feel fine now."

"Enough to peddle a bike?"

"Maybe." She shrugs calmly.

With the dresser in place blocking the hole, they stand back to admire the barricade. "I don't know how to disable the security system," Jim asserts.

"Maybe it is best that it stays on. That way we'll be safe from outsiders."

"Sure." Jim smiles, resting his hand gently on her shoulder.

Oil lamps burn in the kitchen, illuminating the room with a warm glow. Jim pulls a steaming pot from the stove and places it gently on the table. He doles out generous helpings of stewed meats into waiting bowls.

"How long will it take to get home?" Emily insouciantly asks.

"It's hard to tell. Normally it should take about six hours or so by car. It can't take much longer than a few more on bikes I suppose."

Emily fiddles in her chair, eating the hearty meal with a lackluster gaze. Her thoughts keep circling around sharp words like "What will we find there?"

and "Suppose there is nothing, then what?" But she keeps her thoughts hidden, trying not to offend Jim. "I hope we make it there by tomorrow," she breathes.

"We will," Jim insists with an eager grin. "Either way, we can stop running once we get there."

"I don't remember how it feels to be safe anymore. My life as a child seems like a distant memory."

"We've both been through a lot. You were a child when we first met. Now, in only a few months, you are a seasoned woman. You're not the same little girl I had set eyes on back in that traffic jam."

"I've gotten more cynical too. I still have nothing to live for." She stares at her fork contemptuously.

"For now, live for me. My only goal is to take care of you and see you grow up."

"For what? I have no future. All that went away when I lost my family."

"We have each other remember?"

"That's not good enough. I need something more. Some reason to wake up in the morning. Something that makes me want to pop out of bed with a smile. There is nothing left for me to get excited about." She sighs, pausing to concentrate on what she just said.

"I'm sorry Jim. I'm just depressed."

"I know, and we both have every right to be depressed, but if we keep focusing on it, then nothing will matter. The only thing we can do is try to set small achievable goals. The most prominent one is getting to my birth home. Try not to say 'Then what'. Let's take it one step at a time."

She smiles passively.
"You can read my mind."

"It's not hard. I wrestle with the same thoughts every day, but I know we cannot take the easy way out and just give up. We must keep hope alive."

"Why?" she asks intensely, hoping he will depart wisdom to alley her despondency. He poses, "We are products of our loving families. We owe it to them to persevere and keep their legacy alive."

"Oh." She eyes him contemptuously, as if those words did not live up to expectation. Now the seed is planted, sparking imagination. Her thoughts propel back to years past.

"I'm proud of you," her father says after shuttling Emily back from school on a warm June afternoon. "Your exam scores this year are phenomenal. You are in the top one percent of your class."

She bristles in the passenger's seat as the air conditioning flares her fine golden hair. "It was hard, but thanks to you and Mom, I made it through."

"Have you given thought about a meaningful career?"

"There are so many things I'm interested in, like a doctor, pilot and architect, and every day I keep thinking of new things that excite me."

"The world is at your fingertips and that is a marvelous thing. No matter what you choose, remember we love you."

"I will Dad. I will never forget my family. I will make you proud."

"I know you will."

Her thoughts fade. The flickering lamp eases her back into grim reality.

"You're pretty handy with a knife," Jim states.

"I was expecting him to do something, so I hid it under the covers."

A detailed review of what happened leaves Jim speechless.

"Your instincts were right." He sighs. "I must trust your insight more."

She bows her head in recognition. Emily's thoughts focus on a pending topic. "I'm not sleeping in that room ever again."

"You can stay in mine and I'll find another place."

She nods agreeably.

After dinner, the two venture upstairs. Emily has a firm grip on her clean knife, while Jim shoulders his axe. They scale the stairs and crest the landing, each carrying an active lamp in their left hands.

Emily gravitates towards Jim's room then searches for the ingress. Her eyes scan every area. "I need my bag," she states with a sense of nervous urgency.

"I'll get it from your room." He rushes out and returns in seconds.

She plunges her hand deep inside the satchel, searching feverously in the dark cavity for a precious item. She fumbles until a sigh of relief escapes her lips. A paper picture of her family is pulled from the backpack with eager delight.

She clutches it in her palm before pressing it tightly against her chest.

"This is all I have of them," she issues with a fading voice. The picture unfolds in her hand, until it rests gently for Jim to see.

"I understand," he answers, staring at the image solemnly. A picture of Alisha unfurls in his hand.

Emily stares at Alisha, offering a sublime smile.

"Will you be alright in here?" Jim asks.

"I'll be fine. Are you sure you want to sleep all the way down there on the couch?"

"There are no other beds and I don't want his." He ponders. "Maybe I'll take your room. I could clean it up a little and call it home." He smiles.

"Either that or you can stay in here with me," she responds bashfully.

Jim glowers.
"Wake me in the morning when you're ready to try out the bikes." He turns and strolls wearily down the hallway into his new room, where Otis met his demise.

Chapter 36: Monsters In The Night

Hours before first light, Jim struggles to remain asleep. Tormented by visions of his crying daughter, he awakens in a cold sweat. "Insensitive bastards," he slurs at the imagery still lingering in his subconscious.

His eyes flutter until they remain open, gazing into the dull room lit by the oil lamp. It sits to his left atop a wooden nightstand, revealing just a few teaspoons of accelerant that remain in the glass belly.

He scrutinizes the room to get his bearings but lays motionless atop a bare mattress, gawking carelessly at the ceiling.

Suddenly an unexpected sound invades the calm, catching his attention. It had come from outside the room, a muffled thump followed by a short human moan.

"Someone is in the house," he whispers anxiously. Jim springs into action, clutching his axe for safety. He peers into the hallway toward Emily's room with tepidness, expecting to eye an unsavory sight.

But the corridor is quiet and dark, revealing no clues to the momentary sound. Jim grabs the resting oil lamp from the table and turns up the wick key. The soft glow gives way to a brighter flame.

The hallway floods with the warm orange intensity of the lamp as he makes his way out of his room.   Like a firefighter ready to strike at perceived danger, the axe rests between both hands. He cautiously walks down the corridor.

The lamp dangles precariously in his left hand by a thin wire, swaying to his rhythmic stride.

Jim quietly opens Emily's door to spy a sleeping beauty undisturbed by the sound. After sealing the entryway, he sneaks down the stairs in an effort to find the cause of the errant sound.

He slithers like a cat onto the wooden planks.   His heels barely touch the steps, creeping on tip toe in an effort to remain quiet until reaching the bottom.

The glowing lamp glistens like a halo around the epicenter, scattering light in every direction. Devoid of a beam, Jim strains to see beyond the initial cone of light. Undaunted, he pushes ahead, gravitating toward the back foyer where he had forged a hole through the house.

He leaves the lamp at the stairs to disguise his approach to any waiting specters. A cautious stride into the looming darkness sends cold shivers down his spine. He grips the axe handle for courage as he peers into the foyer.

Standing like a stone monument against the onslaught of uncertainty rests the sturdy dresser, blocking the hole. It has not moved.

In the dead of night, the dim outside light shines from around the edges of the dresser with a bluish hue. Crickets and natural sounds seep between the slivers, but they remain outside, separate from the abode.

"Haw." A slow heavy breath whispers in the air from behind Jim. He freezes with fright. Each hair on the back of his neck wavers like wheat in a drying field. He peers over his shoulder to spot a fleeting shadow obscured by the lamp sitting on the banister. A click of a distant door latch snaps shut, forcing a hard gulp. Something indeed has crossed his path.

Jim spins, facing the faraway orange glow, but the obstruction has vanished, leaving a concerned gaze on his fearful face. He anxiously retraces his steps back to the lamp and stares warily at the glowing flame.

His attention waivers and focuses on a heavy door beneath the stairs. Its partially concealed frame sports a French handle. The outlines of the ingress are barely visible, shrouded with ornate molding protruding from the wall.

Jim presses the lever and slowly pulls the door outward, forcing the hinges to creak. He stops, revealing just a sliver into the abyss beneath the stairs.

"The cellar," Jim whispers gingerly while stepping away from the partially opened door. He retrieves the blazing lantern perched atop the banister and presses inward toward the void.

The lamp dangles in his left hand along with the axe blade. The light pierces the darkness instilling courage into his frighten body. He descends a flight of rickety wooden steps. One rung emits a loud squeak, reverberating through the basement.

"Haw." A breath flows crisply in the basement air. "Otis?" Jim expounds, cognizant that he is not alone. "I have a weapon. Come out and show yourself!" he blares in all directions. But the sound evaporates as Jim's right foot lands on the stone basement floor.

Long tables are filled with tubes and beakers along with indistinguishable rubbish. But a far more interesting distraction lingers in the air. A pungent odor flares Jim's nostrils forcing him to quell his continued exploration. The smell of decaying flesh inhibits his advance.

Suddenly a metal pipe bounces on the hard ground, resonating like a mechanical bell in a distant corner of the basement. Jim freezes in fear. His eyes relentlessly search for the sound.

Support columns and equipment skew his reconnaissance. "I know you are in here. Come out now."

A human head rises on cue from beyond a remote table. It continues ascending until a full form stands erect, backlit by the rising dawn shining through a basement window. Jim's lamp barely casts its luminance onto the standing specter.

"Who are you?" Jim expounds, anxiously standing at the base of the steps.

"Haw." A low gargle escapes the specter. The image walks slowly towards Jim.

"Stop!" Jim exclaims.

The lamp blankets the lumbering mass until features begin to appear. Broad shoulders and a head of thin hair reveal a man in his fifties.

The unrecognized figure stands motionless in the warm glowing hue.

"Who are you?"

"Haw?"

"Is that your name?"

"Haw." The man says again with an outstretched hand. He holds a thin black slate resembling a handheld blackboard.

Like an indecisive squirrel, Jim timidly edges forward to gently grasp the chalkboard. As soon as his fingers pinch the slate, Jim falls back a few feet toward the stairs.

His eyes strain to understand the scribbling until words begin to appear beneath the lamp.

"I am Dan. Where is Otis?" the etching asks.

Jim looks up.
"He is gone and not coming back."

Dan feverously pulls a long piece of chalk from behind his ear and requests his slate back. Jim complies as Dan begins to write.

"Then why did you call his name?" the writing bears.

"I suppose it was out of habit," says Jim to disguise Otis' true demise. "I didn't know that anyone lived down here."

Dan reclaims the board and words flow far beyond the initial question before handing his answer back.

"I was his test subject. I came to this house looking for food and he took me in about a month ago. I would give him blood and tissue samples. Then he infected me with something. I am now a Carrier."

"Can you talk?" Jim asks after reading the message.

"I could until he cut my vocal cords" Dan scribbles. "He didn't want to hear me complain. Since then I have been voiceless."

"He never spoke about you."

"I was just a lab rat to him, nothing more. I went looking for food since he didn't feed me tonight. I can often get out of the restraints and he knew it."

"Then why don't you leave?"

"To go where?" He writes. "I've been wandering outside for months until finding this place. Have you seen his pantry? It is filled with food."

"Yes. He has an impressive stash."

"So you have my answer to why I didn't leave."

The morning light fully penetrates the basement windows illuminating the void beyond the lamp. Drab features become apparent as striking reminders of what had transpired down here.

Human remains lay in vats of semi-clear solutions. Arms, legs, noses, ears and eyes scream of atrocities conducted within these walls.

In one jar rests an entire severed head floating in rust colored liquid.   The young female cranium is layered with tight skin, yet her hair has all been removed. Her mouth remains open as does her wide eyes, suggesting a scream forever frozen.

"I'm leaving for home," Jim affirms, lowering the axe to his side. He stares deep into Dan's eyes. He is no longer a beast to be feared, but a victim of opportunistic immorality. The squelching of his voice goes beyond mere scientific exploration and into a realm of perfunctory insensitivity.

"I envy you," Dan writes. "You have a home to go to."

"You don't have to be alone, you can come with us."

"Us? Dan writes. "He spoke of a girl. I wouldn't trust Otis with anything female. Did he hurt her?"

"He tried and she fought him off and killed him."

"Killed?"

"In self-defense, she stabbed him. She is shaken by the ordeal."

Dan squints, prompting Jim to eye the axe for protection. "Otis hurt you, didn't he? Now you are free."

"Free?" Dan scribbles, holding the slate squarely on his chest for Jim to read. "I suppose... At least she didn't become his next victim."

Chapter 37: Awakening

The morning light penetrates the partially opened venetian blinds. Streaks of warm summer sun cascade like jail cell bars over Emily's unconscious face.

One eye pops open followed by the other until a pleasant yawn forms on her drowsy lips. Though fresh from a restful sleep, thoughts quickly flood in from yesterday's ordeal.

With a fearful guise, she reaches for a washcloth atop a nightstand and pulls her trusty knife from underneath.

The clean blade sparkles in the morning sun, brandishing a slight grin upon her glowing face. She hobbles off the bed, carrying the knife horizontally through the air until finding a suitable resting place on top of a tall brown dresser.

The handle is balanced at the edge, allowing her attention to reflect on the immediate environment. Adorned in a long pink flannel gown, Emily locates her backpack.

Rummaging through the bag, she extracts a wrinkled pair of jeans and a crumpled t-shirt embroidered with "I'm with stupid" in blue comic letters; a gift she had received from her classmates at Haldane High in Cold Springs New York.

She unfolds the two garments on the bed, eyeing

them with a playful giggle, trying to anticipate what Jim would say about the injurious statement.

The flannel gown is lifted over her head in one continuous motion. Her partially nude body is covered only by a delicate white panty.

She looks down to examine the scab near her bellybutton. Around the hardened skin is a red ring surrounding the damaged area like a bull's-eye target.

Swelling has gone down and the affected area is now cool to the touch, signifying the infection is under control.

While hunched over, her hands gravitate inside her undies. She winces slightly as soft fingers rub against her tender vagina. "A little sore today," she whispers.

Unfazed, she pulls the jeans from the bed and hops into the legs one at a time. A quick threading of the copper button at the waist secures the pants around her shapely hips. The short sleeved shirt drapes over her shoulders like an oversized tent.

Together the garments are a bit large for her delicate frame, but she wears them with confidence. A pair of clean socks adorns her feet, followed by sneakers rounding out her traveling ensemble.

The knife is plucked from the dresser and stowed inside her backpack with care. She closes the door on her former room without looking back.

Emily prances down the stairs like a galloping gazelle, skipping to the bottom rung. Her buoyant stride quickly ceases. She pauses in the hallway, listening to Jim's voice. It lingers on the air as if a distant conversation is in progress.

She peers down the hall but sees no one. Creeping closer to the kitchen, Jim's sole voice continues to echo.

"How come." He pauses.

"Oh, I get it."

"Jim?" Emily whispers forcefully from the corridor. "Is everything alright?" She stands in the shadows motionless, waiting for his response.

Footsteps emanate from the kitchen and scamper down the hall. Jim finds her in the shade. "You're up early," he offers cheerfully. "Nice shirt."

She brushes aside the comment. "It sounds like you were talking to someone."

He places both hands on her shoulders. "We are not alone in this house."

"What?" She winces with budding concern.

"Otis kept a test subject in his lab down stairs. I found him last night. He can't talk so communication is done by writing."

Emily gulps, prompting Jim to console her. "Don't be afraid. He is a victim like us. Come, meet Dan."

"I don't want to. Can't we just go? I want to leave this awful place."

"We will leave today, I promise."

"Is he coming with us?" She fidgets impatiently.

"No, he has his own plans."

"So why do I need to meet him then?"

"Emily, please. Trust me. Come."

Her tight frown softens, allowing a nudge to propel her reluctantly into the kitchen.

Dan sits at the small table with a clean face and fresh clothes. His fleeting hair is neatly combed to one side. He gets up and smiles politely.

"This is my daughter Emily."

She grins politely while Jim pulls out a chair for her. The backpack she has carried from the room is placed guardedly by her feet. She peers down from time to time, anticipating the quickest way to retrieve the knife handle.

But her anxiety fades as Dan gently hands her his writing tablet.

"I am happy to meet you. I like your shirt, but your father is not stupid." He smiles. "I hear it was you who saved me from Otis."

She looks up at him curiously.
"I was protecting myself," she rattles.

Dan takes back the slate and scribbles more before handing it gingerly to her.

"I heard he saved you from a deadly infection, but don't be fooled. He had a thing for little girls. You were lucky to escape his advances."

"I don't want to talk about it." She squints.

"I understand. Again, thank you for setting me free," he concludes.

"Did he touch you?" Jim interjects.

"Leave me alone," she seethes. "I don't want to think about anything."

"Emily, tell me. There is no need to be ashamed."

"I stopped him, didn't I?" she answers coarsely, effectively ending the conversation.

A hot bowl of dense brown liquid steams at each setting. Dan digs in first, followed immediately by Jim. Emily watches the two enjoy their food before joining them.

"Dan is staying behind to occupy this house," says

Jim between spoon sips. "He packed us enough food for several days."

"Days?" she replies sarcastically.

"It shouldn't take that long," Jim placates. "But at least we have enough just in case."

After breakfast, the three gather at the back foyer where the ingress cage doors have been retraced and locked open.

"I have disabled the security systems," Dan writes.

Sitting next to the cage is Jim's backpack bursting with supplies. He picks up the heavy load and shoulders one strap. "How about that hole I left in the side of the house?"

"I'll board it up before winter."

"Do you have enough wood?"

"I would say so, at least for burning. Between what Otis had and those you chopped, there's enough for three winters at least."

"That was the agreement I made with Otis for taking us in."

"Jim, you are a man of your word," Dan writes. "I hope you find the rest of your family. Remember, you are always welcome here if things go wrong."

"Thanks." Jim smiles.

Dan extends his hand toward Jim then Emily. She hesitates before cautiously reciprocating.

"Whatever Otis tried to do to you," Dan writes, "I am truly sorry."

"He wasn't the first and won't be the last," she snaps.

"That's the spirit!" says Jim with a bold grin.

Jim leads the procession outside under a bright morning sun. The three congregate under the back deck where two bikes rest against a support post.

"They're in good shape," Jim boasts after inspecting the tires. His backpack is flung atop the handle bars. Emily hops on her bike toting her bag. But it weighs far less, offering little hindrance.

Dan presses both of his hands together in a praying gesture as the two settle onto the main road and vanish over the horizon.

"How are you doing?" Jim asks, peddling slowly alongside her. The house fades behind them.

"I think I'll be fine."

The tires rumble and kick up small pebbles along the asphalt.

"Please let me know when you get tired. You gave

me a big scare back there. I could have lost you."

She stares at him with timid eyes from across a ten foot parallel void.

"I'm so sorry. I didn't think anything would happen."

"You have to tell me everything no matter how trivial you think it is. That gash in your stomach was not minor."

They take another road and push hard across the flat plains, putting miles between them and Dan. The blaring sun crests, forcing a respite under a roadside tree. The large oak provides ample shade.

They slump against the massive trunk, brushing elbows while drinking bottled water.

"Not so fast," Jim suggests. "Save some for later."

"How much farther is your home?"

Jim gazes at the range with resolute intent. "I know these roads well. I say a couple more hours at most. Regardless, we should make it there well before sunset."

Jim pulls two cans of baked beans from his backpack along with a manual opener. He hands her two metal forks.

"I'm not hungry," Emily insists.

"It's been hours since breakfast. You need to keep up your strength. Eat even if you are not hungry."

Her eyes roll before reluctantly taking the utensils. With both hands free, Jim punctures the lid with the shiny claw then rotates the container until the top is dislodged. "Eat the whole thing," he prods while handing her the canister. Emily waits until Jim removes his lid before eating her own meal.

Beneath the oak tree, the two travelers quietly consume lunch. Jim gazes at the vanishing road melting in the distance with a vaporous haze. "Just look at it Emily." He points. "All is right in the world from this vantage point. Isn't it beautiful?"

The asphalt ribbon is cradled by tall green grass flanking the two lane thoroughfare. A few trees dot the landscape. It remains a virgin vista, unobstructed by manmade structures.

The sounds of summer fill the air as birds fly overhead. A gentle breeze causes branches to rub against each other, adding to the picturesque scene.

Emily gazes down the road with a blank stare. "It's just a road." She shrugs.

"Look closer. This hasn't changed for decades. From here, the world is at peace."

Her eyes perk with awareness, but the vision

deviates from his. "There is danger lurking around every tree waiting to pounce," she injects. "That doesn't fill me with serenity but fear. I don't see your peaceful world."

"You've been through a lot," he concedes. "Nothing I say can negate what has happened."

Jim pauses with downtrodden eyes. "My heart broke when the soldiers pulled you away from me. I thought I had lost you."

Her eyes glaze.

"Me too. They put me in a brick room; I think it was a jail cell. Then the Sergeant came and released me. If it wasn't for him, I wouldn't be here right now." Instantly, a reciprocating hug binds the two together under the tree.

Their embrace remains tight until a distant sound shatters the warmth.

"What is it?" Emily squints down the road.

Jim looks ahead to spot an approaching obstruction. "Take the bikes and hide!" he commands. Instantly, they maneuver behind the trees, away from the roadside.

Constant bangs pound the asphalt. In the distance a faint specter materializes from the wavy heat. An open horse drawn carriage speeds by with a sole occupant. The driver lashes the reigns, spurring the lone horse to go faster. The wagon passes in a blur.

"I think we should stay off the road," Jim suggests.

"Agreed."

Chapter 38: Peripatetic Ride

They peddle in muck and tall grass. Bumps and gouges rattle their bones, but they persist.

"How much further?" she asks.

"See that tall tree up ahead? I use to play there when I was younger than you."

"That still doesn't answer my question. A farm can have hundreds of acres. So how far are we from the house?"

"At current speed, I'd say about an hour."

"I thought so," she glowers. "Can't we just hop on the main road? We'll go a lot faster."

"What road? We left that a mile back. We will soon come to a dirt path leading to the house. Do you want to stop and rest before we reach the long driveway?"

"No, let's keep going," she moans.

The sun wanes with the approach of late afternoon. Up ahead, a dirt road that has been mostly reclaimed by nature snakes through the wilderness. Small parallel tire paths lead through rising grass while a strip of narrow growth sprouts between them.

"It wasn't like this last year," Jim remarks as the

two navigate through the right side track. They peddle single file with Jim in the lead.

They pass by a large mailbox resembling an oversized plastic fish. Vibrant green scales are molded into the thick polymer, extending two feet toward its grey tail. Its large open mouth hides a doorway into the expansive belly.

A house appears on the horizon about a quarter mile away.
"There it is," Jim beams. "My childhood home."

He peddles faster, pushing over the even plain with enthusiastic vigor. Emily struggles to keep up, forcing the gap to widen.

Sweat pours from Jim's face in a hurried frenzy to reach the house expeditiously. His emotions have left Emily nearly a half mile behind.

On reaching the foot of the massive porch, Jim drops his bike and races up three steps to the front door.

The classic white farmhouse stands majestically against the encroaching environment. A stoic barn painted red vaults a few hundred feet alongside the house. It beckons back to a simpler time, when Jim would tend his chores.

"Jimmy." His mother appears spontaneously, sitting on her porch bound chair in her youthful glory. "Have you finished cleaning the mud traps?"

"Yes." He frowns at the prospect. Cleaning these bins sends loathing through his adolescent bones.

Along the crop fields are basins that collect sediment and organic residue. Periodically they need cleaning to keep fresh water flowing to the fields.

Twice a month, Jim is relegated to getting his arms deep into the muck, pulling clogged weeds and organic matter out of the system. Two entire days are spent on his knees, covered in sludge.

But looking back, his heart fills with contentment at the days spent in the lush green fields. The chores are overshadowed by happier times spent here in his childhood.

Soon her image fades into a misty cloud. Two tarnished chairs sit idle, decaying in time on the porch.

Jim gawks at the two seats with a shameful wince. Seeing the bare rockers chills his soul. "Can it be? Can they really both be gone?" he whispers.

"Mom!" he yells at the large double wooden doors. A pull of the handles finds them securely locked. "Mama, its Jim, your son. I've come home."

A breeze forces a pair of pinecones to sweep halfway across the porch. One rolls by his right shoe. As he bends to pick it up, his eyes widen with expectation. Movement from within the house squeaks the dry wooden floors.

"Ma?" he waits anxiously at the pending encounter.

"Go away," a groggy female voice exclaims.

"Ma, it's me, Jim from New York."

The doorknob rattles while bolts and latches snap inside. Slowly, the heavy thick door creaks open just a crack. One single eye peers through the sliver with eager interest. A blink then another, until the door pulls back further, revealing a stoic woman with silver hair.

"Jimmy?" she breathes awestruck. "Is that you? My Jimmy?"

"Yes. It's me Ma. I've come home."

Her eyes shine joyously, as she flings the door open nearly tearing it off of its hinges in ecstasy. She bolts from the threshold and into the waiting arms of her son.

"I thought I would never see you again," she cries with watery eyes, clutching him tightly.

His emotions bubble to the surface, balling with pain, clutching the last remnant of his family.

He squeezes her tightly, towering over the stout woman. After a few moments, their heads lift. The woman looks up and gazes into her son's watery eyes.

"Where's the family?" she asks guardedly.

"I buried Tommy."

She frowns tearfully, trying unsuccessfully to thwart an onslaught of continued emotions. "Alisha and Karen?"

"Missing," Jim emits sorrowfully.

Those expectant words force a torrent of despair to gush from her already haggard eyes. "I lost my grandkids and everyone that I held dear. I lost them all." She sighs, but her moist eyes focus on Jim with unwavering love. "Except for you my dear. You are a cool breeze on a hot summer day."

She glances past his shoulders at an approaching bike.

"Who is that?"

"Emily." He turns. "She is my adopted daughter. We escaped New York together."

His mother beams.
"You've came a long way Jimmy."

"I had no other place to go but home Ma."

Her eyes sag.
"Your Father is out back under the Great Oak

tree."

"You buried him?"

"No. My hands don't work like that anymore. He
is beneath a pile of rocks that took weeks to
gather. I can't believe he is gone. When I laid the
last stone over his precious face, I could instantly
see all the years we had spent together like a spark
of lightening. I saw our first kiss and everything in
between right up until the last word he spoke."

Emily strolls over submissively and stands below
the porch with cupped hands in a reverent pose.

"But that's all in the past. Come child." Ma
motions with a loving smile "The both of you come
inside."

Emily's shoulders slump while climbing the four
short steps to the porch. She walks as if weights
are attached to her feet. The backpack straddles
her right shoulder but it is not the cause of her
distress.

Passing the threshold, the three enter a long
hallway. The air inside is clean and brisk with a
slight scent of candles. Wooden floors that had
once gleamed are now dull reminders of a fruitful
life.   Remnants of past glory lurk in the shadows
of this old farmhouse. Paper pictures and trophies
languish in obscurity.

The group emerges into a bright airy living room
that exhibits a plush sectional couch dancing with

antiquated pink paisley fabric. At the opposite end of the expansive room is a bare wall that once manifested vibrant images.

The thin layer of wallpaper spans from floor to ceiling along a fifty foot space, delivering a four hundred foot viewing surface. It now sits dormant like most electric devices.

"Come, rest." Ma motions toward the sectional couch. She plants herself daintily near an armrest. Exterior light bathes the room through translucent white curtains extruding frilly accents.

Jim sits in the middle curve that separates the two portions while Emily rests between them, facing the matriarch.

"Welcome into our family Emily." Ma smiles. "You are my new granddaughter."

"Thank you."

"You both can call me Ma." She nods. "You two have no doubt seen a lot in your travels and I want to hear all about them over supper. "Come." She motions toward the kitchen.

The bright spacious area exudes modern living. Multiple island surfaces mingle in open space where pots and pans dangle from the ceiling. Ma gathers foods packed in glass jars and instructs the two toward the formal dining room.

They race diligently multiple times between the

kitchen and the long elegant table below dual swaying chandeliers.   Massive framed pictures hang from the walls depicting static scenes of heroic glory. Tall wooden sailing ships mingle with jet carriers and navy vessels sharing the same wall space.

With the table set, the three are seated. Jim reaches for a ladle prompting Ma to clear her throat in a scolding tone.

"Let's bow our heads," she says, "and rejoice in this meal... Lord, I welcome my son and Emily into my family. Thank you for bringing them home safely."

A quick nod from Ma's head signals it is time to eat. Between the fork rattling, Jim chronicles the journey. Emily interjects small tidbits of information along the timeline but it is mostly Jim recanting the events.

Ma listens intensely, offering a nod where appropriate and wincing in sympathy at ghastly events.

"My poor granddaughter was taken?"

"Yes Mama. I watched as they dragged her away through the monitor."

Ma's eyes squint distressingly.
"When you called from your office, I just knew things were not going to be alright. I could feel it."

Words from their adventure sing on the air like a sad violin.

"And that's how we got here," Jim concludes.

"My word! You two have seen a lot indeed. I never heard of Dr. Otis Miller but we use Dr. Igby and he is nothing like that. You remember him, don't cha, Dear?"

"Yes."

"Well, him and others come around now and again to check up on me."

"So you have visitors." Jim smiles.

"Oh my yes, but it wasn't always like this. For months after your father died, I was alone and thought I was the only one left in the world. So I made do until some old friends started coming around. Seeing them was like a breath of fresh air." She smiles. "Today I wasn't expecting anybody. You gave me quite a scare showing up on my doorstep." She nods.

"Being out here all alone can be bleak and downright risky," Jim utters.

"Most of my friends are still here and we take care of each other."

"How do you get around?" Jim asks perplexingly.

"Nowadays I take the horse drawn wagon into

town," Ma pragmatically explains. "It is like a bus, making stops along a predefined route. Every three days it comes to these parts and ferries me and my friends into town. Tomorrow it will pass by our house between noon and one."

"It is wonderful to be home," Jim remarks. "I want to be a part of this community again." He sighs blissfully. "I haven't felt at ease in such a long time."

"You have been quiet, my Dear." Ma smiles toward Emily.

"I'm fine, just a little tired."

"Ah, you both must be tired. Jimmy, you know where your room is. I'll show Emily to hers. Just leave everything where it is. I'll clean up later since I know where things go."

Plates remain on the expansive table with a sea of empty containers. All the food prepared for the meal has been diligently consumed.

Ma leads the way up to the second level of the old farmhouse where Jim scurries into his boyhood room. He disappears behind the door with a childlike grin.

Ma gently takes Emily down the hall.
"This was where my youngest son slept." She walks over to a bold dresser constructed from mahogany. The dresser drawer is pulled open to expose neatly arranged clothes.

"I'm sorry to say that these garments do not befit a young woman."

"I don't mind." She smiles politely.

"You are a gem," Ma lavishes. "Your parents would be proud."

"Thank you."

"But that shirt." Ma grins. "My word. Where did you get such a thing?"

"Friends at school."

"No doubt that it holds a special meaning for you. Those are treasured moments, my Dear. That shirt will be cleaned and washed so that it can continue serving its purpose as a reminder of happier times."

"Thank you." Emily smiles. "Can I take a shower? I feel dirty after the long ride."

"The electric pump hasn't worked in months. The only way to get clean is outside beneath the cistern."

"What's a cistern?"

"Ah," Ma laughs. "That's a water tank collecting rain. If you really want to use it I'll show you. Find some clean clothes first to take with you, then I'll meet you down stairs."

With Ma slowly descending the rungs, Emily pulls a pair of denim jeans and a plaid shirt from adjacent drawers. Each successive find does little to spark her fashion interest.

She meanders over the dull offerings until settling on a pair of black jeans and a long sleeved blue and white checkered shirt. They lay heavily in her arms like a sack of wet potatoes.

"Ah, you found something, my Dear." Ma smiles from the bottom step. "I wish I could offer you more womanly apparel. Tomorrow we'll bring some of these old clothes into town as a trade." A thick towel drapes over Ma's arm. "Come," she motions cheerfully.

The setting sun bleeds into the horizon like a fluttering ribbon. It is just enough to illuminate the shadows with a golden glow to scare away the approaching night for a few minutes longer.

Standing by the barn is a tall rusted water tower supported by four wooden stilts. It vaults thirty feet above the grassy ground like a tin spider with pipes leading into untended fields.

Another pipe, many times smaller than the others extends through the barn roof. It terminates inside, where a small white plastic stall abuts against a wooden wall. The top of the booth is completely exposed, allowing the water pipe to hover inside.

"The spray is powerful," Ma explains. "So just open the spigot slowly."

"Where is the hot water faucet?"

"There is none, my Dear. But I can confirm that the water temperature is not too bad this time of year."

"What happens in the winter?"

"That is when it really gets interesting... Well, for now there is a bar of soap inside the stall."

A frosted glass door swings outward with a towel rack on both sides. Ma hands Emily the towel she had been carrying from the house. "You have about ten minutes my Dear before the sun fades. I suggest just a few minutes under the spray. When you're done, just come inside the house." Ma turns toward the door.

"Don't go," Emily insists. She places her hand delicately on Ma's arm. "I don't like to be alone."

"You want me to stay until you're done?"

"Yes, please."

"Alright, I suppose if it'll make you feel better."

Emily drapes the clean clothes she had gotten out of the dresser drawer and places them neatly over the outside door rod. The towel hangs inside.

Instantly the frosted glass hatchway closes. After a few quick groans, her old clothes are flung atop the door.

Her hand breaches the enclosure toward the suspended water spout. Emily's fingers grasp then twists the warm spigot. It squeaks under the instant turn until a cold spray cascades down.

"Ow!" Emily winces under the icy water.

"Is everything alright, Dear?"

"Yes." She shivers while grabbing for the soap, not wanting to make a fuss about the chilly spray.

The lather builds over her supple body forming a creamy sheen, but she doesn't linger under the cold spray. Quick darts in and out of the flow dissolve the froth.

"Jim is like a father to me," she emits from the stall.

"Yes, I can see that, my Dear."

"He told me that there were two other brothers but he is the only one left."

"Did he tell you what happened to them?"

"No, and I didn't want to ask."

"You are such a polite child. Since you are a part of our family now, it is only right that you know our history."

Ma finds an old dusty chair and plants her weary body on the wooden seat. "Each of my three boys was born about 2 years apart. Tommy was the youngest and Evan was the middle child. Those three were a handful and God knows I wanted more to help out around the farm. But that never happened.

As the eldest, Jim would be in charge when I or my husband weren't available. Heck, he would act like his father sometimes, thinking beyond the situation. I always felt safe leaving him in charge."

Emily extinguishes the chilly spray and dries herself inside the stall. She reaches around the door to pull her new clothes inside and adorns them expeditiously.

"We would grow a couple of different crops but through it all, corn was our mainstay," Ma continues as Emily steps out from the stall. "The boys loved to play in those tall stalks."

Ma's eyes begin to squint reminiscently. "One day when Jim was 10, the three boys were in the fields playing like innocent lads. Little Tommy was always curious. And when it came to animals he was even more inquisitive.

Just beyond the edge of the cornfield was a newborn puppy. Tommy walked over and started petting it, but little did he know it wasn't a domesticated dog. It was a coyote pup. In fact, the parents were resting nearby. When they saw what Tommy was doing, they came over immediately. That's when all hell broke loose.

Evan tried to help but he was caught in the frenzy and was tackled by the mother. Jim froze for a moment, watching his brothers being ripped apart. By the time he realized what was happening, the damage was already done. The pack vanished into the woods leaving pieces of Tommy splattered between the cornstalks. As for Evan, we could never find his body."

"How awful!" Emily gasps. "Poor Jim."

"Yes," she sighs. "Jim was traumatized for years. He never strayed from the house by himself. And he would always be fearful of large dogs."

"Do you blame him for what happened?"

"I used to," she glowers shamefully. "But there was nothing Jimmy could have done without being killed himself. I forgave him decades ago."

"He is a good man."

"I know, my child. I know."

Emily drapes the wet towel and old clothes over her right arm.

Back in the house, Ma and Emily climb to the second floor. "There is a candle and matches in your room. Just mind the flame and douse it before you get into bed. We don't want any unexpected fires."

"Of course." Emily smiles.

"Good night, my Dear. If you need anything, just holler."

Ma peeks into Jim's room to find him fast asleep, snuggled beneath the covers like he belonged there; and indeed he does. A brimming smile on his face melts into the pillow.

Chapter 39: Solicitous Memories

A full moon shines down on the wistful farm as the three lay in their beds dreaming of happier days. Emily visits with her parents while Ma plays with her three boys before their calamity, all in the confines of their minds.

Across the otherwise silent night, a distant sound radiates over the plains and in through an open window to lodge in Jim's restful ear. It stirs his memories until he wakes in a cold sweat. The bright moon bathes his childhood room with a cool glow. For a moment, Jim is young again gazing around his chamber with ardent wonder.

He is jolted back to reality while peering past his covered feet. "Mama," he whispers. A low cough clears his raspy throat. The sound that had wakened him resurfaces. It pierces the air with a distant howl.

"Coyote," Jim hisses. He gets up and plants himself by the open window, drawing little breath. Again the sound expands over the land. "It is a coyote." Jim shudders, recalling his childhood fears. A bead of sweat trickles down his cheek.

The event that caused the demise of his brothers had happened differently than his mother had perceived. "Tommy!" Jim whispers to his youngest brother. The two adult dogs lay quietly in the woods. "Get away," Jim spouts.

His brother continues petting the pup. Hearing Jim's plea, Evan vaults toward Tommy, but his advance is quickly spotted by the dogs.

Evan is attacked first, thrown to the ground with a horrific bang, knocking him unconscious. His lifeless body is dragged deep into the forest by one of the coyotes.

Not a moment passes before little Tommy is eyed by the remaining parent. The female coyote bares her sharp menacing fangs at the young scared boy, but Tommy becomes even more protective of his new furry pet.

"Leave my puppy alone," the child expounds.

The parent does not take kindly to her offspring being manhandled by humans. She pounces on Tommy with a ferocious growl, lurching at his neck. Blood spatters everywhere. The horrific blur lasts just seconds before the coyote leaves with her pup.

Jimmy races over to his twitching brother lying on the blood soaked ground. Chunks of flesh and a detached arm rest a few feet away. With mangled fingers, Tommy reaches up Jim. "Did it hurt my puppy?" he wheezes in relative calm.

"What?" Jim stresses, peering down at his maimed brother. "That wasn't yours. It was hers." Tommy's eyes roll up into his head as the last gasp of air leaves his body.

A tear rolls down Jim's cheek as he stares at his lifeless brother at the edge of the cornfield.

Chapter 40: Remembrance

Bright morning sun warms the farmhouse, shining through every window like a ray of lightening.   Each room glows in the radiance of a new day.

Emily and Ma assemble around the kitchen table waiting for Jim.

"We made a nice meal together." Ma smiles. "Now where's my boy? Can you go and see what's keeping him?"

"Sure."
Emily bolts innocently from the table and vaults up the staircase.

"Jim?" she emits at his door followed by a knock. "Jim, it's time for breakfast." She persists, but her virtuous eyes quickly swell with concern.

A slow twist of the knob unlatches the door.   It opens with a slight squeak onto a barren room. The mattress swirls with jagged sheets vaulting like islands in a sea of cloth. The unmade bed is still warm as Emily examines the chamber.

Her attention is drawn to the window. She peers down from her second story perch onto a pristine landscape where a large majestic tree shadows the ground.

Beyond her audio perception, Jim kneels near a

long pile of stones. "Pa," he whispers with watery eyes. "I missed your birthday this year." His weary hand trembles on the cold stacked stones.

A metal pole marks the gravesite where the stones form a steep slope. A small wooden plaque is wrapped around the pole with wire, designating the tomb's occupant. His full name is etched by a felt tipped pen along with birth and death dates, leaving no room for anything else.

"What an end to a colorful life. No sign can do justice for all that you have given me. I miss you." A tear trickles down his right cheek. "I am so sorry for everything I have done to you and Ma over the years."

A soul curdling cry emanates from his distraught face. It echoes over the land like the howl from a wounded animal. Events leading up to this moment flare into clarity, hovering around his now defunct family. He bawls in agony, doubling over in pain near his father's grave. All that he had held inside his heart over the months breaches the surface.

His mother slowly advances on the site with Emily trailing behind. Ma stops a few hundred yards away, but Emily passes her. "Wait child," she whispers. "Let him be, Dear."

"But he is crying."

"I know. Sometimes a good cry can cleanse the soul. Be patient."

Jim continues wailing until only sniffles
remain. Spurts of whimpering signal the worst is
over.

"Go to him child."

Emily creeps gently toward the mound of stones
and kneels to the right of Jim. He turns to her
with a soaked face. "This is my Pa."

"I know." Her eyes bulge with compassion.

"What's the point of living when everyone you hold
dear dies concurrently?"

"Stop that," she admonishes with a grin. "You are
starting to sound like me."

His eyes brighten.

A strong resolute face rises above the
site. Standing like a pillar of hope, he gazes at his
father's grave before turning toward Ma.

"It is a different world, my son, and life will get
harder."

"How hard?" Emily asks.

"Let's go inside, my Dears and discuss it over
breakfast." She smiles. The three back away from
the grave and return inside.

Seated around the old table, they consume a light

meal.

"When I was all alone here," Ma states, "I could figure that these preserves would last until next summer and perhaps further. Now I'm not so sure."

"You have enough firewood," Emily interjects. "I've seen stacks of logs outside."

"Yes, my Dear. We will all be warm for the winter."

"Surely we can make a trade for some food," Jim deduces.

"Maybe," says Ma with a cold stare. "But food is scarce everywhere, especially now when most of the farms are idle wasteland."

"Come spring we can grow our own garden," Emily announces.

"Yes, my Dear, but until then we have a long winter ahead of us."

"It doesn't get that cold here, Ma," Jim dismisses. "Maybe we can start growing things now?"

"It's not that easy, my Dear. The ground still freezes by late October and we get occasional winter storms. Growing this late in the season is out of the question."

Chapter 41: Hamlet of Hope

The three assemble on the porch, each with a clothes bag by their feet. Emily's satchel is the largest, filled with dull male attire.

"That looks heavy," Jim comments.

"We cleaned out most of the drawers," Ma explains. "A young girl needs pretty clothes." She smiles at Emily.

Behind the matriarch sits a large black rolling suitcase with a telescoping handle fully extended. Jim's bag is the smallest of the group, resting like a loaf of bread next to his loosely tied boot laces.

"Let's get moving!" Ma exclaims. "We best be at our mailbox before the express gets there."

With a brisk stride, Ma leads the pack down the dirt driveway toward the distinctive postbox.

The quarter mile journey terminates at the fish shaped mailbox.

Ma arrives first and rests against the post. Emily and Jim take second and third place, dropping their bundles on the dusty ground.

"Why do you have a fish for a mailbox?" Emily inquires, staring at the exaggerated proportions.

"He won that," Jim replies. "I was here when he put that up."

"It's hideous," Ma balks.

"I kinda like it." Emily smiles.

A faint sound rumbles in the distance. It draws closer with a thunderous roar. Two horses breach a clump of trees pulling a four wheeled open truck behind. Large tires support a modified frame with its engine compartment removed. Two leather reigns snake their way inside to the driver's seat behind pristine glass windows.

It slows before coming to a quick and silent stop in front of the mailbox. The driver exits the cab from the passenger seat. A portly bald man sporting wide blue suspenders and a red plaid shirt stares at the three with curiosity.

In the back of the open air bed is an elderly couple atop a wooden bench, but there is room for a lot more. The entire deck can support a total of eight patrons like a small school bus. The two customers look down with active interest.

"So who do we have here?" The portly driver squints.

Ma stands proudly in front of her clan.

"This is my son Jim and granddaughter Emily."

"Welcome," says the driver while loading Ma's

luggage into the back first. "Your bag?" he grumbles at Jim who eagerly hands it over.

Emily struggles to lift her satchel for the driver. "I'll take that, my Dear."

Helped atop the back by the portly busman, the three find seats near the elderly couple.

"This is Martha and Ed," says Ma to her family.

The couple politely smiles.
"I remember you." Martha grins at Jim. He nods in recognition but his eyes say otherwise. It has been a long time since he has conversed with the locals.

On most trips back to his parents, Jim would stay just a few days, engrossed in the family events. Seldom did he venture into town.

The carriage picks up speed, pulled by two galloping horses along the paved road. A few miles away, the chariot stops at another driveway to take on more passengers.

The conveyance continues along its appointed route, stopping at various waypoints until nearly all the benches are filled. Names that have been thrown at Jim and Emily are long forgotten, culminating in a hodgepodge of indistinguishable sounds.

A normal trip into town takes about ten minutes, but this involved journey has squandered nearly forty along back roads and far flung rural venues.

Jim and Emily listen blissfully to the abounding conversations blossoming around them. Close by, Ma and Martha strike up a conversation.

"You must be so happy to have your son home," Martha comments with a glistening smile.

"In all my dreams I thought I would never see him again," Ma contends.

"Your granddaughter is quite different then I had remembered."

Ma smiles blankly while the chariot rolls across a wood decked bridge. The short span leads into town from a back road.

Clean paved venues glide straight through town and melt into the distance. On either side of the main thoroughfare are black and white clapboard buildings reminiscent of federalist architecture.

Parking spaces angle inward toward the curb where a few dusty cars still remain. Some shiny bicycles rest on sidewalks, but by far the most prominent form of conveyance are horse drawn wagons.

Each equine is tied to dormant parking meters around a cluster of stores. A farmers market and feed shop garner the most activity.

However, the arriving bus has pulled up in front of

'Trader Joes'. Dark wood siding seems out of place in this mostly white storefront section.

Those at the back of the bus enter first and form a line through the door. "Browse. If you find something you like, hold on to it until you make a trade," says Ma to her clan.

The group dismounts, carrying their precious items along the sidewalk and into the rustic store.

The aroma of antiquities permeates the interior like dry rotting wood. The dark void is only illuminated by outdoor light gleaming in through the storefront windows. Shoppers browse the plethora of goods hanging from every wall and ceiling like a circus gone wild. Makeshift displays fill most of the floor space, spewed with used items, evoking the feel of an indoor flea market.

Jim eyes a pair of snowshoes and pulls them from a rack. The tennis racket sized skids are brought up to the glass counter. Behind it stands a gray portly man covered with blue suspenders and a dark flannel shirt. His face bristles with a wiry beard. His wife Mae stands alongside him, haggling with another customer.

The old man eyes Jim and breaks away from his wife's conversation. "Hello, Sir. You seem familiar but I just can't place your face. Are ya new around here?"

"You're Mr. Beadsley?"

"Yes and who might you be?"

"Jim..."

"Wait a minute." His eyes brighten. "Yes, I remember you. You're Kathy's son. You were in New York?"

"Yes, but I found my way home just yesterday."

"Mae, come take a look at this," Mr. Beadsley declares with an exuberant smile. Though still preoccupied by another customer, his wife Mae slowly saunters over.

"Yes, some good trade?" she inquires. Her haggard eyes glance down at the snowshoes and back up to Jim. "What are ya trade'n for these?" she emits before recognizing his face.

"Jimmy?" she bids.

"Yes, I've come home."

"Mae!" another customer shouts. "I'll take your deal," prompting the storekeeper to retain her professionalism. "I'll be right there." She pauses momentarily before lavishing a smile toward Jim.

"Welcome home, my Dear. My husband Joe will take care of you," she exclaims before returning to other customers.

"Well Jim. What do you have to trade for this fine pair of snowshoes?"

Inside the glass counter, a unique talisman catches Jim's eye. Resting on a white background is a silver heart pendent inlaid with gold vines surrounding a golden cross.

"Can I see that?" He points down into the case with interest.

Joe plucks the medallion and hands it to him. On the back reads "Alisha" along with a date. Inside, the picture still remains, depicting his defunct family.

"It's hers," Jim gasps, his eyes showing his excitement. "Where did you get this?"

"I don't remember. Why?"

"This belonged to my daughter Alisha. You must tell me where you got this!"

All conversations abruptly cease, leaving the store in eerie silence. Ma and Emily scurry over. "What is it Jimmy?" Ma cautiously breathes.

"Look, its hers." He reels, handing over the locket.

Ma examines it before gazing into Mae's eyes. "Who traded this?"

"It was about a week ago," Mae replies sternly. "I barely remember it." Her eyes focus on the talisman glistening in Ma's hand.

"It was traded in bulk by a tall bearded man traveling from town to town," Mae cites. "He traded the entire lot of assorted fabrics and trinkets."

"Yes, I remember," says Joe. "It was at the bottom of a wooden box filled with many things. He comes in now and again. I will ask when I see him next."

"When will that be?" Jim begs.

"Gavin, that's what he calls himself. He comes around every four to six weeks. But it may be less frequent as the weather gets colder."

"I must speak with him," Jim pleads.

"I will send him your way." Joe placates.

Soon, the bustle of the store regains its strength as deals fill the air. "I need that back." Joe smiles. "I'll keep it in a safe place so that I can show it to Gavin to jar his memory."

Ma dribbles the chain into Joe's waiting hand. "When we're done with it, I'll give it to you as a gift." Joe smiles at Jim.

But he is no mood for niceties. His face grows somber. "I'll be outside," Jim grumbles. "Do you want me to come with you?" Emily whispers.

"No, I need to be alone." He steps outside toting his bag and sits quietly on the sidewalk, gazing up at the clear blue sky.

"Why do you continue to torment me," he shouts internally. "I was willing to let her go and now you give me this; a strand of hope. I won't sleep until I find her."

Chapter 42: Effectuation

Days melt into weeks as Jim is ferried back to the store. Each subsequent visit leaves his empty heart filled with more questions.

"Jim," says Joe on his third trip to the store. "There is no need to come back fishing for information. I reckon you are heartbroken but there ain't anything I can do for you right now. I promise, when Gavin comes in, I'll send word. Please trust me."

Jim's eyes sag. "Suppose he doesn't come back?"
"Mark my words, he'll make at least one more trip before winter, he survives on trades."

Dejected, Jim waits outside in the windswept air for his family to complete their weekly transactions. A chill blows down the lonely road causing Jim to shiver in his thin coat. The signs of winter blare around him as bundled patrons scurry into nearby stores.

Wagons of firewood race by and dead leaves are blown from the street collecting in sidewalk crevices.

Ma and Emily emerge from the store. The three board the waiting bus.

Back home, the two women unpack their acquisitions in Emily's bedroom.

"I'm worried about Jimmy," Ma whispers gravely. "He's been so preoccupied after setting eyes on that locket."

"It did belong to Alisha, right?"

"Yes, it is most definitely hers, but no good can come from it. He is holding on to a blade of grass in a field filled with weeds, hoping to find from where it came."

"Are you saying he should stop trying to find her?"

"Well, my Dear, there comes a time when even the most determined need to let sleeping dogs lie."

"He loved Alisha so much."

"As did I, but it is time to move on, otherwise I will lose him to insanity."

Emily plucks a newly acquired dress from her bag.

"That will look pretty on you, Dear," says Ma.

"I hope I can wear it. Am I gaining weight?"

Ma glares at Emily's stomach.
"Turn to your side, Dear."

Why, what's wrong?"
"Can I see your tummy?"

Emily lifts her shirt halfway to expose a slight protrusion. "Do you feel sick in the mornings,

Dear?"

"Yes, and my breasts are a little sore too."

"Did you have your period?"

"No," Emily ponders. "Why?"

"Sit down, please." Ma motions to the bed, casting dispersion over Emily's youthful face. Her eyes harden as she stares at Ma.

"There is something wrong, isn't there?"

"Have you and Jim..."

"Have we done what?"

"Have you two been intimate?"

"No!" Emily recoils instantly. "We never did anything like that. He is like a father to me."

"Then you know what I am about to say?"

"I am pregnant right?" Her eyes tear.

"Yes, my child. You have all the signs. But you do not know how?"

Her thoughts search until stopping at a dark region of inequity.

"Dr. Otis," she whispers at first. Then angrily spews, "It was him. That Dr. Otis. I knew it, I just knew it!"

"Calm down, Dear. Nothing will change the fact that you are pregnant regardless of who did it."

"I don't want this in me. Get it out."

"Nonsense, it is not the child's fault. You can't just banish it for being conceived."

"I was raped! I don't even remember it happening. He drugged me."

"He was an evil man and will find justice under God's watchful eyes."

Emily begins to cry and curls into Ma's arms, cradled against her chest. "There child. You are not alone. Together, the three of us will get through this."

Downstairs, Jim feeds the flaming fireplace with fresh chunks of wood. His placid gaze exemplifies hopelessness amidst spiraling despair. The energy that he had once exuded has evaporated.

"Jim," Emily voices from behind.

He turns with dark ringed eyes. "What!" his spiked tongue spews. Emily is startled by his abruptness, causing Jim to soften. "Sorry." He trembles nervously. "I didn't mean to yell at you."

"I know what you are going through," she whispers. "You feel empty like I did when I cut myself with the knife."

Jim hangs his head. "Empty is a feeling and I feel nothing."

"Just like I did," she insists while kneeling beside him, gazing at the flickering embers in the fireplace. Her thoughts gravitate toward her unborn child with detached interest. She resists telling him, opting instead to console him in his agony.

"You are my best friend and I hate to see you this way."

"What would you have me do?"

"Take a deep breath and let fate guide you. Staying up all night thinking about Alisha does nothing. Do you know what you are doing to Ma? She's worried about you."

"I can't help it right now. Above all, you should understand me. We've been through hell together."

"Supper!" Ma yells from the kitchen.

Chapter 43: Resurrection

The days continue to bleed toward winter. A chill in the air signals a snow flurry as Jim sits on the porch, eyeing the frozen precipitation in the early morning light. It is Wednesday, but no one in his family is preparing for a trip into town.

Still, Jim glances down the driveway toward the mailbox in hopes of eyeing Gavin the trader. Sadly all of his attempts to wait for this mythical being have ended in disappointment, be it Wednesday or any other day of the week.

His eyes close while sitting on the porch, wrapped in a thick heavy blanket. Suddenly, a sound disturbs his ear, forcing his head to actively rotate toward the intonation. The noise clatters closer with a slow rumble. It is unlike the galloping open air bus that is scheduled for later today.

Then the tenor abruptly ceases. Jim peers down the road to spot a lumbering wagon propelled by a single horse. It has come to rest at his mailbox.

A spark of excitement fills his soul, prompting an expeditious vault toward the waiting cart. A lone horse is shackled to a covered wagon, controlled by a single occupant mounted inside.

"Hello," Jim exalts nervously upon approaching the cart. "Hello?" he voices tiredly again.

A head pops out from behind the covering to reveal

a white bearded man dressed in black leather. A long brown duster coat and cowboy hat complete his ensemble; a true product of the old west.

He gingerly dismounts the cart. Despite his advanced age, he stands tall, eyeing Jim with a cautious gaze.

"You must be the fella Joe spoke about. Are you Jim?" he asks in a velvety voice.

"Yes, and you must be Gavin the trader?"

"I can't stay long," he offers, while looking up at the snowy sky, depositing more than just flurries on top of the already snow covered surface.

"Please. Why not come in and stay with us until the weather clears," Jim insists.

"I appreciate the offer, I really do but my plans are more pressing. I just stopped by to tell you about the locket." Gavin pulls the shiny jewelry from his pocket and hands it to Jim.

"I acquired that there trinket a while back from a fella named Olsen."

Jim's eyes bulge.
"Sergeant Nathan Olsen?"

"Sergeant? I don't know nothing about that, but I think his first name was Nathan."

"Where can I find him?" Jim snaps.

"I normally don't give out my sources…"

"This belonged to my daughter Alisha," Jim blares with agitation, dangling the locket by its chain.

"Yes I know. Well, I met this guy at his house about 18 miles south of here in Unionville Missouri."

"Was a little girl with him?"

"I don't recall seeing anyone but him. I never went inside his house, though. He traded me a few boxes of clothing and whatnot."

"Can you take me there?" He twitches excitedly.

"Well I'd be lying if I said yes. I'm not going down that way for a while…"

"Please. I need to find her."

"It'll be a few weeks before I make it down there and I don't take passengers."

"Please," Jim petitions.

"How's this. I'll talk to him about this Alisha girl when I get there."

"And how long will I have to wait?"

"If the weather holds, I should be there in about two weeks. Once I find out for sure, I'll shoot right up with the info."

"And if the weather is bad?"

"Well son, I reckon you'll have to wait till spring."

Jim nods amicably, but with mixed emotions.

"Well, I'll be on my way," Gavin signals. He hops on his rig and loosely dangles the horse reigns between his gloved hands.

"Wait!" Jim blares. "Where is Olsen staying in Unionville?"

"I don't remember the address but it is near the only high school in town." A snap of the reigns spurs his horse along the snowy path.

As Jim walks to the house, his eyes burn with desire, melting the falling snow like a steam roller. Each step brings staunch determination, wondering if he can make the trip on his own.

Back inside the house, he sprints toward his room. A fury of emotions emanates from within. An oblong aqua blue suitcase is flung on the bed and haphazardly filled with clothes.

Ma hears the clatter.
"Jimmy, what's going on?" she prods from the doorway. A concerned guise singes his shoulders.

"I'm leaving to catch the bus into town."

"So you are trading all those clothes?" she stammers.

"No Ma. I'm leaving."

"Leaving?"

"I know where Alisha is."

"Where?"

"Unionville, Missouri."

"How do you know that?"

"I spoke with Gavin the trader just a few minutes ago."

"Jimmy, do you know how far that is on foot?"

"I don't care, Ma. I'll find a way to get there."

"Did this Gavin see Alisha?"

Jim hesitates.
"No."

"Then she may not be there."

"But I have to find out."

"Jimmy." She tenderly strokes his back. "I don't want to lose my only child."

"Now you know how I feel Ma. I don't want to lose

Alisha either."

"That's not fair."

"Ma, I need to go."

Emily wanders past the door. "What's going on?"

"Jimmy is leaving us," Ma sternly replies.

"Why?"

"You remember Sergeant Olsen?" Jim emits with his back turned. "He may have Alisha with him just south of here."

"Sergeant Olsen? He is here? How do you know?" Emily asks.

"The Trader was just outside."

"But I was with the Sargent at the base when we were told Alisha had died."

"That could have been a deception."

"So you're just going to leave us?" Emily squeals. "For how long?"

"As long as it takes."

"He could be gone weeks," Ma cites. "If not more."

"You can't leave. Who will take care of us?" Emily pleads.

"You two will be fine. There is enough food, firewood and hot water for the both of you."

Jim turns and faces his constituency with a fully packed bag.

"Listen. This is something I have to do."

"Will you be back before my baby is born?" Emily vacillates.

"Baby?"

"I'm pregnant."

Their eyes meet. Jim drops his bag swiftly before lunging toward her. He grasps Emily's shoulders and stares deep into her soul.

"You're pregnant?" he whispers with shock.

"Yes," Ma injects, causing Jim to blink away his concentration. He pulls back from Emily but maintains eye contact.

"I'm so sorry," he offers glumly. "My little Emily, how I tried to protect you. I failed."

"No Daddy, you didn't fail me," she instinctively emits for the first time.

His arms wrap gently around her. "I'll be back soon," Jim whispers.

"That's what my father said just before he left me all alone in the car. Remember when you found me? He said he would be back soon and that never happened."

Their eyes mutually moisten.
"Who did this to you?"

"It must have been that Dr. Otis," she snarls. "He was keeping me asleep not because of the pain. He raped me when I was drugged."

"Damn him!" Jim bristles angrily. "How long have you known that you were pregnant?"

"I thought something was wrong on the day we left that God awful place, but I wasn't sure and dismissed it. Then Ma took one look at me and knew right away."

"She has all the classic symptoms," Ma interjects.

"I have to go and find my daughter," Jim delicately states.

"I thought I was your daughter."

"You are and will always be, but you know what this means to me."

"Then let me go with you."

"In your condition?" Jim urges. "No, you need rest. This is something I must do alone."

"Why not wait until spring?" Ma tenders.

Jim turns and glares at his mother.
"Every minute breathes anxiety. If I don't know soon, I'll go crazy."

"You do look more alive," Emily concedes. "Until now, I haven't seen fire in your eyes in weeks."

"Jimmy, listen to me," Ma sternly dictates. "I love Alisha with all my heart, but I can't bear to lose both of you."

"You're not losing me Ma. I will come back. And if she is there then we'll both come home."

"And if she is not?" Ma sighs.

Jim cradles his family in a tight embrace. Their heads rest gently on his shoulders. "You two are my strength. I want to remember this feeling wherever I go."

Tears well up, forcing a communal cry before the hug subsides. "I must do this." Jim radiates with a bold and serene smile, grasping his luggage in his right hand.

Chapter 44: Fellowship

The bus arrives just after 12:15pm. It makes the appointed stops but only a few intrepid souls bear the cold. They ride bundled in blankets and oversized coats as snow swirls around them. No one utters a word.

In record time, the coach rolls around the sidewalk, allowing its meager passengers to depart.

Jim bursts into Trader Joes excitedly, carrying his oblong suitcase. He speeds to the counter.

Joe recognizes him instantly.
"Ah, did you meet up with Gavin?"

"I need to get to Unionville, Missouri."

"Gavin said in a few weeks he'll tell us if your daughter is there," says Joe, with a confused gaze.

"I'm not waiting. Can you help me find passage?"

"I don't recommend it," says Mae. "That is a dangerous ride. It should be left to professionals."

"I'm willing to take one person with me in exchange for everything in this case." He parades it on the counter.

"What's inside?" Joe sparkles.

Jim pops the metal latches and swings back the lid

to reveal gold coins, jewelry and fine men's clothing.

"Well, you might not get many takers for those." Joe smiles. "If you had a pair of boots or work gloves, well that might get you somewhere. But I suppose you can try Wade's auto body shop a few stores down. Either Wade himself or maybe others would be interested in the challenge."

Joe stares contentiously at the two shopkeeps before closing the suitcase. He storms out, clutching his treasures in hopes of finding a more receptive audience.

Outside in the crisp air, Jim spies a pair of closed garage doors a few hundred feet away. He sprints toward them with bold strides. Arriving at a glass doorway, he peers inside before pulling it open.

A combination of grease and barn odors permeate from inside the dank waiting room. A row of chairs are centered around a tall empty counter. Atop the dark wood grain veneer sits a mechanical bell. Jim taps the protruding nipple, sending a noticeable vibration off the walls.

"Hello," Jim emits before ringing the bell again.

"Yes," a voice emanates from the garage. A tall grungy man appears in the vestibule. A dirty rag dangles in his hands. Uncombed hair and a scruffy beard protrude about a half inch from his youthful face.

"I'm looking for passage to Unionville, Missouri. Can you help me?"

"Where?" the man grumbles while chewing on something.

"I need to go south to Unionville, Missouri to find my daughter. Trader Joe said I might find someone here willing to accept a challenge."

"Oh he did, did he? We're not chauffeurs mind ya. There's this guy called Gavin that..."

"I know about Gavin," Jim interrupts. "I can't wait weeks. I need to get there quicker. Can you help me?"

The tall man chews like a cow, bulging his hairy cheeks side to side exemplifying his pudgy face.

"What's your name, Mister?"

"I'm Jim. And you?"

"Wade. So you're fix'n to leave soon?"

"Immediately."

"I'd like to help ya, I really would but I have a place to run here. If ya need firewood or a way to heat your home for the winter, I'm your guy. I just can't pick up and haul ya all the way down there on a moment's notice."

"Do you know who can?"

"It's more like who *will* this late in the season. You had a better shot on find'n some fool hardy soul in any other season but this."

"You have to help me. My little girl was last seen there."

Wade shakes his head with a negative swing. "How old is she?"

"Thirteen."

Jim smacks his trunk on the counter and pops it open. "I'll trade this entire case to anyone who brings me and my daughter there and back." He plunges his hand inside the case to expose the stash.

"Well, Sir, my gut says no, but I can see your powerful argument. You're hurting something mighty bad. I'll tell you what, if ya help me deliver a few cords of wood today, I'll set out with you at first light."

"It's a deal." Jim swiftly accepts.

The two walk from the vestibule to the attached garage. Scant outside light penetrates through the grime filled garage door windows.

Mounds of chopped wood are neatly stacked on three waiting carriages. A single horse is shackled to one.

Wade motions for Jim to hop aboard the low lying cart. The small front bench has barely enough room for two. A pair of rubber wheels rest softly on the concrete garage floor.

"You can leave that here." Wade points to Jim's suitcase.

"This holds all my cherished possessions."

"Ya haven't lived in a small town have ya? It will be safe in my office. I give you my word."

Jim tenderly hands it over. Wade gently takes it and disappears. Moments later he plants himself to the right of Jim along the narrow bench.

"Can ya open the bay door?" He motions.

The heavy overhead door is balanced delicately by a pair of massive springs. Jim tugs on a steel handle protruding from the wood facade. The four slat door lifts effortlessly, singing with clanging metal.

Wade presses the lone horse through the threshold and into the snowy air. He waits for Jim to seal the door shut.

"So where do ya come from?" Wade asks as the cart gallops from town.

"I was born in these parts."

"Really? Ya seem outa place."

"I lived most of my adult years in New York."

"Ah, that explains it."

The rubber tires cut a wide path in the accumulating snow. Within ten minutes they arrive at their appointment. A rustic home nestled in the thicket. Ash bellows from the stoic brick chimney, signifying an active dwelling.

Wade leaps from the bench then ties the horse to a tree. "Wait here." He sprints a few hundred feet from the cart and raps on the ground level door. It opens slowly to reveal a diminutive figure standing as a silhouette to a warm glowing fire.

After a quick conversation, Wade returns. "This whole load is for them. Carry as much as ya can around back, close to the door."

Jim nods, then presses three logs against his chest. They are ferried to a covered pile. After a few trips, the cart is emptied, prompting Wade to boldly smile. "Nice job." His eyes beam. "Ya saved me a lota time." A ride back to the garage allows a new haul to be delivered.

The snow has stopped but the air has chilled further. The cold forces the two riders to bundle up tightly as they make their last delivery.

By the time the last horde is transported, the sky darkens. They roll back into the garage just before the sun sets.

Shedding their coats, the duo nestles around a table in a fire lit room. The warm air soothes their frigid bones.

As they sit around a dark table, the back door opens from another room. A young woman enters, carrying a tray with bowls. She stops abruptly, eyeing the two shadows around the table.

"Wade, is that you?" she gulps.

"Yes'um and I have company. Jess meet Jim."

"Hi there," she responds pleasantly and continues walking to the table. "So ya staying for supper I suppose."

"Yup," Wade replies. "Tomorrow we're head'n down to Unionville together."

"What!?" she sternly emits while doling out two bowls of hot steaming food.

"Gavin had found the locket there," Jim explains to the both of them, dangling the chain between his fingers. "This belonged to my thirteen year old daughter. I've been searching for her ever since this whole thing started."

"Unionville is a long ride," Jess laments. "It'll take ya a better part of a day to get through all those miles."

"We're leaving at first light," Wade sings.

"So I suppose ya want me to manage the business."

"You've done it before Jess. Besides, Jim helped me deliver cords today and cut the time in half."

"Don't get lost down there." She nods, sipping her soup in the confines of the soft glowing room.

"Ah, my baby sistar cares," Wade provokes.

Jim's thoughts gravitate toward the journey.
"I don't understand why such a short trip will take most of the day."

"The main roads are blocked by bandits," Jess utters. "And besides, getting there is not like hopping in a car."

"So we're talking hours?" Jim queries.

"A few," Wade responds. "I've been there a couple of times over the summer. And even in that weather, it's a haul."

After the meal, Jim is shown a small dark room where his suitcase rests alongside a cot. "This is yours," Jess states, holding a candle inside the cubbyhole.

Wade stands in the doorway.
"Yup. Get a good nights sleep and I'll wake ya in the morning if you're not up already."

The candle is left on a dresser, sputtering away in the solitary den. The floor is hard and cold, covered by gray brittle laminate. Pieces are chipped and completely missing in some well traveled areas.

Jim takes interest in the surroundings. He quickly hides the suitcase beneath the bed before succumbing to sleep.

Chapter 45: Journey of Faith

Dawn has yet to penetrate the dark room where Jim is sleeping. Yet outside the closed door, Wade prods his guest. "Are ya ready?" he shouts.

With his eyes still shut, Jim rolls over beneath layered blankets.

"What?" he slurs.

"Well the sky is showing. We best be get'n ready."

Despite his swollen eyes, Jim tucks in his shirt and stumbles to the door. "I'll be right there," he emits before stepping into the hall.

"This way," says Wade, staring alertly in the gloomy corridor.

In the garage sits the same horse-drawn cart that was in service yesterday. It is poised and ready for the journey. The sole engine snarls, sending puffs of mist into the cold still air.

In the back of the cart, blankets cover low lying mounds spread across the entire bed.

"We'll take shifts driving," says Wade as he climbs atop the bench.

Still drunk with sleep, Jim nods warily.

"Open the door," Wade instructs, prompting Jim to

walk over and lift the egress. The cart passes through. Jim climbs aboard after securing the gate.

The cart rumbles on a thin layer of fresh powdery snow. The sky continues to brighten until clear blue erupts above them. Covered by blankets, hats and heavy coats, the two riders resemble mountain peaks atop the bench. Wade stares straight ahead with an unwavering gaze.

They bobble with each bump in the road, until an abrupt ditch wakes Jim from his stupor. "We didn't have breakfast," he mumbles from beneath the blanket as the brilliant sun breaches the horizon.

"I brought two hot thermoses and vittles back there." Wade points behind the bench without breaking his gaze. Road signs sprout from beneath the snow, designating speed limits and various pictograms. Yet none of them hold credence for a horse drawn cart.

Jim exhumes a pouch. "Yeah, that's the one," Wade contends, eyeing the bag in Jim's hand. "We'll stop for a break in about ten minutes."

"That all can't be food back there," Jim comments.

"While in Unionville I thought I'd do some trade'n. That's how folks get by, trade'n and such." He pauses, but his focus remains glued to the road. "Remember how snow would stop most cars and trucks when it got too deep. Well, with a horse it's different. I mean galloping through the snow is safer than just four wheels. I'd never thunk it until I started using a horse. I mean just look at her step'n over the snow and all."

"I suppose."

"Well, if it wasn't for old Betsy here, we'd never even chance leave'n home."

A few moments of silence beneath the tree lined path predicates equality. Jim stares ahead eyeing the desolate tundra. He spots some tracks in the snow ahead. Wheels and hoofs trace their path beyond the horizon. "Are these roads safe?" Jim inquires nervously.

"There are always those who want things without working for it. That's why it's best to be ready for anything."

"Are you?"

"Heck, yes. There's a shotgun below the bench filled with buckshot and a smaller rifle for target hunting."

"Did you ever have to use either of them along this road?"

"A couple of times the shotgun blasted through a line of bandits. I usually keep that one loaded with buckshot to drive away those types of herds. The rifle is for accurate shots. Haven't used that on anyone yet. But ya must always be aware of your surroundings. That's why I keep a steady eye out for what's around the next bend. If ya see anything, holler."

Jim stares ahead, eyeing the pristine snow just beyond the prancing horse with renewed interest. "And while you're my second pair of eyes, ya may want to check behind us now and again."

Jim complies by glancing over his shoulder. Behind the cart blows a vicious storm kicked up by speeding wheels and hoofs. The snowy mist obscures most of the view, persuading Jim to focus at the edges, but that too is insufficient. He opts instead to center his attention up front beyond the horse's head.

"There's a covered bridge coming up," Wade announces. "We'll stop under it and break out some grub."

Resembling a house on stilts, the long enclosed bridge emerges from the distance. It spans a frozen stream like a large fallen tree resting on either bank. They speed toward the trestle, eyeing the surrounding tundra for anomalies.

"What's that?" Jim points to his left at a fast approaching snow scrawl. A black specter speeds toward them, kicking up a snowy dust storm behind.

"Another traveler," Wade cautiously replies before plucking the shotgun from below the seat. It rests openly on his lap.

The racer spots their cart and slows, allowing the frozen dust to dissipate. The lone rider sits atop a golden steed. He stops cautiously by the cart.

"How's the road north?" queries the heavily covered horseman. He removes his goggles and scarf to reveal a clean shaven face beneath a large brimming hat.

"Clear through Numa," says Wade. "How's the path to Unionville?"

"Down by 141 there's some yahoos throwing snowballs. Fire off a round and they scatter."

"Thank you." Wade smiles. "Numa is a peaceful town with a trading post on Main Street."

"Much obliged." The lone rider tips his hat. He snaps the reigns, prompting his horse to jolt pass them down the road.

Wade stows the shotgun beneath the seat and edges his steed forward. They enter the mouth of the bridge and rumble over the wooden planks toward the far end. He stops just before the nose of the horse breaches the outside.

"This is a good place to eat." Wade smiles while taking off his coat and hat. He reaches back and pulls out a couple of thermoses. They both moisten their lips on hot coffee, then fill their stomachs with cold bread.

Wade hops off and inspects Betsy while Jim stretches out on the bench.

"What a beautiful spot," says Jim, staring at the wasteland ahead. His eyes crystallize on a dancing leaf attached to a dormant tree high above the fresh snow.

The foliole dangles in the cold chilly air enticing Jim to imagine what life could have been if all of this was negated. An inventive mind can weave scenarios that might have happened, fostering an alternative to reality. Every detail can be meticulously rendered, right down to the smell.

Jim lingers around the kitchen table on that lurid day, saying goodbye to his family for the last time. "They canceled my play this weekend." Alisha frowns as Tommy quietly eats his breakfast. "Don't worry," says Karen, her mother. "We'll find something fun to do instead."

"How about now? Can you stay home today?" Alisha pleads with Jim.

He stares at his loving daughter. "Of course," he submits fancifully, fabricating a day spent with his family instead of what really happened. But this is just a delusion, unlike the sentiments Alisha had uttered sitting around her kitchen table, spewing her emotions into the camera. "I'm all alone now," she coldly bellows before crying.

Jim scrutinizes the imagery through his mind's

eye, lamenting over his crying daughter. Though staring beyond the covered bridge, he remains oblivious to reality.

"Hey! Didn't ya hear me?" Wade stresses, peeking into the bridge from the outside. He grabs the rifle from beneath the bench. "Mind the horse," he snaps before disappearing beyond the side of the bridge.

One pop, then another stings the cold air causing the horse to stir. Jim tightens the reigns, keeping the equine under the canopy.

Wade breaches the mouth of the bridge with a bold grin. Dangling in his right hand is a limp rabbit swaying by its ears. "We'll have a good meal tonight." His eyes gleam.

"I heard two shots."

"Ah yah, the first one missed but I nailed it the second time," Wade proudly announces. He tosses the carcass in the back beneath the blankets.

"Do ya want to take the reins?" Wade smiles.

"I haven't done this before."

"Heck, it's easier than cruise control."

The leather straps rest gently in Jim's gloved hands. "A slight flick will send Betsy forward," Wade explains. "Then a little tug left or right sends her in that direction. Pull both back together and she'll slow."

Jim jiggles the reigns but locomotion remains dormant. "When ya flick, make a sharp sound."

Jim tries again with a forceful snap followed by "Click-click". The horse lunges forward. "Gently now," Wade stresses as the rig picks up speed. "There." He smiles. "Ya got the hang of it."

Behind the reins, Jim speeds down the snowy road. Over time, miles blaze behind them. Eventually they accelerate onto 141st street. The tree lined thoroughfare differs only slightly from their previous path. The anxiety that had plagued other travelers has dissipated. They sail through and onto Route 5 uneventfully where the road widens.

"About five more miles." Wade motions ahead. The straight expanse leads directly into Unionville. They intersect Route 136, most commonly known as Main Street to locals. The heart of the small city bustles with activity.

Pedestrians parade between various stores lining the central corridor. Jim pulls up in front of a stoic sandstone brick building with the words 'Police' etched into the facade. Wade straps Betsy to a street lamp then follows Jim into the building.

A small waiting area is flush against thick glass extending into the ceiling. Behind the shield is a portly civil servant dressed in a tight blue shirt and black pants. A bushy mustache hovers over his upper lip like a woolly worm. A gold badge bulges on top of his meaty right breast.

He eyes the approaching couple with cautious contempt, but remains seated with his legs sprawled wide open, resting on a warn swivel leather chair.

"Excuse me," Jim declares through a small slot in the dense glass. The officer sighs in disgust. His thick stubby hands press against his knees, helping him rise from the chair.

"Yeah," he mouths while slowly approaching the barrier.

"I'm looking for Nathan Olsen."

"Who?" the officer grunts before laying his hands on the counter for support.

"My thirteen year old daughter Alisha might be with him."

"I'm sorry, Sir, I dunno who this fella is."

Jim plucks the locket and dangles the chain in front of the glass. "This belonged to my daughter. Gavin the trader said he got this from Nathan Olsen who is living in Unionville. I must find him."

The officer glides his right index finger across the bottom of his nose ephemerally. "Look, I don't keep tabs on everyone, only those who make trouble.

You're not here to make trouble are you?"

"I only want to find my daughter," Jim appeals.

"Well I suppose if Gavin said he is here, then he must be. Did Gavin tell you anything else like what street this fella lives on?"

"Near the high school."

"That's on 20th street." The officer nods.

"We'll find it," Wade interrupts.

"Now I don't want you making trouble around here knocking on doors just to find this Olsen fella. Why don't you stay in town overnight and let me ask around."

"I don't have any money," Jim offers.

"Money? That went out of fashion a while back. Ask for Mattie at the White House hotel toward the edge of town. Tell her that Officer Larson says to treat you as authorized guests."

"Thank you." Jim smiles.

Larson turns toward his chair but stops midstream.

"By the way," he says coolly, "what is your name?"

"Jim."

"And does Alisha have any siblings?"

"A brother Tommy, but she watched him die back in New York."

"You're a long way from home."

"I'm staying up in Numa with my mother."

Chapter 46: Reflex

The White House Hotel is a majestic structure done in the classical federalist style. It boasts a column entry into a grand foyer where a small front desk straddles an interior doorway. Jim enters alone while Wade endeavors to hawk his wares.

"Hello!" Jim yells beyond the front desk, but no one replies. "Hello? Anyone here?" An elderly woman steps into the doorway. Her white hair and stoic face reminds him of his mother.

"Yes," the woman emits.

"Are you Mattie?"

"Maybe." She smiles.

"Officer Larson suggested that we are authorized guests."

"Oh he did? Well then, I guess that makes you an authorized guest. But you said it in plural. I don't see anyone else with you."

Jim smirks.
"That is true. I have a friend named Wade who will join me shortly."

"You're not from around here are you?"

"I'm from back east."

"Ah, I thought so. I spent some time in Pennsylvania in my youth. How long will you be staying with us?"

"Just the night."

"And you need one or two rooms."

"Preferably two."

She nods with a smile. "And your name?"
"I'm Jim and my friend is Wade."

"Nice to meet you Jim." She etches their monikers in an old paper book.

"Follow me."

Just beyond the front desk is a long hallway dividing the floor. A bright window at the end beams midday sun, basking the corridor with optimism. Mattie swings open a door to reveal a glistening abode.

Clean peach colored sheets and pastel wall paper exemplify the exalted chambers, bringing a smile to Jim's weary face. He sits on the bed. "Thank you."

"I am glad that you like it."

Alone in his room, Jim lies on the bed and closes his eyes. What seems like an instant has transformed into hours. The bright room is now dark. A knock on the door jolts him awake.

"Are ya there?" Wade asks, prompting Jim to jump from the bed. "Come in," he invites.

A faint light creeps from beneath the doorway until it explodes like lightening, blinding him with Wades entrance.

"How was ya nap?" he asks.

"How long have I been sleeping?"

"A few hours. I sold all the goods. Mattie agreed to make us rabbit stew tonight."

"Any word from Officer Larson?"

"Nah. I don't think we'll see him tonight. It is wicked out there. The snow is coming down like a banshee."

"Really?"

"Yeah, something bad. When I came in about an hour ago, there was about a foot or more out there."

"Supper!" Mattie cries from the hallway, sending Wade scurrying to the door. Jim follows until they both arrive in a large dining room.

Two large chandeliers hang from the ceiling, casting the room in a bright glow of flickering candlesticks. Four settings of fine china rest at one end of the long elegant table. Steaming bowls of mashed potatoes and greens fill the air with tantalizing aromas.

Mattie brings out the last piping hot tray and seats herself at the head of the table. "You boys seem hungry." She smiles.

The long table can seat up to twenty-five guests, but tonight there are four settings placed neatly toward one side.

"Is there someone else joining us?" Jim asks, pointing to the vacant seat.

"You never know when an unexpected guest will arrive. It is always prudent to set an empty plate just in case," she comments while unveiling dinner. "Rabbit stew with potatoes and okra." She smiles proudly.

"A meal fit for a king!" Wade salivates.

"Will you say grace?" She points toward Wade.

Like a child in Sunday school, Wade presses his hands together. He closes his eyes reverently. "Lord, thank ya for this meal and the friendship in this room. May my friend Jim find what he is looking for. Amen."

"Amen," Mattie and Jim whisper.

Food is piled high on their plates with restrained excitement, inhibiting conversation. It is not until the meal is nearly consumed before communication resumes.

"By the looks of the meager leftovers, I'd say you two where hungry," says Mattie.

"It was a great meal." Jim smiles. "You are a master cook."

"Nothing pleases me more than seeing those appreciate my cooking."

"Have you lived here long?" Jim asks.

"Most of my adult life, but you can plainly see I'm not a pure-bred local." She pauses, eyeing the two guests. "Wade told me of your plight. I surely hope you find your daughter."

"Then you never heard of Nathan Olsen?" Jim stresses.

"Sorry, I try to keep my nose out of other peoples business, unless of course they willingly volunteer information."

"What happens if ya don't find her here?" Wade asks.
"Then I'll go back to Numa and live with my mother and adoptive daughter."

"So you have another child waiting for you?" Mattie asks.

"Sort of. I found her along the way. She had lost

her parents so we bonded."

"You may not realize it", says Mattie, "but what you already have is unique. No matter what happens in the coming days, you have a family to go home to."

Jim nods.
"But as long as there is a chance that my blood exists beyond my grasp, I will continue the journey."

Mattie smiles.
"Be careful, if you over extend your arm and reach for two donuts, you may drop both."

Mattie gets up and grabs her dirty plate.

"Let us help," Jim insists. The bowls and pans are gathered. Water flows from the sink faucet, allowing the dishes to be cleaned by the soft glow of candles.

"Goodnight gentlemen." She exhales. "I am sure you will find your beds warm and comfortable. I stoked the fire and it should last until breakfast."

Chapter 47: Protracted Intensity

A hint of morning light penetrates Jim's room. His eyes open with excitement. He vaults to the window and peers onto a cold and quiet landscape. The new sun sparkles over the windswept tundra. Last nights storm has left nearly three feet of fresh powder.

There is no activity anywhere on the horizon, prompting Jim to pry open the window. A blast of cold air fills the void, forcing him to abruptly close the pane.

He leaves the room and stares through other windows in the house to find snow piled up against the glass, suggesting a far bigger storm than imagined.

It is not long before Mattie finds Jim sitting on the living room couch.

"You are up early." She smiles, prompting him to follow her to the kitchen. "We had a heap of snow last night."

"Indeed?" he balks.

"I have seen winters come and go and just when you think it will be a mild season, this happens. It is going to be a bad winter this time, mark my words," Mattie stresses.

"But these parts usually don't get massive

snowfalls."

"It's all about cycles. We are due for a real winter this year."

Late, Wade joins them for breakfast.

"It looks like you two may spend at least one more night here," says Mattie.

"Maybe." Wade nods. "But let's take a look and see what it's really like out there."

Wade tugs on the front door.
"I'd be careful." Mattie signals.

But Wade continues pulling until the door abruptly swings inward followed by a pile of snow. Beyond the threshold stands an impassable mound, forcing Wade to reseal the entrance with Jim's assistance.

"Do you have snow shoes?" Jim asks Wade.

"Nah, not with me."

"I'm sure Officer Larson will find his way to us," Mattie insists. "I say we just relax and wait."

Beleaguered, Jim walks back to his room.

The day moves slowly and by night fall, another storm blows across the landscape, burying them in a few more feet. By daybreak, windows on the first floor are completely blocked by snow.

Each subsequent day finds a few more inches of accumulation until only the attic windows can be opened onto the surface.

"I'm not waiting any longer," Jim insists, gazing into the vast nothingness beyond the opened window. Strapped to his booted feet is a pair of makeshift snowshoes fashioned out of wood planking and string. "I've done this before," he agilely maintains.

Bundled in a heavy coat and yellow rubber boots stretching to his knees, Jim steps out onto the barren vista; a desert of snow lay before him. The tops of majestic pine trees vault above the powder with hints of greenery.

As for manmade objects, only small protrusions from other rooves breach the pristine surface. Most of the low lying buildings are completely covered and indistinguishable beneath the hordes of snow.

"See that tall black spire?" asks Mattie, sticking her head out of the third story window. "That is the church. I would try that first."

Jim slowly skims the surface, barely making an indentation in the powdery strata. His stride quickens as he approaches the spire. The base is deep below the pale terrain, yet only the topmost ten feet are exposed. The dark tapered steeple comes to a two inch point, topped with a silvery cap.

Jim knocks on the spear with a loud rap before placing his ear against the sprout. "Hello," he voices quickly before turning his ear to the tower, but no one reciprocates.

Not far from the church is another protrusion poking through the snow. A red brick chimney just breaches the surface. Jim kneels beside it and digs with his hands until a brick chimney is exposed. Snow has filled the tubular cavity making a verbal announcement mute, but he raps on it anyway with the heel of his boot. Moments pass without a reply.

Distraught, he rises to his feet. Nothing but cold barren snow is seen for miles in any direction. "Why?" he whispers. "Why?" he grumbles louder. "Why?" he yells again in desperation, vibrating his vocals off of the absorbing snow. The sound fades quickly, leaving only lonely silence in its wake.

A slow walk back to the hotel fills his thoughts with gloom. To have come so far and not to realize his dream sets him on edge. His knees buckle, then plunge a few inches into the powdery snow. He looks up with a tearful guise toward the silvery sky and lets out a gut wrenching howl.

His soul is emptied, allowing his haggard chin to sag against his deflated chest.

"Why?" he whispers dispassionately, wondering what he had done to deserve this condemnation. His eyes swell with tears, dribbling the essence of life from his chin to his thighs.

"Jim!" Wade yells from the attic window. "Are ya alright?" His voice carries on the air yet he cannot be seen.

Jim snorts, absorbing his emotions. Standing like a puppet held by strings, he bobbles toward the hotel roof.

"Are ya okay?" asks Wade as Jim approaches the window.

"I'm fine," he rebukes dismissively.

"Was that ya scream'n?"

Jim dusts himself off, then climbs through the window, deflecting Wade's question. "Everything is covered in a layer of misery out there," Jim laments.

"As long as we ration our food," Mattie emits, "we will survive."

"It is not the food I am worried about," Jim admonishes. "It is our sanity. Even if it doesn't snow for the rest of the season, it will take months to thaw all this."

Time passes slowly. Weeks trickle into months. December comes and goes with little fanfare.

"We're getting low on wood," Jim notices after returning from the covered porch with a few logs cupped in his arms.

"How much is left?" says Mattie nervously.

"We have to ration these too."

"Alright," Mattie dictates. "It'll be best if we just use one fireplace from now on. Let's all stay here in the living room."

Jim stokes the fire and adds a new log.

"Happy New Year," Wade whispers, staring at the slow burning embers crackling in the hearth.

"Happy New Year to you," says Jim with a momentary smile. He retreats quickly back into a dull gaze, allowing January to blend into February.

The days are filled with boredom, numbing the senses beyond civility. Throughout most of the day, each recedes into their own corners of the house. They come together for lunch, the only daily meal.

A twenty-eight ounce container of meat is heated by the fireplace then portioned out equally. They savor each bite until their bowls sparkle with cleanliness.

"I hate ya all," says Wade staring at Jim with a crazed guise. "Especially you for taking me from my home."

"You did this willingly!" Jim blares.

"Forget you!" Wade snaps.

"Please," Mattie interrupts. "Go to your rooms." Begrudgingly the group disbands.

Numb with boredom, Jim climbs to the attic and stares out of the window onto the barren surface. As mid-March languishes, the church steeple lengthens, indicating that the snow is beginning to melt.

Jim grabs Alisha's locket between his thumb and forefinger. He opens it and peers at his smiling family. Tears flow from his watery eyes.

But his thoughts gravitate toward Ma and Emily, remembering the last embrace they had shared. "You two are my strength," he whispers, hoping he had not made a mistake in abandoning them. "Please forgive me."

Suddenly a speck of humanity emerges on the white tundra. Jim opens the attic window and gapes down at the approaching anomaly.

"Over here!" Jim cries, waving his hands to draw attention. The speck draws closer until a full sized man waddles toward the window.

The commotion has summoned Wade and Mattie to the attic. They stand behind Jim in eager anticipation.

"I think that's Officer Larson," Mattie whispers.

Their hands rest on Jim's shoulders as they peer beyond the window like children eyeing a Christmas store display. Smiles abound.

"Over here!" Wade injects as the meaty mound looks up a few feet from below the window.

"Mattie?" smiles Larson adorned in a heavy overcoat. "It is nice to see that you three made it."

"Did you find my daughter?" Jim erupts impertinently, crystallizing the moment.

"Your daughter? Oh." Larson recalls that day. "I had never made it there and most likely won't for a while."

Jim sighs, allowing Larson to continue. "I'm sure a lot of people lost their lives through all these months. We'll need help to sort through it all."

Jim recedes into the darkness while Wade and Mattie press against the opening.

"How much snow is out there?" Wade asks.

"I'd say about ten feet or so," replies Larson. "It's been warm the last few weeks and if it keeps up like this, it'll all be gone in no time."

"You lost weight." Mattie notices.

"Yeah. Just a little. There's a group of us held up at the station. We're fix'n to explore the food stores. How's your supply?"

"Meager," Mattie offers. "But we will get by. Don't worry about us."

"How about tomorrow you two men come and join us. We can use extra hands."

Wade nods but Jim peers from the darkness of the attic offering nothing to signify his acceptance. Larson does not skip a beat. "Well, I'll see you tomorrow."

Later that night the three gather around the kitchen table for an unscheduled meal.

"We usually only eat lunch," Wade utters as Mattie doles out bowls of hot soup.

"This calls for a special celebration," she submits.

"Indeed," Jim agrees, but his empty gaze says something far different.

"What's wrong?" Mattie inquires, sipping on her hot bowl of soup. "You've been quiet since this afternoon."

"I know what it is," Wade stipulates. "Your daughter, right? We will find her. I'm sure we will."

"But you said..."

"I'm sorry about that. Ya didn't force me to come here." His eyes sag. "I was mad when I said that. Crazy even. I'm sorry."

"Then you will help me?"

"Yup, like I promised."

Chapter 48: Resurgence

The snow melts, allowing access outside through the second floor of the White House Hotel. No longer is the attic the only portal. A bright and sunny morning greets Jim and Wade, huddled in a vacant room. Kneeling below a window, they attach homemade snowshoes.

"You two be careful out there," says Mattie watching her two snowbound companions. "Don't leave me here alone. Come back before dark and let me know the news."

"We promise," says Jim as he steps outside wearing a heavy coat and hood. Walking on ten feet of old snow, they spot other snowshoe prints. "That must be from him," Wade declares.

"Let's follow them," Jim affirms.

They continue trailing the prints, turning occasionally to see their dwelling fade in the distance. Eventually they spot a red traffic cone directly above the covered police station.

A small opening dug into the snow burrows to a submerged window. Jim raps gently on the glass. "Hello?" he cries repeatedly.

A shadow appears, pushing the aperture open.

"Yeah?" a grungy bearded man voices.

"Officer Larson sent for us," Jim explains.

The figure closes the window abruptly then disappears.

"Maybe they killed him," Jim ventures. "We should head back and not let them see where we came from."

"Let's wait a few minutes."

"So they can come at us?"

The window opens, followed immediately by the pudgy officer.

"Welcome." He smiles. Large snowshoes leap out onto the snow. Shovels and large duffel bags are passed through the window along with two other men forming a group of five. One carries a large axe slung over his left shoulder while another holds a miner's pick.

"Follow me," says Larson without offering introductions. He leads his team across the buried street towards a snow covered mound.

"This is the general store," he advocates. His two followers nod in agreement. Larson directs his party to form a circle around a designated area. "Dig down until we hit shingles."

All five cast their shovels into the hardened snow, excavating chunks of frozen debris. A jagged hole is carved into the surface until it resembles a bomb blast.

Wades shovel hits something with a loud thud. "I think I found the roof," he bristles.

They clear away the remaining snow, revealing a tarred roof. "Stand clear!" the pick man warns. He muscles his way past the shovelers, swinging his mighty steel hatchet like a deranged murderer. Pieces of wood splinter and spew in every direction.

"Let me try some," says the axe man. He whacks at the wood surface alongside the pick man, shredding the roof expeditiously until a dark hole appears. "Next." The axe man looks up with a tired gaze.

Wade volunteers and cracks the hole wider with voracity.

"That's enough," says Larson eyeing the gaping hole. "I should go first." He plucks a flashlight from the duffel bag and shines it through the opening.

"Hello. Anyone home?" he queries, kneeling by the hole. His head passes through, pointing the light sporadically inside.

"The floor is about six feet down," he utters before plunging into the abyss. A soft thump echoes from the cavern.

"I'm okay," he voices. Everyone peers in, watching

the flashlight parade across the room. Larson lunges down a stairwell, spouting a friendly tone. The axe man jumps in next.

"Stay here," says the pick man before following his compatriot. The room is dark and quiet, except for the fleeting rumble of feet on the wood stairwell.

"I don't know how we made it through the winter," Jim reminisces. "There were times I didn't think I was going to make it."

"Don't look a gift horse in the mouth. Heck, it's not even April yet. Snow can still fly till May."

"I'm not sticking around that long," Jim affirms. "I'll walk it if I have to."

"Ya, we may have ta. I don't think my old Betsy made it. How could she. That old mare is probably gone," he grieves.

Larson and his gang emerge from the darkness carrying burlap satchels slung over their shoulders. "There's a rope up there in our bag. Send it down so we can pass these up to you," he echoes through the rooftop opening.

"Good old Nelson is still kicking in there," says the pick man. "He gave us a bunch load of vittles."

Fumbling around in the bag, Jim locates the yellow nylon twine mesh. One end of the quarter-inch cable is flung into the hole while Wade and

Jim grasp firmly on the other end. The satchels are hoisted up one by one until only the men remain.

The axe man is plucked first, then the other, until only Officer Larson remains. The topside four strain, trying to lift the portly leader from the darkness. He eventually breaches the opening.

Exhausted from the ordeal, the four pullers sit on the cold snow gasping for breath.

"Do you need any food?" Larson asks Jim.

"Can you spare any?"

"I'd say so. Why don't you take a satchel back with you?"

Jim nods as he rises to his feet. Wade wearily follows.

Together they lift the burlap haversack and head back to Mattie.

Chapter 49: Fist Full of Hope

The days grow warmer, mitigating the remaining snow. Slowly, the buried city is exposed revealing street signs that sprout from the thawing ground, leaving only a few inches of wet snow on grassy surfaces.

But not all has been pleasant as winter claws at spring. Bodies of human and animal alike pile up. Wade's horse Betsy is among the casualties as is nearly a quarter of the anthropod population.

Inching toward his destiny, Jim sets out early one balmy morning with a pair of borrowed bicycles. Wade peddles behind as Jim recants the directions. He speeds down Main Street then takes a right at a designated boulevard.

He coasts onto a private dirt road and eventually emerges into a clearing. A two story house with blue shutters and white siding bristles under the morning sun. Footprints meander around a nearby barn suggesting recent activity.

Jim drops his bike and walks eagerly up to the front porch. "Hello, Sergeant Olsen?" he radiates, followed by a knock on the door.

Rustling emanates from within. Shortly the front door opens, exposing a haggard man. Olsen gapes. "I know you."

"I'm Jim remember?"

"Yes Jim. Jim and Emily, right? But your chopper was shot down."

"It was."

"So you survived? How?"

"Fate," Jim fires impatiently.

"And Emily?"

"We both made it."

"Then my plan worked." Olsen smiles. "You two are reunited."

Jim extracts his daughter's locket.

Olsen stares at the talisman, trying to understand the significance.

"Remember this?" Jim blares maliciously. "It belonged to my daughter Alisha."

A miraculous sight breaches the doorway. "Daddy?" a young girl's head sprouts between Olsen. Their eyes meet, sparkling with joy. Alisha bolts from the door and grabs her father in a consuming embrace.

Jim cries with affirmation, clutching her tightly to his chest. All their fears dissolve, culminating in this lasting moment. Their bond is inseparable, forcing Wade and Olsen to recede into the house.

"I thought I lost you," Jim puffs, running his hands through her silky hair.

"Daddy, I was so afraid that I had lost you too," she wheezes.

"Why didn't you go to Grandma's?"

"I was only here a week before the snow came. Nathan was going to take me in the spring."

"He said you were dead."

"I was." She grimaces.

Inside the house, the four settle around the kitchen table, sipping joyously on steaming mugs of dark liquid.

"You came here because of that locket?" Olsen inquires.

"It was my destiny." He pauses, eyeing the jewelry. "Why did you give it away?"

"Every captive that dies during experimentation is stripped of all non biological objects and thrown into a bin. It is policy that the mementos are transported back to where the captors originated. I had boxes of trinkets and when I got to Unionville I traded them all for much needed goods."

"I would'a done the same," smiles Wade.

"But how did you know Alisha was alive?" Olsen edges.

"I hoped against all hope."

"The initial report that Emily had heard was true, Alisha did die. I requested that her body be flown back with hopes of bringing closure for you. To my surprise, Alisha was alive, though barely."

"Alive?" Wade squints.

"Yes. Test subjects are plentiful so when she was pronounced dead, they just used someone else. Alisha was quickly wrapped up and sent to me as requested. Hours later she arrived and I was astonished to find a pulse. I nursed your daughter back to health secretly off base, all the while planning to reunite the three of you." He pauses.

"I wish I could have been there to see your faces when you and Emily found each other." Olsen smiles. "Then the news came. You were shot down and there were no survivors... It was my intent that we all meet up here in Unionville, the place of my birth... and it seems that in the end, we have."

"This is a glorious day," Wade injects. "But my sister is waiting for me back home. It's been months since I've been there."

"You were here all this time?" Olsen asks.

"Yes," Jim replies. "Trapped in a hotel since November."

Olsen nods.
"Go." He smiles at Jim. "Take your daughter home."

"And you?"

"Don't worry about me, I'll be fine."

"Nonsense," Jim balks. "Emily misses you."

"Blessed be. She is really here?"

"Yes, at my family farm in Numa. It is big enough for all of us."

"That is a tantalizing offer." Olsen smiles, rubbing his forehead in thought. But it doesn't take long for his acceptance to radiate across his face.

In the barn sits an old truck with a pair of horses hitched to the rig, gorged on meager grains. The reigns pass through the engine compartment and weave through air vents. One strap dangles on each side of the steering wheel.

The four venture from the house and into town. Making stops at Mattie's hotel and the Police Station to display their find. Eager eyes greet the four as Wade stows his goods in the back of Olsen's trunk.

They head up Route 5, the same way Jim and Wade had come. The scent of spring permeates the April air. Blossoming flowers serenade the travelers departing Unionville.

Sticking to well paved road, they pass through the covered bridge sailing onto Numa's Main Street with little fanfare. Jim pulls open the overhead garage door to Wade's abode.

His sister Jess gawks at the four from inside the garage.

"Ya back." She smiles. "I thought I'd lost ya." Her arms wrap tightly around her brother. "Where's Betsy?"

Wade wags. "Didn't make it." He turns toward Jim. "Hey, anytime ya need a job, I can sure use a hand."

"You're a good friend Wade. I'm sure we'll see a lot of each other."

"You bet." He smiles.

Chapter 50: Flowers In The Bane

The sun dissolves below the horizon as the truck rolls onto the snow covered driveway of the farm. They stop in front of the porch, prompting Jim to pull his aqua suitcase from the back.

"This is home." He smiles boldly at Alisha and Olsen.

"I can't wait to see Grandma," Alisha beams.

They eagerly climb the steps and push open the door. "Hello, I'm back!" Jim buoyantly expounds.

"Daddy?" Emily counters. "Is that you?" her voice carries from upstairs.

Jim charges in alone and finds Emily lying on the bed with a swollen stomach.

"I'm so happy to see you!" she cries.

"Something wondrous has happened." Jim smiles.

"Alisha?"

"Yes and Sergeant Olsen, together in our home."

Tears begin to dribble onto her rosy cheeks. "I'm so happy for you."

"Where's Ma?"

Her eyes narrow.
"She is dead."

"Dead?"

Emily grimaces.
"One morning she didn't wake up. They took her body away weeks ago. When the ground thaws, she'll be buried out back alongside your father."

Jim gulps, then sits quietly on her bed, staring helplessly at his hands. A slow rumbling inside his chest erupts with a desperate moan, followed by a lamenting cry.

Alisha sheepishly enters, folding her arms around her father. Emily looks on with a loving smile. "I've heard so much about you," she confesses. "We're sisters now."

Alisha reaches out to Emily while one arm still clings to Jim. He turns and eyes his two girls with a serene smile. "I am home for good."

Olsen enters, prompting Emily to smile profusely. They all sit around her bed telling stories of their ordeals.

Days dissolve into weeks as budding plants signal spring. Outside, Ma's body is laid to rest near her husband. The town outpouring lingers by the gravesite, offering condolences. Eventually they dwindle, leaving just Jim kneeling by the dual sites.

"I'm sorry I wasn't there for you Ma," he sniffles. "But you'd be proud of me. I made it home with Alisha. I wish you could see her. We're a family again."

"Jim!" Olsen yells from the second story window. "You better get in here. Emily is having the baby."

He storms up the stairs and into a room filled with well-wishers. "We came for a funeral and left with a birth," one woman beams.

"Out," says Dr. Igby. "Everyone out."

"No!" Emily wails. "Not everyone. Jim, Alisha and Nathan can stay." She strains.

They kneel by her side. Jim grasps her right hand while Nathan holds the other at opposite ends of the bed. Alisha smiles behind Jim, readying a soft cloth to wipe away Emily's stress.

Emily screams as the Doctor gets into position. "Push!" he yells. "Push!"

Her hands squeeze tightly around her two progenitors. They wince with each pulse until a healthy baby boy emerges.

Beaming smiles abound as the newborn nestles by his mother.

"I think..." she stammers. "... I think I will name him ...Kevin James Nathan."